DOUBLE JEOPARDY

By
Malcolm English

Keith Publications, LLC
www.keithpublications.com
©2012

Arizona
USA

DOUBLE JEOPARDY

Copyright© 2012

By Malcolm English

Edited by Patti Brock

Cover art by Elisa Elaine Luevanos
www.ladymaverick81.com

Cover art Keith Publications, LLC © 2012
www.keithpublications.com

ISBN: 978-1-936372-59-1

If you are interested in purchasing more works of this nature, please stop by www.dinkwell.com

Contact information: info@keithpublications.com
Visit us at: www.keithpublications.com

Printed in The United States of America

Acknowledgements

Heartfelt thanks to Diane Nine of Nine Speakers, Inc. for making this book possible, and to Joanna Stampfel-Volpe, whose guidance and inspiration played major roles in its production. Special thanks also to Raven Ventura for allowing me to use her name and to mangle it a little, and to Dr. D. P. Lyle, a phenomenal source of information on forensic medicine.

Prologue

Everything had gone badly. Thank God he was smart enough to come up with a Plan B. The more he thought about it, the more certain he became that it would work out better than Plan A. His life was going to change. Big time!

His headlights knifed through the night like laser beams. Bugs danced with death across their path as the Lexus swept past slash pines and pepper trees on the fringe of the Florida swamp.

He glanced in his rear-view mirror. She was on his tail, doing as he had said. Good.

The fates had made them partners in a way he had not envisaged. She had been cool to his plan, but she would warm up to it when she realized the pitfalls of opposing it.

There was a lot at stake here, like more money than if you'd won the lottery. But there was a lifestyle, too. If he played his cards right he could be King of the World, like Leonardo DiCaprio had proclaimed in that Titanic movie. And she would be his queen, serving no one but him.

He flipped open his cell phone and punched in a number. "Big change of plan, sweetheart," he said, then quickly recapped the night's events.

"Yes, yes, she's right behind me," he said, irritated. "Don't worry about it. It's going to work out fine." He folded up the phone without waiting for a response.

He slowed as he came to narrow side streets on his right that disappeared into the brush. He had to concentrate now.

Suddenly, his headlights picked out a dirt road, little more than a track, snaking north between the trees. He signaled to alert his companion in the other car, then turned right and took another glance back. She was still tethered to his bumper by an invisible cord of fear and apprehension.

He followed the rutted track as it curved through a clearing in the trees and ran parallel to a fetid canal cut deep into the landscape.

He slowed to a crawl and rode the brakes as he abandoned the dirt path and edged the car forward carefully until the front wheels were on the rim of the canal bank.

His companion pulled up two car lengths behind him and sat motionless behind the wheel. She watched as he got out of his car, leaving the lights on, the engine running and the door open. He walked gingerly towards her through a carpet of weeds.

"I need you to help me," he said quietly. "The canal is pretty deep here and there's a steep drop to the water. Come give me a hand."

She said nothing but left her vehicle and followed him. Her headlights illuminated the scene as he popped the trunk on his car. "Grab the feet," he ordered as he reached in and lifted the body of a woman under the arms. He was a small man and the body was a dead weight. A very dead weight.

"We've got to get her behind the wheel," he said. "Hold her legs while I get her into the seat."

He dropped the lifeless form onto the driver's seat and positioned her feet next to the pedals. He wiped the driver's area down with a towel from the trunk, then placed the dead woman's hands on the steering wheel. He was out of breath. Physical exertion was not his forte.

"Are you sure she's dead?" It was the first time his companion had spoken.

"Yeah. Just go wait in the car while I take care of this."

She said nothing more and did as he bid her. She watched as he cracked the driver's side window, fumbled around the dash, and slammed the door shut. He stepped away quickly as the car teetered on the brink of the canal ridge, then toppled forward and disappeared down the bank. There was a splash and the lights were snuffed out as if by an invisible hand.

He waited a few seconds then stepped to the edge of the canal and looked down. In the gloom he could see only part of the trunk visible above the water. That was good enough. If anyone ever drove through here they wouldn't be any the wiser. Only someone fishing or walking alongside the canal would spot the vehicle below and no one in their right mind would be walking or fishing in this neck of the woods. Too many snakes and 'gators.

Mission accomplished!

He walked over to the woman's car and slid behind the wheel.

He reflected on the evening as he pointed the vehicle back toward civilization. Their new life was about to begin. He smiled to himself as he drove. Even though things hadn't worked out as planned, everything was going to be hunky-dory. No one would have envisaged this when the woman at his side had come into his life a couple of weeks ago.

Chapter 1

Ravena Ventura plopped her rear end down on a cane chair and surveyed the view from her screened lanai. She watched a blazing Florida sun turn rivulets of rainwater into steam on the pink and white patio. Somehow, the evaporating water reminded her of herself: from substance to . . . well, nothing much.

Ravena, star of almost two dozen movies at age 39, was super-wealthy, super-idolized, and currently super-bored. She was also soaked in sweat. But it was good to be closeted away from the Hollywood rat race, the media, the fans and the riff-raff, in a part of the good ol' USA that seemed as far removed from mainstream America as Maui.

Her daydreaming came to a sudden halt when the pink phone next to her came to life. She casually checked the caller ID. David Liebovitz. *Shit!* It was her agent in L.A. She lifted the receiver and purred into it.

"David, darling."

"Don't 'darling' me, Ravena," said the voice from twenty-five hundred miles away. "In the last two weeks I've sent you three scripts to look at and what do I hear from you? Nothing! Have you forgotten how to read?"

Ravena grimaced. "No, sweetheart I still know how to read. What I don't know is whether I want to make any movies right now."

"Paramount is expecting you to do that sequel to *The Gray Rain.* And your fans are clamoring for more. If you don't read the scripts, at least you could read the trades."

"Honey, I don't think I, or my fans, are ready for any more *Gray Rain.* It sounds like an extra helping of dog food."

"Okay, but you don't want to let the grass grow under your feet. You're likely to get an Oscar nomination for *A Woman's Desire* if you don't piss off anybody in the Academy. And the world is demanding more. Strike while the iron is hot."

"I'll think about it," said Ravena in a tone that suggested she wouldn't. "I need more R and R here. And winter is coming. I don't want to be on location in Duluth or Timbuktu when the season here gets in full swing."

"Oh God, Ravena! Why the hell don't you give up this Florida nonsense and come back to L.A.? You were set here. You had a good life, lots of friends, lots of people who could put things your way."

"Yeah, things I don't need. The climate is better for me here—and I'm not talking about the weather. I'll look at your damn scripts, but I'm not going to start any new ventures for at least six months. Don't call me, I'll call you." She hung up before he could respond. All they cared about in Hollywood was what they could squeeze out of her. That was why she was here.

Ravena moved out to the pool, shrugged off her peach robe, adjusted her white bikini and perched herself on a lounge chair.

She looked with a jaundiced eye at the row of coconut palms waving languorously on the ridge that dropped off to the beach. It was a view to swoon over . . . if you were a travel agent. But that wasn't what had brought Ravena to South Florida. The reality was six secret weeks in rehab in West Palm Beach, where she could escape from the prying press corps while she fought an addiction to cocaine.

She had been driving closer and closer to a lifestyle she knew would end in her destruction. South Florida put space between her and the money-grubbing people she didn't want to know anymore. No, she wouldn't go back to Hollywood. More movies? Who knows? It's not like she needed the money and she already had enough fame to last two lifetimes.

"Pardon, ma'am."

Ravena's petite Hispanic housekeeper, Marguerita, was standing over her, eyes wide in apprehension. "There's a woman at the door to see you," she said. "Says it is important."

"Who is she?"

"She not say, ma'am. She laugh when I ask her name."

"Where is she?"

"I tell her wait."

"How the hell did she get past the gate? Isn't there anyone from security down there? Or are they asleep at the switch? What the fuck do I pay these people for?"

Marguerita shook her head sympathetically. "She knock on front door. Will only say she need to see you. She look familiar."

"Did she say she knew me? Or is she just some tourist looking for an autograph or a handout?"

"She say you know her very well, ma'am."

Ravena studied her housekeeper. "What does she look like?"

Marguerita shrugged. "Your age and height, ma'am. Dark hair and sunglasses."

"That could be anybody. Never mind. Show her out here. If she's just some fanatic nuisance I can always throw her in the pool. And tell whoever's on the gate I want to talk to him. We can't have people wandering in whenever they feel like it. That's what the gate is for, to keep them on one side of it while I'm on the other."

'Yes, ma'am." Marguerita bowed slightly and disappeared.

She was back in a few seconds, followed by an attractive woman in a blue halter top and white shorts.

The woman tugged on her hair, pulling off a wig of dark curls, ran a hand through shoulder-length blonde locks and swept off her sunglasses.

Ravena gasped in horror. "Oh my God," she stammered, "Wha . . . what the hell are YOU doing here?"

Chapter 2

"Sis, sweetheart! Surprise, surprise! Aren't you glad to see me?"

Ravena stared at her twin sister open-mouthed. It was like looking in a mirror.

"Liz!" It was almost a hiss. "What the hell? Why are you here?"

"Just being neighborly. Aren't you pleased to see me?"

Ravena was uncharacteristically lost for words.

Liz was ten minutes her younger, identical to Ravena in looks but a world removed in personality and life's fortunes. Ravena was successful and wealthy,
Liz was always struggling to stay above the poverty line. Ravena made blockbuster movies and was surrounded by a coterie of sycophants. Liz was a hardened drug-abuser, made bad choices in men and surrounded herself with dubious entrepreneurs who permeated the dark underbelly of Los Angeles.

"Liz, I can't help you anymore," Ravena said at last. "I gave you money. I put you in rehab. I pulled massive strings to keep you out of jail. Now you have to help yourself. And there's nothing in Florida for you. Go home, find an honest job and stop looking to me to pull you out of every mess you find yourself in. Emily found her own way in life and there's no reason why you couldn't."

"Emily? Have you heard from her?"

Ravena shook her head. Emily was the twins' sister, five years older and light years removed from the family. She had turned her back on the lure of Hollywood and escaped to Mexico as soon as she was eighteen. No one had heard from her since except a hurried postcard announcing her marriage to a Guadalajara businessman.

"No, I haven't heard from her. And that's my point. Learn a lesson from Emily's book. Wherever she is and whatever she's doing she's gotten there on her own. She doesn't keep hounding me for handouts. If Em and I can do it, so can you."

"Well, sis," said Liz, dropping into a patio chair, "I came here for the same reasons you did—to start a new life. And I thought you might want to help me. We're products of the same roll in the hay. That's got to count for something; but you wound up with all the movie roles, all the money, and all the studly men. I wound up with shit."

"I worked my butt off and got lucky. You've never done anything to help yourself. How did you get in here, by the way? Isn't security manning the gate?"

Liz smiled. "Sure. One of your minders is down there, trying to look important. I just pulled off the wig before I got to the gate and waved to him as I drove in like I owned the place. He thought I was you. It's a riot."

Ravena's eyes narrowed.

"Don't worry, I'm not stupid," said Liz. "I rented a Lexus so I wouldn't ruin your image."

Ravena stood over her sister. "Liz," she said, "one of the reasons I left L.A. was because of the embarrassing trail you left behind everywhere you went. I need you out of my space."

"Sorry, sis,I know I've let you down. But I really do want to turn things around. I need to start a new life, and what better place than here?"

"Where's here?" Ravena asked stiffly. Hopefully her sister wasn't planning to move in. "You have somewhere to stay?"

"I rented a little apartment a couple of miles up the street in Lake Worth. It's nothing like this place, of course. . ." Her voice trailed off.

"Come with me." Ravena pulled on her robe, turned on her heels and went into the house. She padded barefoot across a marble-floored atrium, opened a door under a sweeping staircase and took Liz into her private study.

She pulled open a desk drawer and scribbled hurriedly on a check.

"There," she said. "Two thousand dollars. It's all I can do for you. I'd like you to spend it on a plane ticket back to L.A. There's nothing here to help you start a new life. For God's sake shuck off those deadbeats you hang around with and look for a decent man, preferably one with lots of money and even more patience."

Liz's hands closed around the check and she gave her sister a crooked smile.

"Thanks, sis," she said. "I'll be in touch."

She folded the check carefully, stuffed it into the pocket of her shorts, and stood for a second, clutching her wig and sunglasses close to her chest. She looked Ravena up and down then strode out of the study toward the front entrance. She opened one of the huge double doors and turned.

"Nice little crib you got here, Raich," she said.

Ravena bristled. She had worked hard to forget that she started out in life as Rachel Thomas of Glendale, California. And she wasn't looking for any reminders.

"Don't call me Raich," she said. "I'm Ravena Ventura now and I've built a lot on that name."

"Sorry, Raich. You can call yourself whatever you like, but we're still the same flesh and blood. When I go to a Ravena Ventura movie, guess who I see on the screen. Myself! You may have legal rights to that name, but it's still phony and you're no more Ravena Ventura than I am. Do you know what it's like to watch yourself in a movie and get nothing out of it but an empty feeling in the stomach?"

The front door closed with a bang, separating Ravena from a past she'd tried to disown. She shook her head slowly. What would it take to be free from the ghost of Rachel Thomas?

Chapter 3

Jane Connally was frustrated. Honey-blonde hair, blue eyes and a winning smile made her the darling of the newsroom at The National Courier. And she knew it. But being the most attractive reporter on America's most notorious, most despised and most revered tabloid wasn't doing a thing for her on the phone.

Three of her colleagues were flying to Los Angeles from Courier headquarters in Delray Beach, Florida, to cover the latest Hollywood scandal. But she was stuck at her desk, assigned to a tedious phone interview with a doctor in Finland on a new miracle pill to beat cancer. Worse, the doctor had little grasp of the English language and Jane's Finnish was limited to the word "sauna."

She hung up the phone in despair, twirled a strand of her hair angrily around a finger and looked across at her editor's desk. It was empty.

She glanced around the newsroom. "Where's Jack?" she said. Then, louder, "Anyone know where Jack is?"

A bald head popped up over the top of a laptop two desks away. "At the airport, picking up the latest Bob Woodward."

Oh, yes. She had forgotten. Jack Iverson's latest addition to his reporting team was getting red-carpet treatment. He was said to be young, energetic and the leading reporter on a big-city daily. He'd even been a Pulitzer nominee for exposing corruption in Detroit politics. Not that that usually meant much in the tabloid business. Reporters arrived and left The Courier like trains at Grand Central, but Jack Iverson had scooped up this one on a recruiting trip and couldn't stop talking about him.

Jane had no choice but to cool her jets and wait for Jack to show up with his protégé. She stared into space, chewed on a pencil and began to speculate on the latest addition to the staff. Was he really that good a reporter? That didn't matter. At The Courier all new hires were rookies with a short shelf life. More importantly, was he married? Did he have a steady girlfriend? Was he a nerd, a jock, an intellectual? That's what enquiring female minds wanted to know.

Jane had found office romances catastrophic, but then, most of her romances had been catastrophic. She'd earned her stripes as a hard-nosed reporter only to discover that most men shrank from girls who were tigers anywhere other than in bed.

She stiffened in her seat and forced a smile when Jack waltzed into the newsroom with a twenty-something man in tow. This had to be Him. He looked overwhelmed and he was the only guy in sight wearing a suit and tie. He had a lot to learn about The Courier. But he did look cute.

Jack led him over to the bullpen, the circle of desks in the center of the newsroom where the senior editors held forth, then began to work the room, introducing him to the editors, reporters and assistants.
When they reached Jane she stuck out a clammy hand and offered her best and brightest smile.

"Jane," boomed Iverson, "this is Michael Hanlon. He'll be joining our reporting staff. You two have something in common. He's from Detroit."

"Oh, really? Well, actually I'm from Cleveland, so I don't— "

"So now I've got two refugees from the Rust Belt on my team," said Jack with a grin.

Michael Hanlon smiled politely and nodded without losing eye contact with Jane. But before she could open her mouth to voice the standard "welcome to The Courier," Jack whisked his recruit away. Obviously no time was to be wasted on chatting up the office chicks.

Jack moved Michael down the line as though he were on a royal visit, then pulled him back to the bullpen.

"Now you need to see Human Resources," he said. "They just want your vital statistics. You know, age, eating habits, sexual preferences, that sort of thing."

Michael stared at him.

"Just kidding. All they really care about is whether you're an illegal or carrying some disease that'll cripple the health insurance plan."

Jack waited for Michael to leave the newsroom, then made a beeline for Jane's desk.

"Jack," she snapped before he could say anything. "I need an interpreter."

"Huh?"

"An interpreter. I can't understand anything that doctor in Helsinki says."

Jack waved the problem aside with his hands. "Don't worry about that. We'll give Michael a shot at it."

"Oh! Really? Does he speak Finnish as well as walk on water?"

"Don't be so pissy-assed. I want you to take him under your wing. You know, show him the ropes. He has a good track record but The Courier system will eat him alive."

Jane stood up, hands on hips, fists and teeth clenched. "What the hell, Jack? You want me to baby-sit him? Is that why you wouldn't let me go to L.A.? I have to take him under my wing? What the cluck!"

Jack fought off a smile. "Come on, Jane. Everyone has to start somewhere. Even you were like a fish out of water when you first came here."

"Maybe, but I've given you more than two years of my life and almost a hundred headlines for the cover. I've put your reporting team at the top of the heap here. Now you want me to play nursemaid? I can't deal with this crap. Why me?"

"I have to team him up with someone, Jane. Who better than my best reporter? Besides, he's young and impressionable, and I think he'll do better with a woman, especially a bulldog like you."

Jane took a deep breath and unclenched her fists. Compliments from Jack Iverson were rare, even back-handed ones.

"When Human Resources is done with him I'm going to get him a room at the Beachcomber and arrange his rental car," said Jack. "You might want to stop by and buy him a drink."

That was an order. She smelled defeat. And pouting wasn't allowed at The Courier. "All right," she sighed. "I could certainly use a drink." And what the heck? He was cute.

Chapter 4

Jack had warned Michael that despite its ocean view, the Beachcomber was no Ritz. Michael soon discovered it was no Holiday Inn either.

The Beachcomber was an old weathered motel a couple of miles south of downtown, sandwiched between high-rise condos whose residents wanted it gone. Somehow it had survived hurricanes and local politics to remain both a haven and an eyesore on the Delray Beach skyline.

As the favorite watering hole of Courier editors and reporters, the place had seen the birth of many memorable headlines and friendships and the death of many dreams and careers.

The reception area was small and stuffy, had a strange odor of salt and mold, and a hodgepodge of furnishings that might have been loss leaders at Goodwill. But Michael could see the water and the beach through a glass door that led out to the back, and he had high hopes that his room would offer a similar view.

It didn't. Michael's ground-floor room overlooked the parking lot.

He threw his bags on the bed and looked around at his temporary quarters. They were small and dark and had the same smell as the lobby.

He shrugged his shoulders and turned on a vintage TV set that was bolted to a battered dresser. He would watch CNN mindlessly until his rental car arrived. Then he could go out and explore. But when it did show up an hour later he decided that what he really needed was a drink.

He found the Beachcomber's restaurant and bar empty except for a baldheaded fifty-ish bartender and one waitress who was falling out of a maroon top in a futile attempt to divert attention from her age.

Michael ordered a beer, added a cheeseburger as an afterthought and threaded his way through the tables to a corner seat that afforded him a view of the beach and an outdoor pool area.

He looked at his beer and his burger for solace. He had been apprehensive over leaving an established mainstream daily for the mysterious world of the tabloids. The Courier was certainly like no other publication he had ever encountered. Its headquarters were sitting on prime real estate, surrounded by lush tropical gardens in a small seaside town. But the news room seemed much like any other, and the paper was certainly offering him big bucks and a chance for adventure.

A figure arriving at his table brought him back to earth with a jolt.

"Hi! It's Michael, right?"

He looked up. It was Jane Something-or-Other, the unforgettable body from the office.

"Uh, hi." His tongue had suddenly become paralyzed. "Have a seat?"

She pulled up a chair opposite him. "I'm glad I found you in the bar," she said.

Michael stared at her, instinctively checking out her cleavage before zeroing in on a warm white-toothed smile.

"Well, I'm glad you found me, too," he said, "though I wasn't really lost. I'm sorry, but I didn't catch your name at the office."

"Jane. Jane Connally."

She stared back, summing him up through twinkling blue eyes. Michael's brain cells began to melt.

"I was hoping you hadn't gone AWOL," she said. "Jack has decided to team us up together and he suggested we start with me buying you a beer."

Oh! He was just an assignment, not an assignation.

Jane beckoned the waitress over. "I'll have a chardonnay and another Heineken for Mr. Hanlon here," she said.

"You don't have to do that," said Michael.

"Yes I do. What Jack wants, Jack gets. Besides, it's a good way for us to get off on the right foot. If I buy you a beer, then you'll be in my debt."

"Sounds like a wonderful place to be."

"Speaking of wonderful places to be, welcome to the graveyard of journalism."

"Huh?"

"When you leave a big-city paper for the tabloids, you're likely to be ending your career. You'll find yourself so tainted you can't go back."

"I don't believe in looking back, or getting tainted."

Jane smiled but said nothing and Michael sensed a certain hostility. He needed to work on breaking the ice.

"Jack told me this place is a Courier hangout," he said, "but it isn't exactly teeming with customers."

"Don't worry, it'll soon be wall-to-wall people," said Jane. "A lot of the editors and reporters come here. And the local hookers and gold-diggers show up regularly. Everyone in town knows what kind of salaries The Courier pays and this place has seen the demise of many good relationships."

"Oh," said Michael feebly. "Well, I don't have to worry about that. Not yet."

Jane studied him for a second. *Did that mean he was available?*

"You have family in Detroit?" she asked.

Michael shook his head. "Not any more. My parents died in a car crash five years ago and I have no brothers or sisters."

Jane looked askance at him. An only child. So he was probably a spoiled brat. Life at The Courier would take care of that.

She took a sip of wine and smiled again. "So," she asked, "what brings you to The Courier besides the hundred-thousand reasons in your paycheck?"

Michael's eyes widened. "Does everyone know my salary?"

"Yeah. All our reporters start off with a hundred K. The problem is not many of them are around long enough to enjoy it. At The Courier everyone is on permanent probation and many new hires don't even last a month."

"Really?" This was not news Michael wanted to hear.

"Don't worry," said Jane. "Just do what you're told, keep a low profile and work at making the boss happy."

"You mean Jack? He seems pretty laid back."

"Jack laid back? Hardly. He's a curmudgeon before his time. But I don't mean Jack. He's just one of four editors with competing teams of reporters. The only person you have to satisfy is JC."

"JC? Er, Jesus Christ?"

"Close, but not quite. Jason Calloway, founder and owner of The Courier and the undisputed ruler of everything remotely connected to it. He's the president, CEO, editor-in-chief and head janitor. He doesn't exactly sweep the floors himself, but he looks under a microscope to make sure it's done to his satisfaction. He'll see every word you write and fly-speck everything you do."

"Busy guy. He sounds like a genius."

"He *is*," said Jane. She looked around furtively as the bar was slowly becoming abuzz with customers. She leaned closer to Michael and lowered her voice. "Like a mad scientist," she said. "He's the reason we sell four million papers a week but he's so driven he won't be happy until it's five. Don't try to understand him, because you won't. If you're lucky it'll be a long time before you get to meet him."

"I wondered why The Courier was being so generous. Jack made it sound as though I'd been picked out for something special. Now I know what he meant. I'm starting to feel like a spy who gets risky assignments because he has no family to miss him if he disappears."

Jane laughed mischievously.

"So what's the secret to making JC happy?" said Michael.

"His philosophy is simple. Stir readers' emotions. Make 'em laugh, cry, angry, proud. It doesn't matter what as long as they feel something."

Michael found himself starting to feel something as Jane leaned toward him again across the table. The scent of her hair was making his head swim.

"You never answered my question," she said. "Why did you give up a career on a metro daily for The Courier?"

Michael sipped his beer. "Largely boredom. The last straw was when an editor told me he wanted a story on grass in the suburbs. I thought he wanted me to expose a drug cartel, but he said, 'No, you idiot. It's the start of summer. Our readers want to know how they can have the best lawn in the neighborhood.' That's when I knew I needed to move on."

Jane laughed again then looked at him earnestly. "You don't have any qualms about the way we do business?"

"No. Should I?"

"No, but some reporters do. They leave journalism school thinking it's all about the First Amendment. Then they discover that The Courier has its own code of ethics. Checkbook journalism, for example. You know, paying sources."

Michael shrugged. He'd never thought about it before. But anything that was okay with Jane was okay with him. The thought of working alongside her every day was making him feel things where he'd forgotten he had things. If only she weren't being so damned businesslike. He wanted to learn more about Jane than about the job.

"When Jack suggested you buy me a drink did he also tell you to give me a pep talk?"

"No, but I want to be sure you succeed here, since I've been appointed your mentor."

Michael raised his glass in a mock salute. "I've never had one of those before. Are all mentors as attractive as you?"

Jane raised her eyebrows. "Are all protégés as pushy as you?"

"Sorry, but I was led to believe that being pushy is a reporter's stock-in-trade."

"I guess it is, but at The Courier you have to learn when and where to push and when not to. Popular journalism isn't brain surgery, you know, but we don't make up stories, despite what some people think. No space aliens, three-headed babies or people terrorized by vampires."

"I figured that. You don't have to pay someone six figures to make up stuff. Any school kid could do that."

Jane finished her wine and stood up. "Anyway, you'll be working with me until Jack decides you're acclimatized. Just remember to make it fun. You've already cost me a trip to the West Coast."

Another hint of hostility. Was she going to be a friend or a foe?

"Sorry," he said. "I would have loved to have gone there with you." *Or anywhere.*

Jane flipped her purse over her shoulder. "Never mind. I've really gotta rush. Got a date with a dog."

Oh! She has a boyfriend, of course. A black cloud had suddenly filled the room.

"His name must be Lucky."

"Actually it's Poopsie. My roommate is out of town so I'm taking care of her Shih-Tzu. He'll be looking for his walk and his dinner."

Jane wiggled her fingers in farewell. "See you in the office," she said with a look that seemed to promise more fun than Michael dared think about.

His eyes were glued to the door long after she had vanished through it. She had left him feeling like a wet noodle. All the guys in the office must be panting after her. He knew he had to beat the odds and succeed at The Courier. Life without this vivacious blonde reporter would be unbearable, but he had to work on that underlying hostility.

He glanced around. The bar was now filling with people and humming with conversation, but he didn't see any Courier faces that he remembered. And no one seemed to remember him.

He downed his beer and decided to take a run up the coast to Palm Beach and capture the feel of the millionaires' playground that had been teasing him.

He nosed his rental car north, skirted an oceanfront golf course and soared over an inlet that connected the Atlantic and the Intracoastal Waterway.

Then he found himself in the miniscule majesty of Manalapan, a tiny ocean-hugging community of exorbitant mansions where America's nouveau-riche hid behind eight-foot walls, wrought-iron gates and security cameras.

Michael could smell the money and the power as he passed the strip of opulent homes. The owner of The Courier lived around here somewhere. And he knew Manalapan was also the home of sports heroes and movie stars. Maybe he would get to write about some of them for his new paper. That's where the untold stories were: hiding behind the walls that guarded the fortresses of the rich and famous.

Chapter 5

Ravena Ventura lay back in her pink Roman tub and soaked up the luxury of a bathroom that would have swallowed most people's living rooms. She looked down at herself, cupping her breasts, then stroking her stomach, running her fingers down under the water, touching herself. Life may suck sometimes, she thought, but the body is good. Healthy, sexy and firm with no help from a plastic surgeon.

She tried to relax, reflecting on her life. She was in limbo, just as her agent had warned her, wary of making any sudden moves in any direction.

The future? Until she did make a move there would be no future. Perhaps Gordon would be the answer. Husband No. 2 maybe Or more likely maybe not.

Gordon Meriwether was the latest in a long string of men who had paraded through her life. As her attorney Meriwether shielded her from the worst of the world, like the tabloids that even made a big deal out of what she had for breakfast. Then there were the stalkers, the fast-talkers, the crazy fans, all the people who wanted a share of her fame, fortune and looks.

As a lover, Ravena rated Meriwether a five on a scale of one to ten. He was twelve years her senior, self-important and self-indulgent— all features that seemed to manifest themselves between the sheets. But he had a sense of humor and he appeared to care, perhaps in too fatherly a way. Unfortunately he also had a wife and he appeared to care about her too.

Ravena and Gordon had disguised their dates in L.A. as business meetings to keep the prying press at bay. But Ravena figured his wife must suspect something and the actress had no desire to be thrown into the spotlight as the "other woman" in a nasty divorce. She could get all the crappy publicity she needed without having to invite it.

Gordon had flown into Palm Beach and arranged a dinner date on the pretext of discussing some nonexistent business. It would be a good opportunity to tell him they should stick to an attorney-client relationship. If he balked at that, what the hell? Attorneys were a dime a dozen in America, weren't they? And Palm Beach County must be oozing with them. That's it! Ravena had decided—the first decision she had made about anything in weeks. A weight had been lifted from her shoulders.

Her thoughts were interrupted by the ringing of the phone on the wall across from the tub. She ignored the call. Someone would pick it up. Someone did, but this was followed by a buzz on the intercom.

"Excuse me, ma'am," said Marguerita, "but that lady is on the phone, the lady who visited you last week. Says it's important she speak with you."

"Okay," grumbled Ravena. "I'll take it in here."

She stepped out of the bath, grabbed a towel and picked up the receiver. "Hi, sis," said the familiar voice with a giggle. "Did you get my present?"

"What present, Liz? I have no idea what you're talking about. I'm in the middle of a bath and I have a dinner engagement. I was hoping you'd gone back to L.A."

"No, Raich," said Liz. "I like it here. And I sent you a package in the mail. You must have gotten it by now."

"I haven't looked at my mail in days. What the hell did you send me?"

"Go check out my gift, then call me. I sent a note with it with my new address and cell number."

Ravena's blood ran cold. Everything her sister did was usually bad news. "All right," she said. "I'll check my mail when I'm through here."

She hung up, found a robe and slippers and went downstairs to her study. If Liz had sent her something it would be on the pile of mail left on her desk. Most of her correspondence was fielded by her secretary, who would have opened and perused any mysterious package.

There it was, a large bubble envelope, sitting amid a heap of letters. She reached inside and pulled out a DVD. As she did a sheet of paper fluttered to the floor.

Curious and anxious, Ravena picked it up and her hand trembled as she read it.

Hi, Raich. How's it going? I thought you'd find this interesting. Take a look, then give me a call as soon as you've seen it. It's important! Love, Liz.

Ravena stared at the disk. What kind of game was her sister playing now? She slid the DVD back into the envelope, took it to her media room and plugged it in. She sat on the edge of a chair as the giant TV screen flickered to life.

She stared at the screen, numbed in horror for a few seconds, then stood and put a fist to her mouth to stifle a scream. She couldn't risk arousing the staff or, worse, her security people. With shaking hands she hurriedly shut off the TV, stuffed the DVD back in the envelope and reached for the phone.

"Well," said Liz. "Did you watch it? What do you think?"

"Oh, my God! What do you expect me to think? What do you think you're doing?"

"I need to see you. Tonight," said Liz curtly. "At my place, as soon as you can get here. It's important. And come alone."

The room was starting to swim. Ravena fought off waves of nausea as she hung up the phone. She sat down and put her head in her hands. She took deep breaths to control herself then threw the DVD in a drawer and dragged herself back upstairs. Gordon would have to wait.

She ignored the cocktail dress that Marguerita had put out for her and bundled herself into a pair of faded jeans and a white T-shirt she didn't even know she had. She grabbed a Hermes purse and hurriedly emptied its contents into a timeworn black shoulder bag she had intended to throw out years ago.

Her heart pounding, she picked up the bedside phone and called Meriwether to tell him she wasn't feeling well. Wasn't *that* the truth?

Then she phoned Marguerita. "I'm going out for a while," she said, "Please tell whoever's on security detail that I don't need anyone with me tonight."

The moonlighting cops who comprised Ravena's security people hated her solo ventures into the outside world. But she certainly didn't want cops around her tonight. She headed for the door, then had a second thought. She turned on her heels, pulled a .38 Special revolver out of the top drawer of her nightstand and dropped it into her bag.

Chapter 6

Jane was chagrined. So much for having fun. It was bad enough being forced to wet-nurse Michael, but he had turned out to be a human dynamo and was running rings around her.

Jack had assigned him to the desk next to her, given him a company laptop and explained the intricacies of an ugly green telephone that belonged in the Smithsonian. Michael had wasted no time using it to find someone who could speak Finnish—a part-time proofreader who had been under Jane's nose all along. It was embarrassing for someone who was supposed to be the star of the show.

Michael, meanwhile, welcomed Jane's attention but was out to demonstrate to Jack, JC and anyone else who cared that he didn't need a baby-sitter. He completed his first two simple assignments with enthusiasm and efficiency and was bent on proving himself to his new colleagues, especially Jane.

For the graveyard of journalism, The Courier was lacking in corpses waiting to be interred. The average age of the editorial staff was lower than Michael had expected. No ink-stained wretches here coasting toward retirement. Jack, who was in his late forties, seemed to be the oldest member of the group.

Michael was enjoying his new life-style and his overblown salary and he was on top of his game. The only problem was Jane. That undercurrent of hostility wouldn't go away. If only she would lighten up. Any hopes he'd had of a relationship beyond the workplace had all but evaporated.

She always had a ready smile, a ready pen to edit his copy, and ready suggestions on how to deal with The Courier's bizarre autocracy. She also had a ready acerbic wit and she used it like a saber in a fencing contest. And right now she was holding forth at Jack's desk.

"It's a pity we don't have a phone booth in the newsroom." she said.

Jack looked up at her, baffled. "Really? Why?"

"Because it would give Michael somewhere to change."

Jack Iverson guffawed, then looked around cautiously.

Michael had heard every word and it showed. What was he doing to piss Jane off? Maybe he should just ask her.

He decided that when she returned to her desk he would lean over her shoulder and whisper in her ear, "Clark Kent would like to invite Lois Lane to the Beachcomber for a drink after work."

He was trying to think of something clever to say if she turned him down when his phone rang. He glanced at it and saw that Line One was flickering. That was for Jack, who was frowning at his computer screen and thumbing through a sheaf of papers with his left hand. "Get that for me, will ya?" he asked across the aisle.

Michael put Superman on the back burner, picked up the handset, listened intently, then hunted around on his desk for a legal pad and a pencil. He scribbled for a few seconds, then covered the mouthpiece.

"Jack," he said in a stage whisper. "It's a source on Ravena Ventura. You know, the actress. Wanna pick up?"

"What about her?" growled Jack. "We get a million calls a day from people wanting to tell us stories about celebrities. Just get all the information you can and tell 'em we'll get back to them."

Michael shrugged and went back to the phone. His hand shook as he scribbled rapidly. Finally he hung up and turned to his editor again.

"This might be something good, Jack. That was her live-in housekeeper, wanting to sell us a story about Ravena's private life––what goes on behind closed doors in her home, what she's really like, her habits, her love life, all that stuff."

Jack swung around in his chair. "Is the woman crazy?" he said. "She'd lose her job, talking to us about all that. Is she for real?"

"I don't know if she's for real, but she's already lost her job. Says she got fired a couple of days ago and is steaming mad, pushed out into the cold after years of service. Her husband, too. He was the gardener and chauffeur."

Jack looked over his glasses. "What's her name? How much money does she want?"

"She didn't make an opening bid. She asked how much we'd pay for information and I said I'd have to talk to my editor and get back to her. Her name is Cruz. Marguerita Cruz. Husband is Alfonso. Mexicans, I think. She gave me a phone number where I can reach her. They've moved into an apartment somewhere up toward West Palm."

Michael was excited and couldn't understand why his editor wasn't sharing his enthusiasm.

"All right," said Jack after a brief moment of thought. "Call Neil Rowlands. He's chief of the Lantana police and knows everybody and everything in that area. Plus he and a lot of his officers moonlight as security for Ravena Ventura, as well as security for JC. Ask him if he knows this Marguerita Cruz, can verify that someone of that name is, or was, the housekeeper. If you get a positive answer fill out a lead sheet and give it to me."

The police chief didn't seem surprised to be hearing from The Courier. "Yeah," he told Michael. "The Cruzes both worked for Ravena Ventura. I'm amazed they got the ax, though Ravena seems to be cleaning house for some reason. She just laid off some of my men from her security force."

Jack Iverson raised his eyebrows when Michael told him about Ravena's sudden firing of her security cops. That seemed to spark some begrudging interest in the Cruzes' story.

"I'm gonna walk this in," he said. "If I put it through normal channels we could all be dead before it resurfaces. We'll catch up with the obvious questions later."

He disappeared into the glass-walled office of David Peterson, The Courier's executive editor, and was back after less than a minute.

"Peterson is going to rush this in to JC,'" he explained. "We can't do anything without his say-so, but hopefully he'll give us the okay to check this out. So stand by."

A surge of adrenaline roared through Michael's veins. Maybe he was about to get his first big celebrity assignment.

As instructed, he stood by. He sat at his desk and stared at the school of tropical fish swimming around on his screen saver. The Courier really was a strange place to work. A great tip out of the blue for what looked like a hot story and his editor seemed as nervous as a puppy that had just peed on the carpet.

The phone rang again. This time Jack grabbed it anxiously, mumbled something, and vanished from his desk. He was back in five minutes, beckoning Michael to follow him into the executive editor's office. Peterson was at the door, waiting to close it behind them.

"This could be great stuff," Peterson began, "but JC insists that we check these people out properly. It's tough to get information on Ravena Ventura and these Cruzes could be con artists. It's hard to believe that Ravena would suddenly throw a hardworking couple out on the street without good reason."

Jack turned to Michael. "JC asked me who had taken the call and he wanted to know all about you. I told him I was thinking of letting you run with this story, but he was concerned that you may be a little green and—"

"I'm not a little green. I know I've only been here five minutes but I've paid my dues in big-city journalism and, did you tell him, I *was* nominated for a Pulitzer?"

"I told him all that," said Jack. "I stuck my neck out for you. But JC doesn't give a shit about Pulitzer Prizes."

"Doesn't he want to meet me?"

"No. And be careful what you wish for."

Peterson picked up the reins as Michael glared at his editor.

"We need to move quickly on this," he said, "but JC doesn't want it to come back and bite us on the ass. The first thing to do is tie up this woman and her husband so they won't go anywhere else, figure out how much we're going to pay them, run a background check on them, then get them to sign a contract if they're legit. And they have to agree to a lie detector test."

"None of that will be a problem," said Jack, then turned to Michael. "JC agreed to let you work the story. He decided it would be a good test of your mettle. But Jane will be assigned to it as well. This could snowball into a great expose, or fizzle into nothing. If there's nothing there, okay, but if there's a lot of meaty stuff and we fuck it up, we're all in serious trouble, like jobless."

"JC always thought there was something hinky going on at Chez Ravena," said Peterson. "Since she moved to Florida she's become something of a recluse. Is she hiding something? Why did she move here? He's looking for answers to questions like that. You'd better get up to the Cruzes' place and bring them down here while Jack gets Research working on background checks. When they get here stick 'em in that small conference room down the hall from the coffee machine."

"Then call me and let me know," ordered Jack. "Don't leave 'em alone for a second. We don't want them getting cold feet, or calling The Enquirer."

Peterson stood up, indicating that the session was over. Michael felt like a fish that had been caught, gutted and thrown back into the water. But he knew he may have a major story in his back pocket and he was determined not to let it slip away.

Chapter 7

Less than twenty minutes later Michael was pulling up outside a rundown, single-story apartment building. A sign on the corner proclaimed it was F Street. The "F" could have stood for anything from Forgotten to Forlorn, or perhaps even Fuck This. The neighborhood was about six blocks of narrow, ratty streets with weeds clinging to life in broken sidewalks. The music and the aroma of food coming from the tiny homes identified the area as predominantly Hispanic.

The Cruz's apartment was one of six in a building set back from the street behind a parking lot and two stunted queen palms that appeared to be wishing they'd been planted somewhere else.

Michael pulled up at the curb and looked around. He'd just invested in a late-model white Mustang GT and was concerned about its safety, but there seemed to be no one around. He took a deep breath and headed for Apartment D.

Marguerita Cruz answered the door as soon as he reached it. She'd obviously been checking him out through the window.

"Come in, por favor," she said. "You are Senor Hanlon, si?"

"Call me Michael, Mrs. Cruz," he said. His knowledge of Spanish was almost zero and he prayed this wasn't going to be a problem.

"Michael," she repeated, nodding. It came out sounding a lot like "Miguel."

"This my husband, Alfonso," she said, indicating a small, balding man who belatedly tried to get up from the couch in the tiny living room. "*Complace ver que usted. Gracias*," he mumbled as he shook hands. Either he didn't speak English or he was faking it. Mrs. Cruz was undoubtedly going to be the family mouthpiece.

"As I explained on the phone, I need to take you down to The Courier offices," said Michael. "My editor will speak with you and there will be paperwork to complete."

Mrs. Cruz's soft brown eyes widened in alarm.

"Nothing to worry about," said Michael, hoping he was telling the truth. "It's just routine. We pay many of our sources and we will compensate you very well if you have good information we can use."

The woman nodded with a slight smile, but she still looked apprehensive.

Michael pressed on. "Now," he said. "Does Miss Ventura know where you are staying? Does she know you are here?"

"Oh, no, senor," she said. "She just go loco. Had fit about nothing and threw us out on the street. She wrote us check for wages to the end of the month and told us she never wanted to see us again or we would be in trouble."

"What kind of trouble?"

Mrs. Cruz shook her head slowly. "Not know, senor. We make no trouble. We live in United States for eight years, five years with Senora Ravena, Mostly in California."

Michael stared at her. He had to ask. "Are you legal?"

"Oh, si, senor. Senora Ravena herself arranged green cards."

"So she was pretty good to you as an employer?"

"Si, Senor Michael. Very good for long time. But after we move to Florida she change. Very quiet. Recently she get lots of bad temper. Then she start firing people."

"So what did you do to piss her off, er, get her angry?"

"Nada. I was cleaning, tidying up tapes she had left. She came in and saw me, said I was snooping and could not be trusted."

"Snooping at tapes? What kind of tapes?"

"Videotapes and some, what you call them, DVD discs. I not look what they were."

Michael shrugged. "Well, we'd better get going. My editor, Jack Iverson, is anxious to meet you both."

He shepherded the couple to his car and used the time on the drive back to the office to learn what he could about the Cruzes. They had lived in a small town near the California border and had been smuggled across by friends eight years ago. They soon found security, anonymity and no-questions-asked jobs in Los Angeles. Alfonso found work with a landscaping company and Marguerita cleaned homes for a maid service.

It was the latter that brought them to the attention of Ravena Ventura, who hired them both as her live-in housekeeper and gardener-chauffeur. And she pulled strings to make them legal. The Cruzes showed their gratitude with hard work and felt honored at the invitation to move to Florida with her when Ravena pulled up stakes in L.A.

They had been in awe of their employer, her money, lifestyle, influence and her position at the top of Hollywood's pecking order. She paid them six hundred dollars a week, gave them a rent-free apartment in her home, and they believed that, thanks to her, they had achieved the American dream.

Now they were out in the cold, for reasons they did not seem to understand, and the dream had turned into a reality-check nightmare. They were hiding their fear behind anger toward the woman they had trusted with their well-being. Michael was starting to feel sorry for them.

Once in the office, Michael directed them to the little-used conference room as ordered. He did his best to make them feel at home in the small space whose only furnishings were a mahogany table and eight matching chairs. He offered them coffee then called Jack's internal number from the phone at the head of the table.

Within seconds, Iverson was storming through the door with Jane on his heels. He was carrying a yellow legal pad, a tape recorder and an untidy sheaf of papers. He shook hands hurriedly with the Cruzes, dropped heavily into the chair at the head of the table and nodded for Michael and Jane to sit opposite them.

Jack was all business and Michael thought he was treating his potentially valuable sources rather brusquely. After all, they weren't being held captive and they could leave at any time and take their wares, whatever they may be, to other tabloids or one of the glossies.

Jack spread papers on the table in front of him and began machine-gunning questions at the Cruzes. They were looking perturbed and Michael wasn't sure whether they were having trouble with the language or were overwhelmed by his editor's approach.

"How long have you known Ravena Ventura? How long have you been in her employ? How close were you to her? Did you sign a non-disclosure agreement with her? Do you have intimate details about her lifestyle? Do you have names of her friends and associates? Do you know the names of people she doesn't like, especially other celebrities?"

Iverson elicited yes-no responses or a vague shrug to this barrage of questions.

He finally seemed satisfied and pushed a paper across the table toward them. "I need you to read this over," he said, "then sign it. It's a simple contract specifying that you are giving us factual information of your own free will in return for financial considerations. We will pay you five thousand dollars immediately after the first sit-down interview and another five thousand on publication of the story or stories resulting from these interviews. You must agree not to discuss this subject with anyone else, and especially with any other facet of the media. We will need to get these interviews on tape"—he pointed to the small recorder—"and I'm afraid we do have to insist on a lie detector test."

He made it sound as though he was reading them their Miranda rights. The Cruzes had been sitting rigidly until now, trying to focus on what Jack had been saying, but they were visibly startled at the mention of tape recorders and lie detector tests.

"No need to worry," said Jack. "It doesn't involve the police. The lie-detector test will be done by a private expert whom we will hire and pay and it will take place in our offices here. It's necessary to protect all parties, yourselves as much as us."

Alfonso Cruz nodded, but Michael wasn't sure he had a clue about what was going on.

"Si, si," said Marguerita. She was agitated and anxious to get the legalities over with. Jack seized the moment to wave a pen at them, point to sections in the contract and show them where they should sign. He had done everything but accuse them of a crime and Michael wondered if they were going to ask for an attorney. They didn't, but they were obviously hurt, scared and desperate.
Jack was exhibiting feigned authority, as though he did this every day. He scooped up the papers, said, "I'll get these copied and notarized for you," and disappeared through the door, signaling to Michael and Jane to stay put with the bewildered Cruzes.

He was back in less than a minute with a woman whom Michael recognized from Human Resources. "This is Jennifer," he informed the Cruzes. "She's a notary and will verify your signatures."

It was all over in five minutes and Michael's head was reeling. He could figure how the Cruzes felt.

"Now we'd like to take you to a nice place to stay until we're finished with the interviews," said Jack. "How about the Ramada Inn?"

"But we must go home," said Marguerita. "We need—"

"I understand," said Jack softly. "Michael and Jane will take you home to pack something for a few days, and then drive you to the Ramada in Highland Beach. It's on the ocean just a couple of miles south of here. The room and meals will be at our expense. Have a nice dinner at the hotel tonight, and we'll see you tomorrow. We can do the initial interview at the hotel if you like. It will be more pleasant than sitting in here. Let's say we start at ten o'clock."

The Cruzes mumbled agreement and allowed themselves to be shepherded out of the office.

While they walked back to the car Jack took his reporters aside. "Make sure they're comfortable and get everything they need," he whispered. "Use your car, Mikey, so they'll be without transportation and less likely to leave the hotel. Check in with me at the office early tomorrow, and then you and Jane can go down there and interview them. I know you speak Spanish, Jane, but use it only if you have any language problems. We'll evaluate the first day's tape and take it from there."

"Aren't you being a bit heavy handed with them?" ventured Michael. "They seem confused and scared."

"Confused we don't want," said Jack. "Scared is all right. Work on gaining their trust. If they're scared they're more likely to open up to someone they're at ease with. That's gonna be you guys!"

Jane sat in the back seat and exchanged a few words in Spanish with Mrs. Cruz as Michael drove off with his charges and his instructions. It was the first time Jane had opened her mouth since the Cruzes' phone call and Michael couldn't fathom why. Maybe she was currently bad-mouthing him in Spanish. Why the hell were women so difficult to understand?

Michael just wanted to impress his editor with a gossipy exclusive. He might be sitting on a story as explosive as a keg of dynamite. That would cement his position as a Courier reporter.

Chapter 8

Michael walked into The Courier newsroom at eight the next morning to find Jack and Jane tête-à-tête at the editor's desk.

"Good. About time you got here," grunted Jack. "I was just going over a few things with Jane. Make sure you get everything on tape. And find out if they have any pictures. You know, photos of themselves at Ventura's mansion, or, even better, photos of themselves with Miss Superstar herself and any members of her entourage. Managers, lawyers, agents, showbiz friends, and especially men who might be lovers." He paused, then added, "And women who might be lovers, too. That would be great."

Michael's eyes widened. Jack, caught up in the moment, moved on.

"Just make sure you make it sexy. We may be on a wild goose chase but Ravena Ventura really is one of the mysteries of the Hollywood scene. She gets a lot of publicity, but it's mostly generated by her own people to satisfy her own ends. What readers want is the kind of publicity she *doesn't* want to generate. If these Cruzes don't have anything juicy, get whatever nitty-gritty details you can. Background material is always useful and the Cruzes may be able to give us leads to things we can chase down independently.

"For example, make sure you ask 'em about that attorney of hers, Meriwether. He's a heavy hitter on the West Coast and the paparazzi are always catching him and Ravena at restaurants together. And see if you can get any dirt on her ex-husband, Louis Frankel, who also used to be her manager. He was a lying sack of shit who gave us a hard time, but she dumped him about three years ago for two-timing her. Maybe he's still in the mix somewhere. And try to find out why she moved here from L.A."

Jack finally ran out of steam. "Okay kiddies," he barked. "Go get 'em. Call in periodically to let me know how it's going. I've got a chunk of dough and my ass on the line with this. JC thinks Ravena is a tough egg to crack and this is the first chink we've ever found in her armor."

Michael suppressed a smile at the garbled clichés as he and Jane scooped up the audiotape paraphernalia and headed for the parking lot. He suggested they start with breakfast at Denny's, and was surprised when Jane agreed.

After ordering coffee and perusing the menu Michael decided to bite the bullet.

"I'm glad we're finally getting a couple of moments alone," he said. "Something has been bothering me and I need your input."

"Really?" Jane seemed taken aback. "Okay, shoot."

"Actually, I just wanted to tell Lois Lane that Michael Hanlon isn't Superman and is having a tough time just trying to be Clark Kent. I don't know what I've done to piss you off, but we aren't having the fun you talked about when we first met. I'm doing something wrong here, but I don't know what it is."

Jane leaned on her elbows and stared thoughtfully at her coffee cup.

"You aren't doing anything wrong, Michael," she said at last. "And that's the problem. Jack assigned me to show you the ropes, but you know them better than I do. You're a good reporter, a very good reporter, and you don't need me holding your hand. The truth is you're shaking my confidence. When I first came to The Courier all I got was blonde jokes and offers of sex. I had to prove that I was no bimbo, and I did it by becoming aloof and hard-nosed and having the best work ethic in the office. Like you, I work hard not only to keep my job at The Courier but to be the best at it. And now I'm in your shadow. I'm sorry if I've been a bitch. I try to reserve that side of me for the job."

"I see. Look, I can't help being me and you can't help being you. It's just that I don't want to be looking for a whip and a chair every time we work a story together."

Jane gave him a slight smile and stuck out a hand across the table. "I promise not to claw you to death. Can we start over?"

Michael took her hand in both of his and grinned. "Absolutely. And when we get time Clark Kent would like to buy Lois Lane dinner."

"I'll settle for a drink. But right now we've got big fish to fry and we do need to get down to business. I realize the Cruzes' story is really yours, not mine, but I'd appreciate it if you'd let me lead the interview. We'll be toast if we don't come back with something good and I've been in this territory before."

Michael nodded. Jane was a tabloid veteran. He had no problem with her teaching him new tricks.

She seemed to relax over bacon and hash browns and Michael decided that one of his new goals in life was to dine with her more often.

When they made contact with the Cruzes, however, her persona changed again and Michael began to wonder which was the real Jane. She became as abrasive as Jack Iverson—all piss, vinegar and business. While Michael was trying to put the couple at ease with encouraging remarks, Jane was bouncing hard-line questions off them. He was like Mr. Nice Guy in a good cop/bad cop scenario and after two hours he felt as if he'd been put through a wringer. So he suggested a break for lunch.

He and Jane left the Cruzes alone at the hotel and drove up to the Beachcomber to unwind and compare notes. They had gotten a lot of background material, names and profiles of many members of Ravena's support group—her manager, lawyer, agent, financial adviser, publicity maven, and the business consultant who organized her cosmetic and perfume lines. They found out what Ravena liked to eat and where she ate it, where she went and who she went with. What they didn't have was what they were really seeking: intimate details about her personal life.

"Quit worrying," said Jane as Michael swung into the Beachcomber parking lot. "We'll get something. Alfonso drove Ravena around, so he knows everywhere she goes, and probably who she meets. And Marguerita was in a position to know just about everything that went on behind Ravena's walls. Remember, what's important to us may not seem important to the Cruzes. We've got to lead them to where we want them to go."

After a leisurely meal they drove slowly back to the Ramada and parked outside the Cruzes' door. A knock brought no response and panic welled in Michael's breast. He peered through the window and cupped his hands to ward off the glare but he could see no signs of life in the room.

"They've gone!" he exclaimed. "Looks like they've run out on us!"

Chapter 9

Michael turned to find Jane with her arms folded, grinning from ear to ear.

"Don't be silly," she said. "Where the hell are they gonna go? And how are they going to get there?"

"They probably got cold feet after we left and called a cab."

"I doubt it. They're still hurt and angry and looking for revenge against Ravena. We're the only ones who can help them with that. Besides, they could use the money. Let's go check out the restaurant and the pool."

To Michael's relief and embarrassment they found the Cruzes sitting at a patio table under a huge red and white umbrella. He suddenly felt stupid and his confidence took a nosedive. He was desperate to please Jane and terrified that he'd screw up and be tossed out of The Courier on his ear, another victim of Jason Calloway's penchant for perfection.

The Cruzes had strolled briefly on the beach after lunch and were taking a mini siesta by the pool. They seemed relaxed and ripe for the kill as the reporters ushered them back into their room.

Jane and Michael decided to start with Alfonso, who appeared to have spent his lunch hour learning English.

"You were Ravena's chauffeur?" asked Jane.

"Si."

"So you drove her everywhere she went?"

"No, no." He wrinkled his brow, searching for words. "Ravena drive, but I drive when she go potty."

That brought laughter all around, even from Alfonso, though he didn't know why.

"When she go *potty*?"

"*Si. Cuando ella va a las partes.*"

"Ah! When she goes to parties. So you took her to parties, nightclubs, restaurants. Perhaps to a liaison with a friend, like a boyfriend. Did she have any regular boyfriends? Special men?" A pause, then, "Or women?"

Alfonso nodded and Jane snapped to attention.

"In Los Angeles I drive Ravena to meet lawyer in restaurant," he said. "No paparazzi. I wait two hour. They come out, she tell me go, take car home. Say she and lawyer have business."

Apparently Alfonso had been dismissed without so much as a thank you or a doggie bag and was left to watch Ravena depart in Gordon Meriwether's car. Alfonso had been hungry, thirsty, tired and bored . . . and now very pissed off, too. He had deserved better than that, he explained in torturous English, and became determined to tell her so. So, throwing caution to the winds, he had followed Meriwether's car to a motel in Burbank. Then fear got the better of him and he decided to go home after they disappeared into one of the ground-floor rooms.

This was hot stuff. Obviously Ravena liked to live dangerously. Michael stepped in to press for more and Alfonso suddenly remembered taking Ravena to South Beach in the limo, where she hooked up with a group of showbiz names.

"Did she take any minders with her?" asked Jane.

"Miners?"

"No, no. Security. Police. Bodyguards."

Alfonso shook his head. "No," he said, "clubs have plenty bodyguards. They fight with photographers."

According to Alfonso the group skipped from nightclub to nightclub, getting louder and drunker as the evening wore on. It ended with

Ravena and a rapper named Bobo Bolum falling into the back of the limo, laughing hysterically and demanding to be driven to "Ravena's Hideaway."

Before Ravena had the inspiration to close the back-seat partition, she had Bobo in the mother of all lip locks and Alfonso had been hard-pressed to keep his eyes on the road.

Jane and Michael eagerly tried for more, but it was the best Alfonso could do. So Michael turned to Marguerita.

"You must know everything that goes on in Ravena's home," she said, "both here and in L.A."

The housekeeper smiled shyly. "No," she said. "Not everything. But I remember parties in Los Angeles."

"Was this Bobo guy there?" asked Jane.

"No. Never see him before we come to Florida. But sometimes rock stars show up and movie stars like Ashley Browne and Lance McGowen. I remember party in Beverly Hills. It mucho hot, they all go in pool. Senor McGowen take off all clothes and dive in, and soon they all run around naked, laughing and screaming and splashing all over. They all very drunk and keep disappearing into house."

"For sex?" asked Jane.

"Perhaps. I know for coke."

"Did Ravena do coke?" asked Michael.

"Si. I see Miss Ravena doing cocaine. And I'm the one who clean up. Hollywood people have plenty money but not much sense. And very untidy."

"What about parties here in Florida?" asked Michael.

"When Miss Ravena first come here she throw parties," said Marguerita. "She hired plane for Hollywood friends. But they not come anymore, except for her lawyer."

She paused to sip from a glass of wine, then continued. "Miss Ravena changed after she move to Florida. She got very serious and shut herself off from people. I think she wanted to join that Palm Beach group. You know, like the Kennedys and Trumps. But I don't think they want her company. I guess she too, well . . . just an actress."

"What about her husband, Louis Frankel?" asked Michael.

"Oh, we not see him much," said Marguerita. "He did not like us." She shuddered. "Not like anybody, unless they young girls. He tried to fire us but Miss Ravena wouldn't hear of it. And she controlled the money. So he left us alone after that. Think he was embarrassed. Then one day Miss Ravena come home and find him in their bed with young actress. Plenty fireworks that day. Yelling, screaming, throwing things. Girl running around the house with no clothes, screaming and crying. Senor Louis, he pack bags and move out. We never see him again."

Michael was fascinated. It sounded like a scene from one of Ravena's movies.

Finally he and Jane declared the session over. They had depleted the room's minibar in an attempt to oil the Cruzes's lips and revive their memories. How much of their material was usable was questionable. There were libel laws, and how much credence could you give to a couple of fired Mexican domestics? After all, they had circumvented the law to enter the country. And they were being paid good money to tell all. Those were headaches for Iverson and Peterson . . .and Jason Calloway.

* * *

It was getting late when they got back to the office and the newsroom was almost deserted. But Jack was there, waiting to debrief his reporters. They both tried to put an exciting spin on it, but Jack, true to form, didn't seem impressed.

He took the tapes and said, "I'll get these transcribed right away. We'll have hard copy in the morning. Then we're gonna have to dig for backup sources. Did you get any photos?"

"Some," said Jane. She opened her purse and pulled out an envelope. Jack tipped the contents onto his desk. A few fading Polaroids and a dozen drugstore prints. The Cruzes alone, the Cruzes posing separately with a smiling Ravena, the Cruzes with Ravena and her secretary at a birthday party for Marguerita thrown by the staff. And there was one shot of the Cruzes posing at the entrance to Ravena's Beverly Hills mansion, taken by a security guard on the day Alfonso and Marguerita got their green cards.

Jack fanned them out on his desktop. "Not bad, considering," he said. "At least it helps prove they really were there."

"Did you ever doubt it?" asked Michael.

"Sure," said Jack "Don't ever believe anything just because someone tells you it was so. Remember the old newsman's motto: If your mother says she loves you, check it out."

Michael burst out laughing but turned it into a nervous fit of coughing when Jack glared at him, then dismissed his reporters for the day.

"Going over to the Beachcomber?" Michael asked Jane hopefully as they reached their cars.

"No," she sighed. "I'm too bushed. And Jack pisses me off. He never gets excited about anything. To him everything is a problem. I swear he finds issues where they don't exist so he can solve them himself and feel important. I'm going home to wash my hair and sit in a bubble bath."

"Sounds like a plan." *Maybe she'd like company.*

"Guess I'll see you tomorrow then," he added when no invitation was forthcoming.

* * *

The office was already a hive of activity when Michael got there the next morning. As usual, most of the action was centered around Iverson's desk.

Jack dumped copies of the tape transcripts in front of Michael and Jane. "Go through them carefully," he ordered. "There'll be a quiz later."

Michael knew he wasn't joking and thirty minutes later Jack announced, "Conference time. Let's go." He scooped up his paperwork and headed for Peterson's office in a Charlie Chaplin quickstep.

Peterson shuffled papers nervously as the three of them found seats across from his desk and Michael waited for him to lavish praise for a job well done. He was disappointed. Getting dirt on movie stars was all in a day's work at The Courier.

Peterson went through the transcripts line by line, questioning almost everything. Jack jumped on anything Peterson didn't query. Michael likened it to the Spanish Inquisition and let Jane do most of the talking. She'd been through this before.

They were down to the last two pages of the transcripts when the door suddenly burst open. The newsroom buzz flooded into the office as Marty McDonald, one of the paper's veteran reporters, stepped into the room.

Michael's blood ran cold and his heart hit the pit of his stomach as McDonald
announced, "Sorry to interrupt, David, but we just got a call from Fred Wandsworth in the sheriff's office. They've found a car in a canal in Loxahatchee. There's a body in it. And they think it might be that actress, Ravena Ventura."

Chapter 10

Ravena Ventura dead? Shock waves were bouncing off the newsroom walls like ping-pong balls on a springboard.

"I'd better get this under control," said Peterson. "Get all the editors in here right now," he yelled to his secretary.

Then he turned to Jack. "Get the location from Mac and put someone on the scene right now. Let's not go nuts. It's probably bullshit. What the hell would Ravena Ventura be doing up in Loxahatchee?"

Iverson turned to Michael and Jane. "All right, kiddies," he said. "This is your beat. Get up there and report in as soon as you have something."

"I'll drive," said Michael as he and Jane rushed into the parking lot. "But where is this Loxa-something? I've never heard of it."

"It's Loxahatchee," said Jane grimly as she got into the Mustang. "A West Palm suburb, out in the boonies. It's an Indian name for River of something. Turtles, I think."

"Cute. But it sounds like a Jewish breakfast to me."

"I need to figure out where we're going. Do you have a GPS or something?"

Michael nodded toward the glove box. She pulled out a street map and opened it up on her lap. "Very high-tech, I see," she said.

Michael grinned. "I'm working on it. What kind of a neighborhood is this Loxahatchee?"

"Well, like Peterson said, it's not an area where you'd expect to find the likes of Ravena Ventura. It's a little bit of country wedged between suburban cities. The people who live there like to play by their own rules."

"Are we talking hillbillies?"

"No. Far from it. There are some shacks and mobile homes in there but they're outnumbered by large homes and little horse farms on acreage carved out of the swamps. There are a lot of dirt roads and some steep drops into narrow canals that stop the whole place from flooding every time it rains. I can't image why Ravena would be in that area, unless she got lost. Locals used to joke that Loxahatchee was one of those places where all the footprints go in and none come out."

"Great. But if Ravena's footprints don't come out, our big story with the Cruzes could be shitcanned."

"Look on the bright side. We'd have enough stuff to devote a special issue to her. And the dead can't sue."

"We'd run that stuff if she's dead? Isn't that kinda, like, below the belt? I mean, people don't usually speak ill of the dead."

"Of course we'd run it. We report on life as it really is, from the cheesy to the sleazy. People like to know that celebrities are just as vulnerable as anyone else to the crap life throws at you."

Michael looked at Jane out of the corner of his eye. She had looks that could melt steel, but on the job she had ice in her veins and a mouth that could shock a truck driver. What was she really like under all that professional armor?

"Why would the sheriff call and tell us about this?" he asked.

"Sheriff Wandsworth is a big friend of The Courier. He was head of our security for a time when he was a deputy, and JC donated a lot of dough to his election campaign. I told you we can worm our way into most places. Here," she said, "take the next exit and head west on Southern Boulevard."

Michael drove past the perimeter of Palm Beach International Airport as Southern Boulevard took them away from the built-up area. Tacky nudie bars and pawn shops gave way to lumber yards and plant nurseries as the city dissolved into untamed countryside.

Jane pored over the map and directed Michael to a narrow well-worn dirt track that disappeared into the brush. She reminded him that homes lay hidden in the tangle of jungle around them.

Less than a quarter mile from the main road they found the way blocked by four police cruisers where the dirt road skirted an open area of grass and scrub. Beyond the knot of cars was a tow truck that had already pulled a light green Lexus from a canal swollen by recent rains. The car, encased in mud at the front, was now perched precariously near the edge of a steep embankment.

"Hi, Jane," said one of the officers. "Didn't take you long to get here."

"Right, Charlie. You know The Courier. Always first, always right, always on top of things." Jane introduced Michael to Charlie. Like many of his colleagues, Deputy Charles Noonan worked for Courier security when he was off the clock.

"No other press here?" she asked him.

"Not yet," said Charlie, "but I'm sure they won't be long. They'll all be monitoring the scanners. But they aren't going to get any big TV satellite vehicles in here. And I'm afraid you're all going to be in for a great disappointment. The woman in the car isn't that actress after all."

"You mean we came all the way out here for nothing? Why did you guys think it was her?"

The officer looked a little embarrassed. "We got a nine-eleven from a guy who lives around here and was out looking for his dog. He spotted the car in the water. All you could see was the trunk. Obviously, the first thing we did was check for people inside the vehicle. We found one body and Bulldog Drummond over there thought he recognized it as Ravena." Charlie pointed to one of the other deputies, who was chatting with the tow truck driver.

"Bernie Drummond has been moonlighting as Ravena's security," he explained. "He knows she owns a car similar to this one and the woman who was behind the wheel does look like Ravena. But we ran the plate and found it was rented out at the airport two weeks ago to an Elizabeth Thomas. We've since confirmed that Ravena is very much alive. It seems Elizabeth Thomas is Ravena's sister. *Twin* sister. So you can see the confusion. Ravena wanted to come up here but we talked her out of it. She can identify the body later at the morgue. She seems to be in shock anyway and some of our people are at her house with her."

"Where's the body?" asked Michael.

"Still in the car," said Charlie. "The medical examiner has been notified but we can't really make a move until the dickheads get here."

"Dickheads?"

"Detectives are on their way."

Jane wrinkled her nose. "Detectives investigating a car crash?"

"Well, we don't know what happened and we don't really know the cause of death yet. We figure she got trapped in the car and drowned when it went over the bank, but until someone confirms it as an accident we have to treat it as a possible homicide."

Michael caught his breath. "You mean murder?"

"It's doubtful, but the department has to be prepared, especially in such a high-profile case. If the deceased is who we think it is we're dealing with the death of a celebrity's sister."

An approaching siren heralded the arrival of a small black sedan that had seen better days. It kicked up a clod of dirt as it skidded to a stop by one of the patrol cars.

Two men in well-worn suits clambered out. They had to be the detectives. They shot a curious glance at the two reporters, then ignored them.

"What we got here?" one of them asked Charlie.

"Body of a female, age about 35 to 40, wedged behind the wheel." He pointed to the Lexus, which was still dripping fetid canal water from the fenders.

"Fish or gators been at her?" asked the detective. "How long she been in the water?"

"Don't know," said the officer, "but she's not in too bad a shape . . . except for being dead. Being inside the car probably kept some of the bigger predators away. We're still waiting for the ME."

The detective waved toward Michael and Jane. "Who's this?" he asked.

"Two reporters from The Courier. Only press here so far, but I'm sure others are on their way."

"Well, we need to get 'em out of here. We don't want body photos in the papers and we don't need them nosing around." He walked over to the two reporters.

"I'm Detective Harry Henderson," he said, sticking his thumbs in his belt. "This looks like a simple accident but right now it's a crime scene investigation and I'm afraid you'll have to back off while we do what we gotta do. We'll make a statement to the press as soon as we've got something to state."

"We won't get in your way, detective," Jane assured him with a toss of her hair and an overpowering flash of pearly whites. "But can't you just fill us in on the fly? We'll wait quietly over here."

Henderson's order to get lost was cut short by a huge black Suburban that lumbered into view around the bend. The medical examiner was finally on the scene with a vehicle that successfully blocked in all the others, including Michael's Mustang.

Henderson and the ME walked over to the Lexus, where the other detective had the driver's door open and was perusing the body.

Michael and Jane edged over as close as they could, trying to become invisible while they caught fragments of any conversation.

"Head injury," announced Henderson's partner. "Look, around the temple. No other visible sign of serious injury. Maybe she got banged around as she went down the bank. There's been a lot of rain lately so any skid marks have probably been washed away in this crappy mud hole."

"Fingerprints?" asked Henderson.

"We can check for 'em at the pound," said his colleague. "This woman was probably alone when it happened. Maybe got lost or started to doze off behind the wheel. The driver's side window is open a ways. She likely just lost control of the car in the mud, was knocked out when she hit her head as she careened down the bank, and drowned." He turned to the medical examiner. "We just need to take some pictures then I think she's all yours, doc."

The ME nodded. He looked bored. Cars in canals were a common occurrence in South Florida.

Newsmen from the *Palm Beach Post* and two local TV stations arrived just after sheriff's deputies had bagged the body and were loading it into the Suburban.

Detective Henderson was irritated by the invasion of the press corps and tried to shoo them away, back to the main road. Michael wondered if the local reporters knew the deceased appeared to be related to a major movie star. Probably not, or they would have been here sooner. It was just another car in a canal to them, too. Only a good story on a slow news day.

Henderson conferred with the medical examiner as the doctor was getting behind the wheel, then turned to the knot of reporters and cameramen who had stood their ground as long as they could.

"All right, folks," he said. "Party's over. We're all outta here. We're going to let the ME do his job and we'll have a statement for all of you later today."

Everyone piled into their vehicles but Michael was reluctant to leave. "These detectives didn't do much detecting," he said to Jane. "They didn't even check down the bank where the car went over.

Maybe there's nothing to check. But at least they could *look*. And they barely gave the car the once-over."

"I'm sure they'll do that when they get it to the police pound," said Jane. "Anyway, if it's just an accident, who cares? I'll call Jack and fill him in. What we need now is something emotive from, or about, Ravena. She must be beside herself. Don't forget, there's nothing better for us than an out-of-control celebrity."

She paused, deep in thought, and stared at Michael. "It's strange, you know," she said. "The Cruzes never mentioned Ravena's twin sister. I wonder why."

Chapter 11

Jack Iverson seemed undaunted by the news that the body in the car was not a movie star. He was chomping at the bit over new twists in his Ravena Ventura expose.

"We've got to switch our focus to this twin sister," he said. "Obviously the Cruzes didn't think she was very important and we were asleep at the wheel not to jump on it."

Michael knew that "we" meant "you" even though news veteran Jack Iverson hadn't paid much attention to Elizabeth Thomas either.

"Anyway," Jack said, "I had Research run LexisNexis on her. Seems that when they were seven years old Elizabeth and Rachel Thomas had a role on a short-lived TV sitcom called 'Daddy's Darling.' It sounds like crap, and it must have been, because even though the kids were cute it didn't make it through a second season. Remember this was more than thirty years ago—before our time. Well, before yours . . . and almost before mine!

"After the show the Thomas twins disappeared back into obscurity. Their parents, who had been managing them, were unable to find more show business work for them and started squabbling between themselves. The mother took the kids' money and ran. No one has ever heard from her since. She may even be dead by now. We know the father is. George Thomas looked after the twins and their older sister, Emily, for a few years but they went to live with grandparents after he went off the rails and started hitting the sauce. He finally blew his brains out in a hooker motel in South Central L.A.

"Both twins dropped out of school after Emily split. They bummed around and got menial jobs, but Rachel found a way out of her loser lifestyle. She distanced herself from Elizabeth, tried to get acting jobs, and wound up in the bed of that erstwhile producer, Louis Frankel. He eventually became her manager and her mentor, then her husband. He's now her ex, but he's the guy who got her back into show business. She changed her name to Ravena

Ventura and the rest is history. There's a whole generation grown up now that never heard of the Thomas twins."

"But what happened to Elizabeth?" asked Jane.

"The opposite side of the coin, I gather," said Iverson. "What *didn't* happen to her? As she and her sister became estranged, Elizabeth's life went more and more downhill. We found arrest records for DUI, disorderly conduct, resisting arrest, possession of drugs and drug paraphernalia, even soliciting. You name it, she did it. But she was never convicted of anything. Obviously someone was looking after her interests. Maybe Ravena Ventura does have a heart after all."

Michael was impressed. "How did you dig up all this so fast?" he asked.

Iverson smiled. "It wasn't exactly rocket science. I got L.A. out of bed. Most of this stuff is in the public domain. You just have to know where to look for it. In any event, there's a great story here. We need to flesh out details on the accident, find out what Elizabeth was doing in Loxahatchee and whether she'd been in touch with her sister. And we've got to get Ravena's side of this whole thing somehow."

"Ravena Ventura hates the press," Jane reminded him. "She's not going to talk about this incident any more than she has to. And she certainly won't talk to us at all."

"Come on, Jane," said Jack. "You know we can get people to talk. We've just got to find a way to get close to her. With this terrible family tragedy she'll be looking for a shoulder to lean on, and it might as well be ours. We can offer her an outlet for all the sensitive emotions she can dredge up to show the public what a caring, loving human being she really is."

Jane laughed. "You are a cynical bastard, aren't you? You know damn well she's a bitch on wheels and hates us like poison. And with all that stuff from the Cruzes she's going to hate us even more."

"The Cruzes' stuff has to be on hold right now. Once the sister's death has played itself out we'll be able to segue into it." His eyes glazed over. "RAVENA EXPOSED," he announced, stretching his outspread hands across his face to embrace a huge invisible headline. He leaned back in his chair and grinned like a kid with a new toy, then quickly collected himself.

"We need to talk to the Cruzes again," he said. "Maybe Elizabeth hadn't played much of a role in Ravena's life in recent years. But they must know something about her and the whole sibling relationship."

Iverson turned to Michael. "Why don't you and Jane run down to the hotel and find out everything they know about Elizabeth Thomas. Then we should arrange the lie-detector test and front them some more money. But we need to keep 'em under wraps until all this blows over. Persuade them to stay at the Ramada until further notice. I'm sure they'll go for it as long as we're picking up the tab."

* * *

"My turn to drive," Jane told Michael as they left the building. "It'll make me feel useful. Maybe I'm jaded but I see nothing for us but an uphill struggle. All the dailies and networks will be on top of it. I'm bummed because it's taken the edge off our exposé."

"Maybe not," said Michael as Jane clicked the doors open on a small silver Mercedes. "Perhaps the stuff we have on Ravena will be more meaningful, coming on the heels of a tragedy in her life rather than out of the blue."

"I guess. I just hope we can get some inside stuff from the Cruzes on this Cinderella sister. They probably didn't tell us anything about her because we never asked."

Michael and Jane found the Cruzes in their favorite spot by the pool. It was no secret to them that Ravena had a twin sister with a questionable lifestyle, and they were shocked to learn of her death. But they seemed to be short on information about her.

"She didn't visit Ravena at all?" asked Jane.

Marguerita hesitated. "I not sure," she said. "Not in California but I think I see her here once, recently. A woman came to the house to see Miss Ravena. She look a lot like her, but she had dark hair. But two weeks later she called on the phone and I recognized the voice as her sister's. She used to call Miss Ravena all the time in Los Angeles."

"Did you catch any of their conversations?" asked Michael.

"Oh, no! I would never listen to Miss Ravena's private conversations."

I'll bet, thought Michael. *You were fired for snooping.*

"Did you get the idea there wasn't much love lost between Ravena and her sister?" asked Jane.

Marguerita looked confused, as though she didn't understand the question, or didn't want to. "Don't know, ma'am," she said. "But every time the sister called, Miss Ravena had very bad mood. And sometimes, after she call, she go out in her car alone. I often thought she go to meet her sister somewhere."

"She never talked about her sister to you? Never mentioned her in conversation?"

"No. Except once, she told me, very angry, she had to go take care of her 'stupid' sister. She asked me to phone and cancel a meeting with her accountant."

A shrill melody from Jane's cell phone brought the conversation to a halt. It was Jack.

"How's it going?" he asked. "You two had better get moving. Ventura's publicist is going to issue a statement on the death of Ravena's sister and the sheriff's office is planning a press conference at three o'clock. Sheriff Wandsworth is going to handle it himself and he's given us the heads up. Seems there's evidence of foul play!"

Chapter 12

Despite ominous rain clouds, the Sheriff's Department had set up a small podium and a microphone outside their West Palm Beach headquarters on Gun Club Road.

Michael and Jane waited with a score of media people. Most of them were TV crews with trucks that had given birth to miles of cable that snaked around the parking lot.

Michael felt energized. This was how he had imagined life at The Courier would be. He was working on a major story alongside a girl who was giving him serious carnal urges. Things didn't get much better than this.

The two Courier reporters edged their way to the front of the throng just in time for Sheriff Wandsworth's arrival. With silver hair and a navy blue civilian suit he looked more like a savvy businessman than an elected law enforcement officer. To his right was Detective Henderson, who looked like what he was, and gave the impression that he'd rather be someone else and somewhere else . . . anywhere else. A prim-looking woman in horn-rimmed glasses took a position to the sheriff's left.

"Who's the woman?" Michael asked Jane under his breath.

"That's Harriet Usher, Ravena's publicist. We call her Husher because it fits what she does best. She's more of an anti-publicist, hushing up everything we want to know about her clients. She represents most of the celebrities who call Florida home and she's trying to build up a reputation here that she can take to Hollywood."

Michael nodded as the Sheriff took center stage.

"Ladies and gentlemen of the press," he began. "As I believe you know, the body of a woman was found in a car submerged in a canal in Loxahatchee this morning. The victim has been identified as Elizabeth Thomas, most recently of Los Angeles, who happens to be the twin sister of the movie star, Ravena Ventura. At first we thought Miss Thomas drowned when she lost control of her vehicle, a rented Lexus, on the muddy dirt road in Loxahatchee. We figured she was trapped in the car after it skidded over the embankment and down a steep incline into the water. However, a preliminary report from the coroner's office suggests that Miss Thomas may not have met her death in this fashion. The medical officer reports that a head injury, rather than drowning, is the likely cause of her death. And there is evidence that she was dead before the vehicle went into the canal."

There was an audible gasp from the knot of news people and a sudden clamor of questions. Sheriff Wandsworth raised his hand to silence them.

"Our investigation is continuing, and at this time we are treating this case as a homicide. I regret I can take no questions at this time. Our sympathies go to Miss Ventura, and her spokesperson, Ms. Usher, has a statement she would like to make on Miss Ventura's behalf."

Wandsworth smoothly stepped away from the microphone and allowed the publicist to slide in front of him to take charge at the podium.

"Good afternoon," she began. She squinted in the sunlight and assumed the pose of a schoolteacher about to read the riot act to a second-grader.

"Miss Ventura is obviously very distraught and distressed by her sister's death," she announced gravely. "She and Elizabeth were very close and indeed Miss Thomas had recently moved to Florida so they could spend more quality time together. Unfortunately those plans will now never bear fruit." She made it sound as though peace talks to avert World War III had just collapsed.

"Miss Ventura is confident that the perpetrator or perpetrators of this crime will be apprehended and brought to justice," she continued. "She will use all the means at her disposal to assist the police in their investigation and at the appropriate time she will arrange for a private funeral so that her sister may rest in peace. Miss Ventura asks that you please respect her privacy at this difficult time. Thank you."

The crowd erupted in another cacophony of questions, but Usher cut them off. "The sheriff's office will keep you informed of developments in the investigation of this heinous crime as they are warranted."

She stepped away from the podium and Sheriff Wandsworth resumed his position. "I would like to reiterate that we have no more information to impart at this time. Detective Henderson here is in charge of our investigation and will report to you on a regular basis. We will schedule another briefing when we will be in a better position to answer your questions. Thank you for coming."

With that Wandsworth turned tail and was followed back into the building by Usher and his detective, who seemed relieved that he hadn't had to do anything but stand tall and look important.

Michael turned to Jane as the crowd began to disperse. "Wow," he said. "That was much ado about nothing. And what a crock! Contrary to what Usher said, we know Ravena treated her sister like a bothersome gnat and Wandsworth didn't tell us much about Elizabeth's death. They were very vague about why this is a homicide."

"We need to get to the ME's office," said Jane, "and find out what was in his report. Let's go down there and see if we can dig up something from somebody."

Michael turned to head for the car, but Jane stopped him. "We can walk," she said. "It's just around the corner in the complex here—and besides, we might run into someone on the way who could be helpful."

"Sure," said Michael, "or we might run into someone who tells us we need to mind our own business."

Jane gave him the evil eye. "We're reporters," she said. "And we are minding our own business. Our business is to find out what's going on."

Michael gave her a weak smile and got in step beside her. At least she wasn't giving him the silent treatment anymore.

They turned the corner and found themselves at the Medical Officer's center of operations, an unimposing single-story building located in the shadow of the county jail and its razor-wire perimeter.

Jane pulled open the glass door at the main entrance and they stepped into a small tiled foyer that had the atmosphere of a doctor's waiting room and a disturbing smell of cleaning chemicals and decay. Immediately in front of them was a glassed-in reception area, but there was no one in sight. Battleship-gray corridors to the left and right led into the interior of the building.

"Do you think this is where they bring the bodies in?" asked Michael.

'Doubt it," said Jane. "They probably have their own private entrance somewhere in the back."

With no one manning the reception desk, Jane was in no mood to hang around. "Let's go this way," she said, nodding to the left-hand hallway. "The worst thing that can happen is we'll get thrown out."

"Or get dissected," added Michael, but he followed her to the end of the hallway, where it made a sharp right turn and led to a maze of corridors in the medical examiner's windowless kingdom. There was still no one in sight and an eerie silence permeated the malodorous air.

"This is spooky," said Michael but Jane was still on the move.

"Hey, you there!" A voice behind them shattered the silence. "Can I help you?"

The two reporters froze, then turned.

"Charlie!" cried Jane. "Thank God. It's you! What are you doing here?"

Deputy Noonan smiled and shook his head. "That's the question I have to ask you," he said. "I'm here to protect and serve. What are you here for?"

"What do you mean, protect and serve?" Jane gave him her trademark flick of golden hair and a devilish smile.

"You know our motto. Protect and serve. And I'm here to protect the M.E.'s office from intruders like you and to serve you notice to get out of here pronto before you get into real trouble."

"Come on Charlie," said Jane. "You know we're just trying to find out what's going on in the Ravena case."

"I know," said Noonan, "but you really need to talk to Robbery-Homicide. It's Henderson's baby."

"You know Henderson isn't going to tell us squat. I think he hates the press in general, and us in particular."

"That's true. But he answers to Wandsworth, who loves you guys, and Henderson knows which side his bread is buttered."

"Can't you tell us what's going on?" pleaded Michael.

"Didn't you guys go to the press conference?"

"Sure. But we didn't learn much we didn't already know, except that this simple accident appears to be a homicide."

"Come with me," said the deputy, shepherding them back toward the main entrance. "Let's get outta here."

"Look," he said, once they reached the parking lot. "I shouldn't be telling you anything. But just between you and me, the M.E. believes the cause of death was a blow to the head near the right temple. She'd lost quite a bit of blood but very little was found inside the car. Her head could have hit something when she went over the bank but there's not much in the car that could have caused an injury like that. Besides, it's tough to drive a car if you're lying in the trunk."

Michael gasped. "Lying in the trunk?"

"Yeah. Some blood was found in the trunk, which wasn't completely underwater."

Noonan paused and looked at the reporters, wondering if he should say more. "Then there's the blood in the body," he continued. "As you probably know, gravity takes over once you die. Thomas had some lividity toward her back as though she'd been lying down after she died. But she was in a sitting position, slumped over the wheel. Perhaps more importantly, there was no hemorrhaging in the airways and a diatom test was negative. These things suggest that she didn't drown. Seems she'd been dead some time when she went into the water."

The deputy looked grave. "It looks as though someone whacked her on the head, put the body in the car, took her out to what they thought was the middle of nowhere, propped her behind the wheel and . . . bingo! And now I've told you more than I know."

For a second Michael thought Jane was going to kiss the cop. "Thanks, Charlie!" she cried. "We owe you a drink."

"You may owe me more than that," said Noonan. "You may owe me a job for talking out of school."

"Don't worry, Charlie. You know we never reveal our sources." Jane grabbed Michael by the arm. "Let's go, Mikey," she said with newfound exuberance, "time to check in with Jack."

Life was looking up, thought Michael. They had exclusive information on Elizabeth Thomas's death—and Jane had called him Mikey. "Honey" would have been better, but it was a start.

* * *

The sun was doing its disappearing act over the horizon when they arrived back at The Courier building and the newsroom had almost emptied out. Jack Iverson sat alone in the middle of the vast room, surrounded by newspapers and computer printouts as he stared spellbound at his monitor.

"About time you guys got here," he said. "The press conference has already been on CNN, FOX and the networks. I hope you dug around and got something they didn't. I'm sure Nancy Grace will be all over it."

Jane and Michael filled him in on their meeting with Charlie Noonan.

"Good," said Jack. "JC has scheduled a special Page One meeting tomorrow morning and I was wondering what we were going to come up with for a cover headline. C'mon, let's go down to the Beachcomber. I'll buy you a beer and you can repay me with a brainstorming session."

At a booth in the bar, fortified with drinks, Michael dared to ask, "How can we come up with a Page One headline when we don't have a story yet?"

"We aren't working for AP here," said Jack. "I'd like to come up with a potential headline then see if we've got, or can get, the facts that will stand it up. We have to analyze what we have, which isn't really a helluva lot, then see how we can project it."

"What about HOW RAVENA'S SISTER DIED…THE INSIDE STORY?" offered Michael.

"Not bad, but it's a bit vague. And most readers think they already know how she died. Sounds as though we don't really have much."

"Think," said Jane. "Imagine you are Ravena Ventura right now. How would you feel? What would you be thinking?"

"I'd be pretty distraught, I guess. Like her publicist said she was," said Michael.

"Sure, but you'd also be scared. Frightened to death! If I were Ravena right now I'd be surrounding myself with bodyguards and looking for somewhere to hide. What if the murder was a case of mistaken identity? What if the killer was really after Ravena for some reason? There doesn't even have to be a real reason. There are enough crazies out there stalking and threatening stars.

Remember that Ravena's sister was her twin, her *look-alike* twin. At first blush even one of the deputies thought the body might have been Ravena. So . . ." She paused.

"So . . . ?" said Jack. "Go on."

"So the obvious headline is something like RAVENA FEARS FOR HER LIFE...SHE COULD BE REAL TARGET OF SISTER'S KILLER."

Jack beamed. "That's it, Jane! First thing in the morning I want you to call that publicist and see if you can get some quotes about how terrified Ravena is and what she's doing to protect herself. In fact Ravena might have some ideas about possible suspects in the murder.

"Michael, you should call the cops—Manalapan and Lantana Police and the Sheriff's Office—and find out if they're offering special security for Ravena. Then try to hook up with some of the cops who moonlight for her. Find out what they think about her being in danger and how they're likely to deal with it."

Jack sat back and downed his beer." Who knows," he said, "maybe Ravena Ventura even knows who the murderer is."

Chapter 13

It didn't take Jane long to hook up with Harriet Usher who, true to her reputation, would never miss an opportunity to set the press straight about her clients.

"Who did you say you represent?" asked Usher after Jane introduced herself.

"The Courier…The National Courier."

"Oh." Usher made no attempt to hide her disappointment. She'd been hoping it was one of those real newspapers like the *New York Times* or the *Washington Post*. Jane ignored the critical tone of Usher's voice and launched into a line of questioning about the possible danger to Ravena herself.

"To my knowledge Miss Ventura has no concerns that she may be the target of whoever killed her sister," Usher responded haughtily. "She has not expressed such feelings to me, and as far as I know she has made no plans to step up security. As I am sure you know, her home is already well-protected and is in one of the most secure areas of Palm Beach County."

Jane wrinkled her nose. *What an arrogant bitch!* But she hooked onto the words "as far as I know." Could Usher actually be admitting there was something she didn't know?

"It seems to me, Ms. Usher, that anyone whose twin sister is brutally murdered would be alarmed at the possible consequences and couldn't help but feel threatened in some personal way, even if they weren't internationally known celebrities like Miss Ventura."

"All I can tell you is that Miss Ventura is co-operating fully with the police and is satisfied that they will bring this terrible crime to closure quickly."

Blah, blah, blah! More politically correct bullshit. Jane figured she'd go for broke. "Well, Ms. Usher," she said, "it's difficult to believe that her twin sister's sudden and tragic death has not affected her in some way. It's a matter of public record that she has ongoing concerns about her security, as all celebrities do, and should, and we are planning a story on how her life, and her security, have been affected."

"Miss, uh, Connally," said Usher, checking hastily scribbled notes for the caller's name. "I trust you will not publish anything that is inaccurate. I will discuss your comments with Miss Ventura and will get back to you shortly."

A click indicated that the call was over. Jane figured the next one would be from a battery of lawyers demanding that The Courier cease and desist before the paper could get out of the starting gate with any story at all.

She stared at the phone on her desk, then glanced across to where Michael was engrossed in a conversation with one of the local police departments. Jack was nowhere in sight, probably at JC's morning meeting.

When Michael hung up he stepped over to her desk.

"I hope you're getting better news than I am," he said. "FEARING FOR HER LIFE doesn't seem to be happening. Not only is Ravena not beefing up security, she seems to be dismantling her entire security system. As the Lantana police chief said earlier, she'd already let a number of her rental cops go and she's now laid off a whole bunch more. And this is *after* her sister's murder. It makes no sense."

"I'm getting the same feeling from the publicity witch," said Jane. "When I brought up our story line she was adamant that it wasn't true and that Ravena wasn't losing any sleep over the idea that there was a killer on the loose who could be targeting her. Usher promised she'd call me back, but if she does I'm damn sure it will only be to tell us to mind our own business."

She looked up. Jack was marching across the newsroom toward her desk and his smile grew broader the closer he approached. "Great!" he said. "JC loved our angle. What ya got, kiddies?"

We haven't got squat, thought Jane, but she decided to temper it. "We haven't exactly got what you and JC love. How about IS RAVENA'S LIFE AT RISK?"

Jack's enthusiasm evaporated as they related how the morning's phone calls had evolved. He shuffled over to his own desk and slammed his legal pad down on it.

"We're looking for news, not conjecture. And you know JC hates questions for main headlines," he said. "The Courier is supposed to answer questions, not ask them. But if we really wind up that desperate maybe we could do something like RAVENA: KILLER DOESN'T SCARE ME."

Michael was impressed. Their great story angle was in the toilet but Jack was already trying to mold a 180-degree turnaround into something positive. "I
would—"

The sudden ring of Jane's phone caught him in mid-sentence and she pointed a "hold-that-thought" finger at him as she picked up the receiver. After a brief conversation she said, "Thank you. I'll be there. Goodbye," then looked glassy-eyed as she let the instrument dangle in her fingers.

"I don't believe it," she said. "That was Usher. Not only did she actually call me back, she says Ravena wants to see me."

"What?" Jack rocketed out of his seat, then slumped back down in it. "She most likely wants to rip you personally for intruding on her privacy and her grief with a cock-and-bull story. She probably wants to feed *you* to the fishes in some stinking canal."

"Don't think so," said Jane. "Usher told me to be at the estate at two o'clock. Just me. No one else. No substitutes. No cameras. No recording devices. It sounds like I'm being graced with an interview!"

"Why the hell would Ravena Ventura give you, or any of us, an interview? You're the one who reminded us all that she hates us like poison. And she must be getting more publicity than she needs right now from the establishment press."

"Maybe she's more shook by her sister's murder than we figured. But why should we look a gift horse in the mouth?"

"True. Take advantage of your time there. Find out whose shoulders she's crying on and that kind of stuff. That woman has the reputation of being an ice maiden, but there's something incredibly odd going on at Chez Ventura. Meanwhile, bring the Cruzes up to the office for their lie detector test. Michael, you'd better get up to the Sheriff's Office. Wandsworth is planning another press conference. I don't expect we'll learn much we don't already know, but we've got to stay ahead of the pack so try sucking up to that detective in charge and see if he'll give you anything exclusively."

* * *

Without Jane at his side, Michael felt uncomfortably naked as he drove up to Gun Club Road alone. But he had to stay focused. He reminded himself that he didn't need some chick to prop him up. But a dose of her sex appeal might have helped get something out of Detective Henderson, who didn't act as though he had any reporters on his list of six thousand best friends.

He found Wandsworth still very much front and center for the press conference. Prompted by questions, the sheriff brought the media throng up to date to the point where The Courier had been last night, thanks to Deputy Noonan.

Jack had been right, as usual. Unless Michael could squeeze something extra out of Henderson his morning would be wasted. And The Courier wasn't the kind of paper where "nothing new" was an acceptable excuse.

This time Harriet Usher was nowhere in sight and Wandsworth used Henderson and his sidekick to help field questions. After half an hour, the sheriff formally closed the press conference and disappeared inside the building, leaving the two detectives with their heads together as the crowd dispersed.

Michael took a deep breath and approached them. He didn't have to introduce himself. "Oh, it's you," said Henderson, "the first hotshot reporter at the crime scene. Where's your sexy girlfriend today?"

"Unfortunately she couldn't make it," said Michael. "And I know I'm not anywhere near as attractive as she is, but perhaps you could help me instead."

The two cops looked at each other and laughed.

Michael pressed on. "Since we've been told Ravena Ventura is co-operating with the police we wondered if she'd come up with any useful information. Like, has she been able to, uh, give you any leads?"

"Well," said Henderson, "she was able to give us an address where she believed her sister had been living. A little apartment in Lake Worth. We've got forensics over there now going over the place."

"Really? Can you give me the address?" Michael looked hopeful.

"Can't divulge that at this time. It may turn out to be where the crime was committed. It's possible she was killed in her home and her body driven out to the canal in Loxahatchee."

"Any possible motive?"

"Not sure yet."

"But the autopsy did find some evidence of drug use," cut in the other detective.

Henderson waved his hand agitatedly. "Let's not get into that, Bill," he said. "Too premature. Besides, most people are doing something these days."

He turned back to Michael. "Look kid, this is off the record. Traces of cocaine were found during the autopsy, but not a lot. So there's really nothing yet to indicate that the death was drug-related. And that's all we can say for now. Give my regards to your lady. C'mon Bill, we'd better get going."

The two detectives left Michael standing outside the sheriff's headquarters and piled into their unmarked sedan. Michael hurried to his car as they pulled out onto the street. Wherever they were going, he wanted to be there too. He wondered if it was illegal to follow a cop car.

Chapter 14

Jane's Mercedes hummed quietly as she headed north up the two-lane highway that hugged the coast. Between the trees to her right she could see the Atlantic, quietly stretching to the horizon like an iridescent carpet under the Florida sun. The swaying palms and pastel oceanfront buildings were the hallmarks of travel brochures. Yes, all was well with the world . . . all this and an exclusive one-on-one with the great Ravena Ventura.

Jane's thoughts turned to Michael. Was she was being too much of a thorn in his side? He was a nice guy, knew what he was doing, and deserved better. Oddly, he hadn't made a pass at her, though she'd never given him any encouragement. Maybe she would work on that once business was taken care of.

A few miles north of Delray Beach a modest road sign announced Jane's entry into Manalapan. This was a one-stoplight town, but not a one-horse town. You could drive through it in the blink of an eye, which was the way the locals liked it. They were lawyers, surgeons, CEOs . . . and movie stars. This was the home of Hollywood expatriates like Ravena Ventura.

An expanse of water materialized to her left, lapping perilously close to the roadway. This was the Intracoastal Waterway, where yachts of the nouveau riche found harbor and shelter across the street from where their owners lived.

Jane slowed, looking for the huge wrought-iron gate that identified Ravena's mansion. If it were open it meant the rent-a-cops were on duty. But it wasn't. Her presence barred, she pulled off the road and picked up a phone set in the wall.

It rang four or five times. Jane was beginning to wonder if the whole arrangement had been some kind of joke when a male voice answered. "Please drive up, Miss Connally. You will be met at the front entrance."

The gates silently swung open as if by magic and Jane followed a pink cement-block driveway on a circuitous path through a tropical wonderland. The driveway led her to a turning circle around a majestic eight-foot stone fountain. To her right was a classical portico with massive Grecian columns standing like sentinels at the main entrance to the house.

She parked outside the door, which was opened before she could step out of the car.

"Please follow me," said her greeter. "I am David Ellerby, Miss Ventura's manager."

Jane gave him the once-over and was not impressed. He was short, and oily. And he seemed a little edgy.

Ellerby held the door open and Jane stifled a gasp as she crossed the threshold into the huge marble entrance hall. Chez Ventura was a palace.

She looked around wide-eyed, but Ellerby didn't give her time to take in the scenery. He ushered her through a doorway to her left and she found herself in a room almost as large as The Courier newsroom.

The room was dominated by an ornate marble fireplace and a gigantic flower arrangement that sat on a burnished oak coffee table. On one corner of the table were glossy books that were never meant to be read. They were well out of reach from a richly embroidered sofa that seemed to say "don't sit here." A couple of high-backed armchairs shared space with massive potted palms, adding emphasis to the feeling that no one ever parked their rear ends in this room. Nice stuff, but not very homely.

"Please have a seat," said Ellerby, waving vaguely at all the furnishings. "Miss Ventura will be with you shortly."

Jane selected the corner chair that would give her the best view of the room and its entranceways. As she smoothed her skirt and sat down, Ellerby slid through a set of double doors in the far wall and carefully closed them behind him. Jane was alone inside Ravena Ventura's pink palace.

She tried to get her mind to absorb what she saw—the glitzy flamboyant chandelier, the plush but barren bar by the wall, the top-of-the-line maple flooring, the intricately patterned Persian carpet and the original paintings that looked down on her. She wondered if they were Old Masters. She didn't have a clue about paintings. But whatever they were, and whatever they were worth, she knew that Ravena Ventura would have paid an arm and a leg for them.

Muffled voices were coming from behind the door where Ellerby had disappeared. Jane strained to listen. She couldn't make out the words but there appeared to be some kind of argument taking place.

* * *

In the adjoining room, Ellerby was making a last-ditch attempt to cancel Ravena's meeting with the reporter as the actress applied a final touch of lipstick.

"Are you sure you want to go through with this?" he asked.

"Yes, Damn sure. I know what I'm doing. I want to get the press off our backs and you catch more flies with honey than with vinegar."

"All right, Ravvvennna!" spat Ellerby. "But just remember we're a team. We're in this together."

"How could I ever forget? You never let me."

"Just don't forget one important thing. If you fuck this up we'll go down together, and you have more to lose than I do."

"Yes, I know that, Ellie, but I'm sure you'll be working on balancing the scales."

Ellerby brushed off the sarcasm. "Come on, sweetheart," he said, "you know I want what's best for both of us. You do look like shit by the way."

"Thank you very much. I'm supposed to look like shit. I'm in mourning, remember? Enough of this crap. Let's get this over with."

The actress rose and headed for the double doors. Jane, who had left her seat and moved closer in hopes of catching some of the conversation rushed back to the sanctuary of the corner armchair.

"Miss Connally," said Ravena, not even looking at the reporter as she swept into the room with Ellerby hard on her heels. "Thank you for coming."

"My pleasure," said Jane. "It's not often I get an invitation to meet a movie star."

Ravena sat down at one end of the sofa and glanced across at Ellerby, who was lurking uncomfortably by the bar. No drinks were in sight and none were being offered.

"I know you're wondering why I agreed to meet with you," said Ravena. She was choosing her words carefully. "This is a terrible time for me and I really can't deal with any extra harassment from the press. To be honest I thought a conversation with you, and you alone, would help get the media off my back. I want peace and privacy and a dignified private funeral for my poor sister. I am prepared to make one statement, and make it exclusively to you. To be frank, I chose The Courier because I know you are the most aggressive of all the media and I really didn't relish the thought of The Courier breathing down my neck."

"I understand," said Jane. "You said no tape recorders, but may I take notes?"

"Of course, if it will help you get it right."

Jane fumbled in her purse and pulled out a small notepad and a pen.

"Mr. Ellerby and Miss Usher didn't exactly approve of this meeting," continued Ravena, "but it makes sense to me. I have one stipulation in return for your right to publish what I tell you."

Jane raised her eyebrows but said nothing.

"Usher tells me you want to write a story about how I'm living in fear for my life. That is not true. I certainly don't want a story like that seeing the light of day. I am not in fear of anything except losing my privacy and I want assurances from you that you will not publish anything negative about me, or even anything at all without my approval."

"Miss Ventura," said Jane, "I can assure you that I wouldn't, but I can only speak for myself. I'm not authorized to make commitments on behalf of The Courier's editorial board."

Ellerby snorted from his vantage point by the bar. "I told you this was a mistake."

"Ignore him," said Ravena with a curt shake of her head. "I know The Courier has had 'arrangements' with other people in Hollywood and I don't see why we can't come to some similar agreement. Have your editor call Usher. I expect you to call your dogs off if you intend to publish the information I give you. I don't think anyone else's dogs will be of much consequence."

"Sure," said Jane. Ravena obviously didn't know how fierce the story wars could be in Tabloid Valley.

"First," said Ravena, "I want you to know that I am totally mortified by Liz's death, even though it should not have come as a shock to me. Liz and I were very close, as all identical twins are, I guess. As you probably know, we even acted together many years ago. We were seven years old at the time but our mother thought we were cute and talented. Whatever we were, we were lucky. We landed a role on a sitcom. Child labor laws wouldn't let either one of us work enough hours, so being identical twins we were hired to share the leading role. Actually, I thought Liz was a more natural actress than me, but it didn't matter. The show didn't last too long and the work dried up after that. The networks went through a phase where they decided that child stars were too much of a headache to cast and didn't do much for the ratings anyway.

"In any event, our young foray into show business didn't help our family life. Mom and Dad started to squabble about money—most of it *our* money, since we earned more in a week than Dad could make in a year. Then they split and we were pretty much left to fend for ourselves. Survival can bring out the best and the worst in people, and we were no exception.

"I was very lucky. I was 'rediscovered' at age eighteen by a talent agent. Unfortunately Liz wasn't so lucky. She was discovered by some disreputable people long before she reached eighteen. She started using drugs and alcohol to numb the pain as I found success and she found nothing but failure. It wasn't her fault. It's just the way of the world.

"I did everything I could for her. I loaned her money, I *gave* her money. I even tried to get her movie roles, but the fact that she looked like me was a detriment. I guess she could have been my stunt double, but as I'm sure you know, the stunts I perform on the screen don't really require a double.

"When I decided to move to Florida, Liz came with me. She couldn't handle L.A. alone, poor thing. But things were no better for her here and she got involved with more unsavory people. Those scumbags are everywhere.

"Ironically, that's why I am not afraid of being targeted by her killer. I never knew any of the people she hung around with, and I certainly didn't want to. I just tried to help her, financially and emotionally, as much as I could. But she was caught in a cruel vice. I don't know who killed her, or even why, but I know it has to be some seedy underworld character. Maybe she learned too much about them and had to be silenced. Maybe it was an accident and they didn't really mean for her to die. We may never know. But I do know that these people have no interest in me. They and I live in different worlds and I have nothing to offer them.

"As I believe Usher told the press, I'm using all my resources to work with the authorities to bring the killer or killers to justice. I have told the police all I know about my sister and her life. It's not much. A number of local police officers have worked on my security staff, as I am sure you know, and I am confident they will devote as much of their time and energy to this case as possible.

"And this is also why I have also decided to offer a reward of two hundred thousand dollars to anyone who provides information that leads to the conviction of Liz's killer. Usher will give you the details. I've told the police that I am doing this and that I am announcing it through The Courier. The rest of the press will learn of it from you and when they contact me I will confirm it. After that I wish to say nothing about this case until it is resolved."

Ravena paused and sighed, and Jane stopped scribbling. She had enough for a cover story without having said a word, but she felt compelled to ask a question, even though she got the feeling that questions weren't part of the deal.

"That's a very noble gesture and a very moving story," she said, "but just how close were you and Elizabeth? After all, you did grow up together. And don't identical twins have a lot of things in common besides looks?"

"Yes, they do, and Liz and I did. When we were young we took delight in switching identities to play jokes on people. I guess all identical twins do that. We seemed to be able to read each other's minds and when one of us was sick, the other would suffer too.

"Around the time my sister was killed I got a terrible sense of foreboding, but I didn't realize why at the time. She was often getting into trouble but I always knew about it instinctively and I was always flying to her side to help her out."

And to prevent her from embarrassing you. "Exactly what kind of problems did Liz get into that she needed your help?"

Ravena bristled. "I really don't want to go there," she said, "but it's common knowledge that she became very dependent on drugs. I put her in rehab twice but it didn't work out. In fact she met some people in there that maybe made things worse for her when she got out. Sometimes my helping her had more of a negative impact than a positive one. She thought I was flaunting my wealth, my success, my abilities to make things happen. It made her feel even lower on the food chain.

"Now at least I believe she is happy at last. When they release her body to me I intend to have a private funeral and spread her ashes over the ocean. She always loved the sea and wanted to live by it. But she never did. Now, in death, she will be able to fulfill her dreams."

Jane felt a tight band in her chest. *This was great stuff!*

"Thank you, Miss Ventura," she said and looked slowly around the room. "I will have my editor contact Miss Usher as soon as possible. I think everything will be fine. But I have just one more request."

Ravena raised her eyebrows.

"I wondered if . . . well, do you think I could look around your, uh, house? It's magnificent. I've never been anywhere like it and— "

Ravena smiled. "Come with me," she said. "Five minutes. But all this is off the record. No hidden cameras, I hope? And no flowery descriptions to appear in the press."

"Of course."

Ravena stood up. "Wait here, Ellie," she said to her manager, who still stood tight-lipped, leaning with his back to the bar. "I'll only be a minute or two."

Jane followed her back into the cathedral-like entrance hall where hallways led to both sides of the house. About thirty feet from the front door two plushly carpeted winding staircases joined on the second floor to create a balcony overlooking the hall.

"There are six bedrooms and six baths upstairs," said Ravena, "plus a master suite, of course." She obviously didn't intend to take Jane up there but opened a small door under the right-hand staircase.

"This is my personal study and library," she said, allowing Jane to peer into a dark wood-paneled room that bore the comforting aroma of paper, coffee and dusty books. French doors provided a view of a small palm-fringed courtyard, and the foliage shielded the room from Florida's glaring sun. Books lined two walls and a huge polished mahogany desk was the piece de resistance.

Ravena stood by the door as Jane glanced around the room, the private lair of a world-famous celebrity. How she would love a hiding place like this.

Moving at a brisk pace, Ravena led Jane through hallways to the north and south, past or through endless huge rooms—living rooms, formal and intimate dining rooms, a restaurant-size kitchen, various bathrooms, a recreation room, an exercise room and, inevitably, a media center that would have made Cinemark proud.

The far end of the main hallway was glass, two stories high, that looked out onto a pink patio and an azure pool. Beyond that, Jane could see the beach and the ocean behind stands of tropical greenery. A screened lanai to the left led out to the pool area.

The building took Jane's breath away. "This is magnificent," she gasped. "It must take a lot of upkeep. You must have a huge staff to take care of it all."

"Actually, no. Right now it's a bit of a problem. I had a live-in couple, a housekeeper and gardener, but I had to let them go and I haven't had time to replace them yet. An agency is working on that for me and I do have a maid service, plus a cook who comes in every day. I can assure you, not for publication, that I don't do any cleaning. Or cooking.

"I loved this house when I first saw it, so I bought it. It sounds so simple. But my life is complicated, and it takes a lot of people to uncomplicate it for me. Too many people, so now I'm in the process of scaling back. I guess my sister's death has made me recognize my mortality and I want to kick back and enjoy life."

She stopped. "None of those personal comments are for publication. If you print any of that all deals will be off and I will sue you. Now you must excuse me. Ellerby will be wondering where I am. As I'm sure you've figured, he's not a big fan of the press."

Ravena led the way back down the hallway to the front door and opened it in invitation for the reporter to leave. "Thank you, Miss Ventura," said Jane. "And thank you for the tour of your house. I'm sorry for the loss of your sister. We will be in touch."

She turned toward her car, not looking back until she reached it. When she did, the door to the pink palace had closed behind her. It was the end of the most exciting hour in her life. But there were still so many questions. And she felt she'd been fed a pack of lies.

Chapter 15

The detectives' car had disappeared by the time Michael exited the Sheriff's Department parking lot, but it didn't take him long to get them back in view. He tried to stay three or four vehicles back as he trailed them through a maze of strip-mall thoroughfares. Michael decided he was spending too much time in areas that had never made it on the *Money* magazine list of Top Ten Places for Anything.

The further east they traveled the heavier the traffic became and Michael was having trouble keeping them in sight. Maybe it didn't matter. Perhaps they weren't going anywhere important, though this seemed to be a long trip for doughnuts.

The road divided and became one-way as they reached the business section of the city of Lake Worth, then the cops turned south down Federal Highway, where mom-and-pop businesses gave way to modest condominiums and apartment buildings. Now there were no vehicles between the Mustang and the detectives' wrapper and Michael held back as much as he could, praying that Henderson and his buddy wouldn't spot him.

Suddenly they slowed to a crawl. The cops were looking for somewhere, or for somebody. Then they made a sharp right turn. Whatever their quarry, they had found it.

They pulled into the parking lot of a small rundown apartment building where a couple of sheriff's cruisers and an unmarked van were already positioned at angles designed to deter other vehicles. Michael had no option but to drive by and hope Henderson hadn't seen him.

He remembered what the detective had just told him. Ravena's sister had been staying at a little apartment in Lake Worth. This had to be it. Forensics was on the scene, they said, and now so were they. And so was Michael. But he knew better than to gatecrash their party.

He drove slowly around the block and retraced his path down Federal Highway. There was no street parking so he pulled into a condo parking lot across from where the police were congregated and found a space where he could sit behind a low hedge, facing the street.

He didn't know what he was going to do, but the cops were on the hunt for clues, and clues meant news. Michael decided to sit and wait them out, then try to surprise them into giving him a few tidbits when they were ready to leave.

It didn't take him long to discover that, unlike on TV, surveillance is a tedious enterprise. TV likes to cut to the chase. Real life takes its own sweet time. After an uncomfortable half-hour staring at the corner apartment which had seemed to interest the sheriff's officers, Michael was squirming in his seat. The steering wheel appeared to be getting closer and closer and squeezing on his belly. Plus, he was getting hungry. Now he knew why cops were doughnut hounds.

The heat and the boredom were making him sleepy and he kept jerking himself awake whenever he thought he saw movement across the street.

After thirty minutes dragged by in what seemed like eight hours, he noticed the law enforcement personnel piling into their vehicles. They were leaving.

Michael started his engine. He wanted to appear to be nonchalantly arriving at the scene just in the nick of time to meet them. His plans were thwarted by a sudden stream of traffic that blocked his exit from the parking lot. By the time he swung onto the street he was too late. All the police cars were gone.

There was no point trying to follow them. They were probably going back to headquarters anyway. He decided to stop and check out the apartment complex.

He parked in front of the apartment doorway which had been the focus of the cops' attention and was surprised to find the door a few inches ajar. Maybe the officers had just gone down the street to get a burger. Perhaps they'd left a deputy on the premises. Heck, he was on the scene now so he might as well keep going.

Michael got out of his car and knocked gingerly on the door. There was no response. He tried to peer through the windows on each side of the door, but partly closed blinds and the sun's reflection off the glass blocked his view.

He eyed the door and the enticing three-inch gap between it and the jamb, and took a deep breath. He pushed the door with his fingertip and it swung open far enough for him to put his head around the frame and peer into the room.

There wasn't a lot to see—a battered sofa, a huge metal coffee table and a small television set perched on a tiny stand. The room was dark, dusty and malodorous. A movie star's sister had lived in this dump? Was this where she had met her death?

Michael stepped boldly into the room, being careful not to touch anything. But there wasn't anything interesting to see. If this Spartan furniture and faded carpet were holding any secrets, they weren't about to divulge them to him.

Michael weighed the dangers of venturing into the other rooms. There was a kitchenette to one side of the door and a small hallway at the back that presumably led to a bathroom and a bedroom. But he was already on thin ice for entering the premises. He was contemplating his options when a human figure cast a shadow across the half-open doorway.

"Can I help you?"

The voice didn't sound too helpful or too friendly.

"Er, um, ye–, yes," he stammered. The cops must be back. And he was in trouble. All he could do was 'fess up, so he hurriedly pulled out his press pass, a card that read "PRESS" in large black letters and "The National Courier" in smaller type.

He held up the card and waved it at the man stepping across the threshold. He didn't look like a cop, but you never know.

"I'm looking for Detective Henderson," said Michael, hoping that name-dropping might legitimize his presence.

"Are you a detective?" asked the man. He obviously hadn't paid much attention to Michael's credentials.

"No," said Michael. This man didn't seem to be a detective either, so he relaxed a little. "I'm with the press, and I wanted to speak with Detective Henderson. I thought he might be here."

"Cops wuz here, but they gone now," said the man. He was short, and in his sixties. And the years had not been kind. Faded beige slacks and a gray T-shirt that had once been white hung on his skinny frame.

"They asked me to lock up when they left, but they never done tol' me when they were goin'."

"Do you live here then?" Michael asked.

"I lives here and works here. Vinnie Povnik. I'm the resident manager." The man looked annoyed. Maybe his happy hour had been rudely interrupted. "My place is around the back, so I don't always know what's going on around the front here. Which," he added philosophically, "can sometimes be a good thing and sometimes a bad thing."

"Do you know if the Sheriff's Department is coming back?"

"Beats me. Like I tol' you, I didn't even know they'd gone. Looks like they left a heck of a mess though." He started to peer around the room, then glanced in the kitchen and paddled down the hallway before returning to the tiny living room.
"Look here," he said, wiping his finger on the coffee table and the TV stand. "Soot! What a fuckin' mess."

"I don't think it's soot," said Michael. "Looks like the cops have been dusting for fingerprints."

"Well I'm sure they found plenty. Don't know when this place was last cleaned properly. Can't get no good cleanin' help anymore. The cops coulda cleaned up after themselves, ya know. An' what about this?" The manager pointed to a couple of holes in the wall near the front window. "What the fuck has been goin' on here?"

"Wish I knew," said Michael, moving closer to examine the wall. The place was certainly a mess, and the cops hadn't made it any better.

"Perhaps you can help me," said Michael. "I guess you knew Miss Thomas?"

"The dame who lived here? Sure. Stupid bitch ran off the road and wound up in a canal, I hear. Now they think somebody done 'er in. I think she was probably tanked up or high on sumthin' and did herself in."

"Why do you say that?"

"She kinda looked the type. Pretty gal, somehow looked familiar, but she seemed a bit wasted when she came here lookin' for a place to stay. Didn't turn her down though. She paid a month up front, had a nice car and there ain't no other tenants here. Not this time of year. Owners would be pissed off if I turned away cash-money rent like that before the season picks up."

"How long had she lived here?"

"Coupla weeks. Said she'd just moved here from California and needed a little place until she got established."

"Was she alone when she moved in?"

"She was alone when I saw her."

"Did she have any visitors while she was here?"

"Not sure. I live around the back so I don't have to know. And I don't spy on the renters. What they do and how they live is their business . . . as long as they pay and don't give me no trouble."

"Did you ever see anyone else here since she moved in?"

"Well the other night, the night the cops say she died, I heard something that sounded like a gunshot. Don't have no time for guns so I went out and looked around. Probably punks in the neighborhood, ya know? Didn't see nothin' but there was three cars parked out front. Maybe she did have guests, though sometimes folks at the bar next door park in my lot when things get busy."

"Did you notice what kind of cars?"

"Oh yeah, I'm good at that. Managers need to have trained eyes for that kind of stuff," he said proudly. "There was Miss Thomas's Lexus, and another Lexus. Very similar cars. An' there was another car, a Lincoln. Not one of them humongous Town Cars, though. It was smaller. Beige it was. All them cars looked pretty fancy to me, so I figured everything musta been hunky dory."

"What about the gunshot?"

"Like I said, probably punks in the neighborhood. Or it might have been fireworks or a car backfiring."

"You didn't investigate it any further?"

"No. Nothing wrong that I could see, so it weren't my business."

"Did you tell the police all this?"

"Sure I did. Like I tol' em, anything I can do to help. But I still think her death was an accident. Told 'em that, too, but they ain't gonna listen to me. Anyway, gotta get back now. There's always a shitload of stuff to do around here, even when there ain't no tenants."

He jangled a bunch of keys in the direction of the front door, and Michael got the message.

"Don't know if them cops are comin' back," said Povnik, "but if they do they'll have to hunt me down and beg for me to let 'em in." He cackled at the thought.

"Thanks for your help. It was nice talking to you."

The manager said nothing, just stared as Michael got into his car. Obviously not many people had ever thanked Vinnie Povnik for anything. Michael waved farewell but the man was already shuffling off around the corner, out of sight of the apartment, the parking lot and the world that passed by on Federal Highway.

Michael turned south toward The Courier offices and pulled out his cell phone. The apartment hadn't yielded many answers. It was time to play hardball with Detective Henderson.

Chapter 16

Henderson picked up the phone on the first ring. But if he'd been eager to talk to the press he didn't show it.

"Mr. Hanlon," he groaned. "And what can I do for you now?"

"I was just at Elizabeth Thomas's apartment," said Michael, "and I wondered what you'd found there. It seemed to be a real mess."

"Waddya mean you were *at* her apartment? And how did you find out where it was?"

"Oh, come on detective, you know I can't reveal my sources."

"Don't gimme that bullshit. How d'ya know it was a mess? Were you in there? Because if you were you were trespassing on a crime scene and that—"

"Some crime scene," retorted Michael. "You didn't tape it off, you didn't secure it in any way. You left the door open, and I don't just mean unlocked. I mean O-P-E-N, open! I was there looking for you, figured that's where you shot off to this morning, but I think I just missed you." *It was more or less true, anyway.*

"We told the super to lock up when we left," said Henderson defensively. "And there was no need to tape the place. Forensics had wrapped up there. There wasn't much to see, anyway."

"Except you forgot to let the super know when you'd finished," said Michael. "Anybody could have gone in there and messed with stuff."

"Like you?"

"I didn't mess with anything. I just looked around. Do you think it was where she was killed?"

"Look, son, I don't have to tell you anything. This is an ongoing murder investigation and the last thing we need is nosy reporters sniffing around in things that don't concern them. If you impede our investigation in any way I'll— "

"I'm not out to impede your investigation. Remember how the cops screwed things up in the O.J. and Jon Benet cases? I'm trying to help you. You tell me what you know and I'll tell you what I know."

"What could you possibly know that we don't?"

"I know that you're risking allowing a likely crime scene to be contaminated," said Michael, "and I know you wouldn't want that broadcast."

"Don't be an asshole. If you have any information that would help us in our investigation you're duty bound to tell us about it."

"Don't worry, I will. But it would be nice if it worked both ways. I have a job to do too and the public has a right to know. Plus, you know Sheriff Wandsworth loves The Courier and neither of us would like to piss him off."

The silence lasted long enough for Michael know he'd hit a nerve. He wondered if Henderson had hung up. "You still there?" he asked at last.

"Yeah, I'm here," said the detective. "Look, there are things in the investigation that can't be made public, at least not yet. Some loose ends, and lots of question marks. So how are you going to help us?"

"Well, did you know that Elizabeth apparently had a number of visitors the night she died? She was apparently the building's only tenant and the super told me he'd gone to check gunshots and found three cars parked near her apartment."

"Yeah, so?" said Henderson. "We know all that."

"How about the gunshots?" asked Michael.

"What makes you so sure there were any gunshots?"

"Did you check out the holes in the wall by the window?"

There was another brief silence. "What about 'em?" said the detective.

"They could have been bullet holes."

"Look Columbo, they might have been, they might not have been. And what's that got to do with the price of eggs? The deceased didn't die from gunshot wounds. She died from a blow to the head."

"Did you find any evidence that she got that blow in her apartment?"

"Maybe. There was no visible evidence of blood anywhere but we ran a Luminol test that showed quite a lot that you couldn't see with the naked eye. There was blood in that living room—on the floor, the carpet and on that ugly-ass coffee table."

"Which means someone had tried to clean it up," said Michael. "Looks like it. And a funny thing, we found a number of prints, including the deceased's, in the living room but nobody's prints in the rest of the place. Somebody had wiped the whole apartment clean, except the room where the vic appears to have met her death."

"That's weird. Do you have any theories as to why?"

"Not yet. But you tell me. I thought you were playing detective."

"I'll give it some thought," said Michael. He thanked Henderson and hung up. What Henderson had told him was interesting. But what did it mean?

* * *

When he reached the office, Jane was pounding away on her keyboard and Jack was up to his neck in paperwork as usual. Michael began to fill him in with a torrent of words that he couldn't get out fast enough.

"All right, all right. Calm down," said Jack. "I need this stuff in writing. Jane's already in the middle of hers. I need you to type up everything you've got, from day one, even if it might duplicate Jane's stuff. Don't try to write a story. Just the facts, and all the facts. When you're done print out four copies. When we all have hard copy to look at we'll see what we've got and where we can go with it. I've picked up some interesting information myself."

Michael raised his eyebrows.

"What's the matter?" snorted Iverson. "You think I just sit here with my finger up my ass? This is a hot story and we're short of personnel. I'm doing some reporting on this myself—and trying to handle three other stories at the same time."

Michael nodded sympathetically and got to work. He didn't want to merely type up facts. He wanted to craft a story, to meld everything he'd learned about Ravena Ventura, her sister and the sister's death. That's how he'd been trained as a reporter. But that wasn't the way The Courier worked. They had a team of writers who honed reporters' copy into Courier style.

With deadline fast approaching and his editor anxious for a banner story, Michael finished his report and had it printed out in twenty minutes. Jack gathered up all the paperwork and scurried into Peterson's office.

In less than five minutes Michael and Jane were summoned to join them.

"Shut the door," Peterson ordered. "I've been on the phone with Harriet Usher, Ventura's publicist, and we hammered out an unwritten agreement. Usher didn't like it at all, but Ventura okayed it. Ravena doesn't get copy approval, per se, but we have to call her with a synopsis of anything we plan to run and give her time to respond to it. Frankly, we'd do that anyway."

"Jane, I think you've got enough support material for this week's main story. We have enough good quotes from Ravena about how she loved her sister, tried to help her but couldn't, and now is torn apart because she's gone."

The executive editor was winding himself up, slicing the air with his hands as he constructed the story in his mind. "We can do the two-hundred-thousand reward as a separate piece. I got some details and a cookie-cutter quote from Usher that will flesh it out. That will give us a couple of strong headlines on the cover. People like to see dollar signs in headlines. I just wish we had a stronger main line."

"Well," said Jane. "How about RAVENA: I KNOW WHO KILLED MY SISTER?"

Jack frowned. "Did she say that?"

"Kinda. Look at my notes."

Jack thumbed through the stack of papers on his lap and shook his head. "She actually told you she didn't know specifically who killed her, or why. We'd be conning the readers. She thinks it was some unidentified lowlife druggie. We could try RAVENA: UNDERWORLD KILLED MY SISTER but it's not very sexy, and I don't think Ventura would agree to it anyway. She's going to want us to soft-pedal with anything quoting her."

"True," said Peterson, "but she doesn't have headline approval. "The executive editor shuffled his papers. He was agitated and wanted to move on.

But something was needling Michael. Things that didn't seem to add up were being ignored.

"You know," he said, "Jane has a pretty good sob story and we have some solid background material, but all our given facts don't gel. Ravena told Jane how she's falling apart over her sister's death, but the Cruzes didn't give us that impression. According to them the two sisters rarely got together. I don't think there was much love lost between Ravena and Elizabeth. Ravena found her sister to be weak-willed, wasting her life, and an embarrassment to Ravena's star status."

Peterson looked around the room in search of a consensus of opinion.

"You're right, Michael," he said, "but we're fast approaching deadline. Let's work on the sister's death and hunt down an original angle for next week."

Michael was being put on a back burner, and he knew it. He thumbed through his notes. "As you can see," he said, "I've already discovered where Elizabeth was living and where, apparently, she was killed. That information hasn't been given to TV or the dailies yet."

"Yes," said Peterson. "That was good work, Michael, though that detective has probably put out a press release to everyone by now. How did you get him to open up?"

Michael shrugged. "I pointed out to him that the crime scene had probably been contaminated and reminded him how the press had jumped all over the cops in similar circumstances."

Jack laughed. "But you were the one who probably contaminated it."

Michael shuffled in his chair. "I was careful not to touch anything and there was nothing to suggest it was a crime scene. There was no police presence and the door was open. I just wandered in looking for Henderson and stumbled onto what he had left behind. I'll bet he rushed back there as soon as I hung up the phone with him."

"Henderson will be running scared," said Peterson, "and he's not going to love us for it. It's a good job Wandsworth and JC have some sort of mutual admiration society. I suspect the sheriff's department is out of its depth in a case like this. But they won't want it to show."

Jack stood up in an attempt to wind up the meeting. "I've already got L.A. working on a comprehensive Elizabeth Thomas backgrounder," he said. "What we really need is in-depth stuff on Miss High and Mighty Ventura, not the shit those public relations flacks churn out about her. We've got some decent anecdotes from the Cruzes, but we need more. We need someone to go underground at her place. We need a fly on the wall."

Chapter 17

Michael sat at his desk and opened his hard-copy file. It didn't take Jack long to be fixated on Ravena again, but Michael wanted to know more about Elizabeth Thomas. It sounded as though she was the one who could have benefited from a fly on the wall in her life. Or a guardian angel.

The Courier's Los Angeles bureau had done a thorough job in producing a profile on Elizabeth. The document was a depressing read, a fact-filled litany that chronicled the downfall of a woman living in the dark reaches of her twin sister's shadow.

The report was devoid of emotion. But it would help lay the foundation for a great sob story for Courier readers. Michael was surprised that none of the tabs had zeroed in on it before.

While Rachel Thomas changed her name and soared to great heights on the thermals of Hollywood hubris, Elizabeth went the other way. The same looks, the same feelings and the same background weren't enough to save her from the abyss that was the antithesis of her famous sister's life.

Wasn't there always a strong twin and a weak twin? In the case of the Thomas girls their differences weren't so much physical as emotional. Rachel found ways to step out, upward and forward. Elizabeth was in lockstep with her, but going in the opposite direction. When Elizabeth got into trouble, Ravena would reel her in, hose her down, shoo off the predators, then throw her back into the troubled waters to go through all the motions again.

Ravena had ladled it on thick to Jane about how close the two of them were, but there was no evidence that the Thomas twins had much of a relationship. Stardom had its privileges and the sanitized, squeaky clean Ravena Ventura was not about to let a wayward sister ruin her image. Whatever it took she did, whatever it cost she paid.

The dossier left Michael feeling frustrated. He wasn't sure what he was looking for but he knew he hadn't found it. Just more holes to fill.

Ravena had told Jane that she and her sister relocated to Florida together, but Ravena had been in town for eight months and Elizabeth had just arrived.

She'd been driving a rented car that she'd picked up at the airport on a two-week contract. She never seemed to have any money, but she'd been able to spring for a Lexus. Then she'd moved to a ratty apartment.

Ravena had told the cops where her sister was living. Had she ever been there? Two people with high-end cars had apparently visited Elizabeth on the night of her death, according to the super. A Lexus and a Lincoln. He knew Ravena had a Lexus registered in her name. Maybe she had been one of the visitors. But who owned the Lincoln?

Ravena seemed anxious to help the police close the case but she hadn't really been that forthcoming, only suggesting vaguely that the killer was probably some underworld figure who'd tracked Elizabeth from L.A. So why was she promoting a two-hundred-thousand-dollar reward for serious information? Did she really expect that would lure some obscure criminal element out of the woodwork to drop the dime on one of his peers?

And why was Ravena suddenly getting rid of her staff? Surely she needed her security people more than ever.

She was in high demand in Hollywood but had distanced herself from the movie industry both geographically and mentally. She hadn't made a film in more than a year and seemed intent on dropping out of the limelight. She was wealthy and attractive but appeared to have few, if any, male friends unless you counted her old-fart lawyer, or perhaps that new manager, David Ellerby. And where did he suddenly come from? Her last manager was a guy she abandoned when she left Los Angeles. Michael made a note to get a LexisNexis check on Ellerby.

Then there were questions about the crime scene. Why would the killer wipe down prints all over the apartment except in the room where the murder actually occurred? After all, pains had been taken to clean up the blood.

Then there were the gunshots, if there actually had been any gunshots. If the killer was a professional criminal like Ravena theorized, a gun would be the natural weapon of choice. And those two holes in the wall could have been made by bullets. But if you had a gun, why bother doing something messy like beating your victim to death?

Michael turned to his editor. "I think we should get Research to run a make on this manager, David Ellerby," he said. "And I'd like to go back to Elizabeth's apartment. I could look around some more and chat with the super again."

"All right," said Iverson, "but take some pictures this time. You can use your cell phone."

"My cell doesn't take pictures. I'm lucky it takes phone calls."

Iverson sighed and reached into a desk drawer. "Then take this fuckin' camera with you. I don't want you trespassing on the crime scene again but you could get some shots of the exterior of the apartment building."

"Don't worry," Michael assured him. "I'll be careful where I tread. I've no desire to get arrested."

But he sensed that getting a fresh lead on this story would mean stepping on thin ice.

Chapter 18

Michael arrived at the apartment to find the detectives' unmarked vehicle in the parking lot, but no cops in sight. There was still no crime-scene tape in sight either, but the door to the apartment was now closed. Michael rapped on it, with no response, then tried the knob. The door was locked.

He decided to check around the back of the building where the super, Vinnie Povnik, hung out, and wasn't surprised to find him sharing his views on life with Henderson and his partner, Bill Gregory.

"Hey, look what the tide washed up," said Henderson as Michael rounded the corner. "Well, hotshot, come to tell us how to do our jobs again? Or have you found the killer?"

"Just thought I'd see how you guys were doing," replied Michael. "Hi, Mr. Povnik. How are you?"

Povnik saw an opportunity to rant and went for it. "To tell you the truth I'm pissed off. Between the police and the press always around here I can't get fuckall done. An' now I've got a big hole in the wall to fix."

Michael tried to suppress a smile. *No big deal. The whole place is a hole in the wall.* "What happened?" he asked.

"There was them two itty-bitty holes in the wall and these guys turned it into the fuckin' Grand Canyon."

"We already apologized for that, Mr. Povnik," said Henderson. "But we've got our jobs to do. Afraid we had to do that."

"Just what did you do?" asked Michael.

"Those holes in the living room wall, near the window. We looked at 'em again and decided they might be bullet holes, so we checked 'em out."

Michael stared at him in disbelief. "Yes, detective. I'm the one who told you they could be bullet holes."

Henderson glared daggers at him. "Like I keep saying, the deceased didn't die of a gunshot wound so it's probably not that important, but we did find two slugs in the wall. Thirty-eights."

"And now I've got a hell of a re-plastering job," complained Povnik.

Henderson stared him down. "Look on the bright side," he said. "A few more inches and those slugs would have gone through the window and you'd have had a bigger mess and a ton of glass to replace."

"That's strange, detective," said Michael. "If the killer had a gun why didn't he shoot the victim? Why bother to hit her over the head?"

"Well, first of all, sonny, we don't know whose gun it was, or whose possession it was in when all this was going down. It may have been the victim's gun and it could have gone off in a struggle. Or the victim might have been whacked by an accomplice when she tried to disarm the gunman. Or the slugs might even be from a previous situation."

Michael nodded in agreement. "You obviously haven't found the gun, then," he said.

Henderson shook his head.

"And we still haven't discovered the actual murder weapon either," added Gregory. "It might be that gun. The vic could have been pistol-whipped."

Henderson turned to the super. "Anyway, Mr. Povnik, I think we're all through here," he said. "You're free to go ahead and fix up the place. Just give it a real good cleaning, a nice fresh coat of paint and air it out some. It'll be as good as new."

"I know my job," said the super. "I'm gonna have to throw out all that furniture, too. You said you found blood on it."

Henderson raised his hands to stave off more complaints. "We're outta here," he said, heading for the corner and the car.

"One more quick question, detective," asked Michael, breaking into a trot to catch him up. "Don't you find it strange that Ravena Ventura hasn't been able to shed any more light on this?"

The cop stopped and turned. "Look," he said, "I know you tabloid guys are hot
to put a celebrity angle on this crime, but apart from the fact that the deceased was related to a movie star, there isn't one. Miss Ventura thinks some criminal element from California sent someone here to take care of her sister. Most likely some drug deal gone bad on the West Coast. Elizabeth Thomas probably thought she'd be safe in Florida. Anyway, we'd love to stop and chat but we gotta go."

Michael waited until their car had left, then returned to Povnik, who was fidgeting nervously in the rear parking lot. Michael figured he was probably looking for an opportunity to crack open a cold beer.

"Do you mind if I have one last look around the apartment?" he asked him.

Povnik shrugged. "Don't see why not," he said. "Maybe I could charge admission. Might be worth a dollar a pop to see where the movie star's sister was bludgeoned to death."

He cackled, pulled a hefty jangling key ring off his belt and headed for the front of the building.

Again, Michael didn't know what he was looking for. The place looked pretty much unchanged from his last visit, except for the wall under the window. The police had exposed the studs in a sudden fit of enthusiasm.

He smiled to himself. He was getting under Henderson's skin. Then he remembered something he'd forgotten to ask him.

"Do you know if the cops found any drugs?" he asked Povnik, who was hovering near the door, waiting to close up.

The super shook his head. "Doubt it," he said. "We don't allow no drugs here."

Of course not.

Michael nodded, stepped into the tiny kitchen and began looking through the cabinets. There was nothing there but a few hand-me-down plates and glasses
and meager food rations. It had never occurred to him that some people lived on a steady diet of macaroni and cheese and silent desperation.

It was all too depressing. Time to leave. He slammed the last cabinet door in frustration, and then pulled out the camera. Povnik didn't object when Michael asked if he could take photos of the living room. And he agreed to stand still for a head shot.

"Thanks, Mr. Povnik," he said. "Hopefully you won't be bothered again. You've been very helpful."

"Okay," said the super. "Just remember to spell my name right, though I'd 'preciate it if you didn't give out the full address. Bad for business, you know. And I need the job."

Michael smiled but said nothing. He wasn't about to promise something he couldn't make good.

He high-tailed it back to the office, where Jack immediately dropped a bombshell on him.

"Good news, Mikey," he said. "I said we needed a fly on the wall at Chez Ventura and I've been working on it. How would you like a cushy job working for Miss Movie Star herself?"

Chapter 19

Michael was dumbfounded. And his editor was grinning like the cat that got the canary.

"While you were gone I had Research run that check on Ventura's manager," said Jack. "Seems David Ellerby isn't his only name. He's got aka's up the wazoo."

Jack consulted a two-page printout. "Like David Elfman, porn producer, Desmond Emerson, small-time loan shark, and Derek Edmunds, the name he used when he did two years in Pasco County for dealing. He has so many names in his portfolio I'm surprised he can remember who the fuck he's supposed to be from one minute to the next.

"Now, I want to know what a movie star like Ravena Ventura wants with a man like that if she knows his background. And if she doesn't know his background why doesn't she? I don't think she's such a stupid bitch she'd hire a new manager without checking out his credentials. And Ellerby, by any known name, has no legitimate positions listed in his resume.

"Jane has met the guy. And she says he's creepy. Of course you can't judge a book by its cover. And Jane has pretty high standards. She sometimes thinks I'm creepy. However, all this leads me to think our Miss Movie Star knows a lot more about her sister's death than she's letting on. So I started thinking about that fly on the wall and called in a marker.

"Seems Miss Ventura has hired a private security company to replace all the moonlighting cops at her place; Blackwell Security Services. Which—bingo!—happens to be owned by my buddy Richard Blackwell. You'll like him!"

Michael was speechless. "You mean you want to send me undercover to Ravena's house?" he stammered at last. "Like, in disguise?"

"Well, there won't be any disguise involved. You don't have to wear a false mustache. And you won't be wearing a uniform either, if that's what you mean. Just your own clothes, trying to look like a normal human being. I know that's not going to be easy for you." He paused melodramatically for laughter but none materialized.

"Anyway, it's a great opportunity for us to get in on the ground floor and find out what's really going on in her life and perhaps get some answers in this case. Whaddya think?"

Michael took a deep breath. He didn't know what to think. "Look," he said, "I appreciate that you've picked me, the new kid on the block, for this. But it's risky. And is it legal?"

"Actually, Michael, I chose you *because* you're the new kid on the block. You haven't been in town long enough for anyone to know you and your name has yet to make The Courier masthead. It's almost like you don't exist!"

"Thank you very much." *There was that lonely-spy allusion again.*

"I don't mean it like that. It's just that right now no one can finger you as a Courier reporter."

"How about the risks? You're not talking about that."

"What risks? You're just a reporter doing his job."

"Do I have a choice in this? Can I think about it overnight?"

Iverson was clearly miffed. "Sure," he shrugged, "but we don't have time to waste on this." He put his hand comfortingly on Michael's shoulder. "This could be great for you, son . . . and for the paper."

Michael looked around for Jane, his only possible security blanket. She wasn't at her desk but he hunted her down at the copying machine.

"I'm finished for the day," he said, "but I need to bounce something off you. Do you, uh, have time for a drink after work?"

Jane stared at him quizzically. "Sure," she said slowly. "I'll be about ten minutes here. Do you want to go ahead to the Beachcomber? I'll meet you there."

Michael hesitated. "I'd rather somewhere more quiet," he said. "Somewhere that isn't going to be full of Courier people." *Maybe she'd think he was hitting on her. Not that it was a bad idea.*

"There's something I need your opinion on," he added hastily.

"I see," she said with a coy smile that put Michael's heart into overdrive. "In that case I'll meet you at the Bull and Bear. Know it?"

"Yes, I think so; that English pub off Atlantic Avenue, just down from the ocean?"

"That's it. There won't be anyone in there at this hour, except perhaps a few Brit tourists looking for early-bird fish and chips. Just order me a glass of white wine."

* * *

The Bull & Bear had an old-world British atmosphere with a Dickensian façade on the outside, a huge well-stocked bar and a sizeable wood-paneled dining area. The place appeared to be in a time warp from the Victorian era and was rumored to be haunted.

The pub was empty except for one older couple with strange accents and a gay bartender who was doing nothing to hide his sexual preferences.

Michael perched on a stool at the bar but when the drinks arrived he escaped to the sanctuary of a booth tucked away in an alcove.

Jane bounced in and shot him another smile. He felt better already.

"I think I know what you want to talk to me about," she said. "It's the job at Ravena's, isn't it?"

"Yeah; I guess Jack told you all about it. I suppose I should feel honored that he wants me to do it, but frankly it bothers me."

"Don't see why. We do this sort of thing all the time. We've had reporters posing as pizza delivery guys and as waiters at wedding receptions." She laughed. "We once had an L.A. reporter get a job as an actress's pool guy and she seduced him. I guess it's true what they say about pool guys."

"Or about actresses. But I'm supposed to go in there as a security guard; as in, protecting her from the likes of us. And what's going to happen when, or if, they find out who I really am?"

"Nothing much," said Jane. "First, it's not likely to happen. But if it did, you'd just get thrown out on your ear and threatened with all kinds of things that will come to nothing. Blackwell will be hauled onto the Ventura carpet, he'll apologize humbly and ensure Ravena that he will deal with you. He'll tell her you've been fired for misrepresenting yourself to his company and she'll be satisfied. She'll also feel more secure, knowing that the mole has been caught."

"Would there be another mole?" Michael asked warily.

"That depends," said Jane. "Personally I doubt it. I don't think Blackwell would want to risk putting in another reporter. That could cost him his company's reputation."

"Why would Blackwell risk getting involved in this in the first place?"

Jane cocked her head. "Jack has a lot of contacts he does 'favors' for and he remembers who owes him. Besides, Blackwell is his brother-in-law."

"Oh." Michael reached for his beer.

"Look," said Jane. "It's a no-brainer. If you do this and get away with it just long enough to find out something useful you'll be a Courier hero. It'll be worth a bonus and perhaps a promotion and a raise. If you don't do it, you could be out on your ear. JC expects his staffers to go to the mat for his paper. He demands loyalty, dedication and hard work. That's why we all make the big bucks."

Michael gulped at his beer. "I get the picture," he said. "Thanks."

"Don't think these undercover assignments are taken lightly," she said. "We only go to these measures when we feel there's a real need for it. And Jack senses that Ravena Ventura may be much more involved in her sister's murder than we think. While you were up at the apartment I went back and talked to the Cruzes again. It seems that the last time Mrs. Cruz thought she'd recognized Elizabeth's voice on the phone, Ravena cancelled a dinner date with her attorney and took off alone in her car. She hadn't returned by the time the Cruzes went to bed around eleven. Ravena did tell the cops that she'd been to her sister's apartment once, and that might have been the occasion. If so it was the night Elizabeth died."

"Yes. That ties in with what Povnik said about the cars in the parking lot."

Michael knew what he had to do.

* * *

Jane was right. It *was* a no-brainer—and he received an ear-to-ear grin when he told Jack so the next morning.

"Come on then," said Jack eagerly. "Let's go see Richard."

Iverson drove Michael south of Delray to a strip mall shopping center in Boca Raton, then ushered him into a small storefront office sandwiched between a Thai restaurant and a dry cleaner's. Michael was not impressed but Jack took him into the back through a tiny reception area that had no receptionist. He led Michael into a spacious modern office with flashy furnishings that might have just been delivered by Rooms to Go.

Richard Blackwell rose from behind his desk. He looked to be pushing sixty, but he was tall and muscular with a full mane of snow-white hair, and he carried a stiff military bearing that denoted authority.

"Hello, Richard," said Jack. "This is Michael, the guy I was telling you about."

"Good to meet you, Michael," said Blackwell, offering his hand. "Have a seat."

Michael plopped down on a gray velour chair next to the desk, wondering what Jack had been telling this man about him. Or not telling him. Jack had already made himself at home on a sofa that lined the wall behind him.

Blackwell pulled out a sheaf of paperwork from a desk drawer and studied it. "So, Michael," he said at last. "I gather you want to be a security guard."

"Well, uh." Michael wasn't sure what to say. "Jack wants me to be a security guard. He thinks it would, uh—"

"That's all right, Michael." Blackwell cut him off. "I know what's going on here. Jack thinks you could use a job on the Ravena Ventura estate."

"Uh, yes." Michael wasn't sure if he was walking on quicksand, but Blackwell was giving him a knowing smile.

"I'm told you have no arrest record," he said. "No felonies, no misdemeanors. Not even a parking ticket. Have you ever done any work in security?"

"No."

"Doesn't matter; the work in question is really pretty simple. Celebrities find there's a downside to being rich and famous. They're human, too, and they only want adulation on their own terms. They're always trying to maintain a barrier between themselves and their fans and that's where we come in. At Ravena's estate you wouldn't be guarding Fort Knox, just a client's ego.

"I'm prepared to take you on part-time on the basis of Jack's recommendation. I desperately need young, bright security people because I'm short-staffed right now. I just signed a contract with Ravena Ventura's manager to provide her with round-the-clock security and she wants a five-man team on her turf at all times."

"But, but," Michael stammered, "didn't Jack tell you that —"

"Yes, of course, but as far as I am concerned you are a good candidate for the job with acceptable credentials and no priors. If someone discovers that this isn't so I'll summarily fire you and offer my sincere apologies to my client. I'll also assure her that I intend to make sure you never get a security job anywhere again."

It was exactly as Jane had predicted.

Blackwell winked. "Don't worry, Michael, I've traveled down this road before. It's fun having a Courier editor in the family. All you have to do is fill out this brief human-resources form, and then get to work. You'll be scheduled for two or three days a week at the Ventura estate and I'll pay you fifteen dollars an hour with a check every two weeks."

Michael was flabbergasted. "I'm actually going to be paid for this?"

"Of course," said Blackwell. "As long as you're working for me I'm obligated to pay you. What you do with the money is up to you."

"No it's not," snapped Iverson from across the room. "You hand it over to The Courier. It will eventually be returned to Richard as one of our investigation expenses."

"All right," sighed Michael. "When do I start my new career?"

"Tomorrow morning would be good," said Blackwell. "I'll alert Paul Hendrix that you're coming. He's my crew chief at the Ventura estate and he'll show you the ropes. No one up there knows your connection to The Courier."

"Good," said Michael. *And hopefully no one ever will.*

Chapter 20

It was dark, foggy and unseasonably cool. A heavy mist was drifting in from the ocean, but Ravena was sitting out by the pool in a pink thong bikini which left nothing to the imagination.

Michael came around the corner of the house and faltered in his stride when he saw her. But she smiled and beckoned him over.

"You're the new security guard," she said.

"Yes, I'm Michael." He didn't know what else to say. He stood paralyzed as she eyed him up and down. He felt like a piece of meat.

"Well, well, Michael," she said as she stood up from the lounge chair. "We know who you really are. Do you like what you've seen so far?"

Michael licked his lips but said nothing. There didn't seem to be an appropriate answer.

"What's the matter? Cat got your tongue?" The smile faded and she spat at him.

Then suddenly she was on him like a frenzied wild animal, clawing at him with two-inch nails, ripping at his shirt, then his flesh, slashing at his face.

Michael started to scream—and sat up in bed shouting hysterically. He was wreathed in sweat but alone in his own bedroom. There were no scratches, no cuts, no blood, and no Ravena Ventura. Just the hangover left by a nightmare.

He looked over at the clock by his bed. Five after four. Three more hours before he had to be up, but he knew sleep would be elusive for the rest of the night. He didn't want to be doing this. Yes, he wanted to do a good job for The Courier and he craved the admiration of his peers, especially Jane's. But he had an uneasy feeling about this assignment and it wasn't clear to him how he was going to get anything out of it.

He ordered himself to get it together. *The night always magnifies problems. Most reporters would give their eyeteeth for a chance to do this!*

Michael lay back down and pulled the sheets around him to form a protective cocoon. But he gave up on sleep before dawn. By six-thirty he had showered, shaved and was studying his modest closet for appropriate clothing. Nothing too formal, nothing too grungy, Blackwell had told him. "We don't want you looking like an FBI agent, or like a homeless person." Michael finally settled on a white polo shirt and khaki pants. Cool chic, he told himself hopefully.
He pushed his wallet into his pants pocket, then paused and pulled it out again. He had to be careful what was in it, just in case things fell apart. He had sixty-two dollars, a Michigan driver's license, his car registration, one Visa card . . . and his press pass!

Thank God he had remembered to check his billfold. He plucked out the press card, stuck it into a nightstand drawer, then picked up the little camera Jack had given him.

"Why do I need to carry this?" Michael had asked him. "God knows what I can take pictures of. Anyway, we wouldn't be able to use them without Ravena's permission, since I'd be taking them while on her property."

"You never know what you might want to photograph," Jack had explained patiently. "And don't worry about the legalities of using anything you get. We have attorneys to worry about stuff like that. Just don't let anyone spot you getting snap-happy. Of course," he'd added with a leer, "Ravena might want you to take a few intimate shots of her."

"Asshole," Michael muttered reflectively. He tucked the tiny camera into a side pocket of his pants and checked to make sure there was no incriminating bulge.

He eyed himself in the mirror. Mr. Private Security Guard. He was ready. As ready as he would ever be. He locked the door to his apartment after a careful look around, wondering what would transpire that day before he would see it again, if he were to see it again. *It's easy for you, Jack, but what if I wind up in the slammer?*

He forced such thoughts out of his mind, slid into the Mustang, and headed for his debut with his new career. He would be rubbing shoulders with the glitterati of show-business while secretly looking for . . . what?

* * *

The gates to the Ventura estate were open when Michael arrived, and he turned in and pulled up at the tiny guardhouse. A man with a bear-like physique and a look of boredom on his face rolled out of his chair and leaned in the window of the Mustang. Michael made an effort to be nonchalant and pulled out his driver's license by way of ID. At least that was genuine.

"Michael Hanlon," he announced. "Just signed on with Blackwell Security. This is my first assignment."

The burly guard eyed him up and down, then returned the driver's license. "Welcome to my world," he said. "This is about as close to Club Med as you can get. My name is Harris, Jonathan Harris. You'll find me down here most of the time."

Harris pointed up the driveway. "Follow the driveway up around the bend there," he said, "and you'll come to a small branch off to the left. That will take you to the north side of the house where we have a security office. You can park there. If you find yourself at the front door of the house you missed the turn. Try not to go there. Milady is very picky. Hendrix will meet you at the office and fill you in. I'll call and let him know you're on the way."

Michael thanked him and drove up the driveway of pink pavers, sweeping through tropical foliage that shielded the house from view. He found the cut-off, a narrower pink ribbon, and suddenly found himself at the back of the house. He had reached the far side of the mansion without ever seeing the front.

The pink pavement ended at a small parking lot that already embraced two cars, and Michael pulled in alongside them. He was greeted before he could get out of his vehicle.

"Hello, Michael, I'm Paul Hendrix," said a dapper middle-aged man, extending his hand. He looked like the stereotype of a seasoned surfer—buff, bold and confident. He seemed friendly enough, but he was Michael's new boss, and he didn't know about Michael's double life.

"Come on into our operations room," said Hendrix. "This is where we all hang out. It serves as my office, but it's also our security break room." He pointed to the amenities. "There's a bathroom, shower, TV, kitchen area, even a small place to bunk."

Finally he pointed to a door with the word "PRIVATE" stenciled on it. "That will take you into the house, if necessary," he said, "but the interior of the house is off-limits unless you're invited or assigned there for some reason. I called Ellerby, Ravena's business manager, and he'll be down to see you in a few. He wants to meet all the new security people personally."

"Makes sense to me," said Michael, "or you might get somebody claiming to be security when they're not." *Like me!*

"Ellerby is Number Two in our pecking order," explained Hendrix. "Ravena, of course is Numero Uno, and Ellerby acts like her mother hen. He spends a lot of time on the premises and has an apartment on the second floor. I'm Number Three in your pecking order but I'm the guy you report to. I get my orders from Ellerby. It's okay if he gives you an assignment personally, but I need to know about it. We can't have security personnel running around willy-nilly or we'd be in a hell of a mess if we ever had to deal with something serious."

"Have you ever had a security breach?"

"No, but we're still just settling in here. And I think security has been pretty lax. A place this size could use some video cameras. I guess Ravena felt safe with an army of cops, but she laid them off for some reason. We're still working out the details of just how visible our presence should be, but—"

Hendrix paused as the forbidden private door opened and a small figure in a business suit stepped into the room. Michael knew from Jane's description that it was Ellerby. Short, quiet, creepy and yes, even slimy.

After perfunctory handshakes Ellerby and Michael eyed each other up and down, then Ellerby made small talk with Hendrix that was obviously designed to show Michael who was where on the totem pole.

After five minutes of acting out these pre-planned motions, Ellerby quietly excused himself and disappeared into the house.

"Strange guy," said Michael after a comfortable time lapse.

"You can say that again," said Hendrix, "but I guess it takes all kinds. Most of these Hollywood types are weird anyway.

"Have you met Ravena herself?"

"Yes. Ellerby took me into the house to introduce me. She wasn't how I imagined. Very quiet, very nervous actually, and not big on the social graces, which surprised me. You'll probably get to meet her in due course. You may even get to see more of her than you'd like. Ellerby told me that she may need a driver from time to time and it will be our responsibility to chauffeur her around and provide security for her while she's out. You can have that assignment if you feel star-struck."

"No, I'm not star-struck, but I wouldn't mind taking a turn at the wheel of her limo. It might prove interesting." *And informative.*

Hendrix sniffed. "Obviously you've never been anyone's driver," he said. "It can get pretty boring, sitting or standing around for hours while they're out having a good time. Then when they get drunk or high you have to protect them from themselves as well as the press and the public."

Michael didn't care. It might be fun to give the paparazzi a run for their money. After all, he would have the inside track. And he even had a hidden camera.

Chapter 21

Michael soon discovered that being a security guard could be tedious work, especially when everything seemed secure. The minutes dragged by like hours and it was tough to stay awake, let alone focused. This, he decided, was not going to be a permanent career move. At least he had been assigned to cover the grounds, which kept him on his feet and enabled him to reconnoiter the landscape.

He hadn't realized just how immense Ravena's estate was. The house was more than ten thousand square feet under air conditioning, plus a covered lanai and an outdoor pool and patio that overlooked the ocean. It all sat on three acres of some of the most desirable and expensive real estate in America. And on the other side of the highway which ran by the front gate was another quarter-acre on the Intracoastal Waterway, Here Ravena had a modest thirty-foot yacht waiting at her private dock. He wondered if she ever used it.

The grounds had been meticulously landscaped and were maintained in immaculate condition. A landscaping service came every week to "mow, blow and go" as they liked to put it, and Michael wondered what Alfonso Cruz's duties had been as Ravena's gardener.

Michael walked around the white and pink stucco building, careful to stay at a safe distance. Around the back he strolled along the far edge of the patio where it ended at a five-foot seawall with steps down to the beach.

Across the water to the left, Michael could see a headland, a sandy promontory that stretched out defiantly into the ocean. It was almost barren, dotted with a few coconut palms spared by builders who had been clearing the property for yet another architectural masterpiece.

Ravena's beach was considered private, though anyone with a boat or the swimming talents of Michael Phelps could infiltrate the property from the sea, if they had the need or the desire. But why would they? Ravena had given every indication that she didn't feel threatened by her sister's killer or killers.

Hendrix had advised Michael to stay out of Ravena and Ellerby's sight as much as possible, but when he turned the northeast corner on his second circuit of the property he spotted the actress lounging by the pool. He looked around quickly for a detour and discovered a path that took him down the ridge. Then he found himself on sugar sand in the shadow of the seawall. A tightly manicured hedge atop the wall helped keep him out of sight, only a few feet away from Ravena but well below the patio level.

He was busy mapping out a route through the shrubbery that would take him back up to the house level unseen when he heard voices. They were muffled by the surf crashing ashore, but strident enough to alert him. He stopped and strained to listen.

It wasn't too difficult to recognize Ellerby's voice. He had a hoarse, nasal tone and a slight lisp. It somehow complemented the man's physical stature.

Michael hugged the seawall to make sure he wouldn't be spotted. Jack had wanted a fly on the wall. Well, how about a sand fly?

"I don't like it," grumbled Ellerby. "It's not necessary."

"Oh shut up, Ellie." For a syrupy movie queen, Ravena Ventura wasn't exactly sweetness and light when there was no one around. "I know what I'm doing."

"I'm tired of falling over these half-baked amateur security guards wherever I go. Maybe we should have kept a few real cops around."

"The real cops need all hands on deck to find my sister's killer. This security firm will keep out fans and the rest of the nosy public, and that's really all we need."

"But we can't sit around here forever, drinking and sunbathing. People are already starting to talk."

"What people? And about what?"

"Well for starters you got a call this morning from Liebovitz, that agent in L.A. He's heard about your sister and wants to know why you haven't called him. This movie-star-turned-recluse stuff can't go on until the end of time, you know. The whole of Hollywood has been wondering where you've gone, and why—and now that the headlines are linking you to a murder you're back at the top of the Tinsel Town hit parade."

"I know. Just chill, will you? The next time Liebovitz calls let me know. I need to talk to him. And I need to deal with Meriwether, too."

"You need to tread carefully with him. He's been calling from L.A. too, wanting to know if you need his services."

"What for? He's an entertainment attorney."

"He obviously thinks it's his duty to protect you. I've told him that as your manager that's what I'm here for. He's not happy about that and is still threatening to fly over here. I think he's just missing a little extra nookie."

Ravena glared at him. "You really are a stupid asshole. Why don't you do something useful and get me a drink. Better still, go up to West Palm and see if you can score some quality coke. Maybe someone will mug you."

"You need me, Ravvvennna," Ellerby hissed through clenched teeth. "Just remember, we're a team. An inseparable team. Whatever happens to me happens to you, too."

"Go fuck yourself!"

There was a sudden silence from the patio above Michael's head. He waited and listened carefully, but heard nothing. Maybe Ellerby had taken the hint and left. If so, where had he gone? And was Ravena still sitting by the pool? Either one of them could decide to come down to the beach. He had to get out of there.

His Loafers weren't designed for beachwear and he was about to step carefully through the sand when he froze. Ellerby was suddenly back by the pool.

"There's a woman at the gate to see you," he told Ravena gravely. "Says she's your sister."

Chapter 22

"My sister? How could—?"

"I have no idea. I'll go down there and check her out. Maybe it's a crazy fan who thinks she's been reincarnated or something."

Ellerby marched quickly into the house but Ravena appeared to be staying put. So Michael continued to flatten himself against the seawall and pray.

After five long minutes a female cry broke the tension and the silence.

"Rachel, sweetheart!"

"Em!" gasped Ravena. "I don't believe it."

Ravena stood up, opened her arms, hugged her older sister, then held her at arm's length and stared at her open-mouthed. The woman was slightly taller and heavier than Ravena, blonde hair in a pageboy cut, her body poured into a tight-fitting navy blue pantsuit that was defying the heat index. Careful makeup helped give her sex appeal, but the gene pool had shortchanged her at the side of her twin sisters.

"Em! It's really you?"

"None other. I heard about poor Liz and just had to see you. I was in town anyway, passing through, and couldn't let the opportunity slip by."

"Em, it's been, what, twenty years? How have you been? Where have you been?"

"Everywhere and back. More importantly, how are you? I've been reading the papers and watching the news on TV. You're back in the headlines, though not in the best of circumstances."

"I know. But I'm doing okay. Here, sit down." Then, as an afterthought, "Ellie, this is my sister, my long-lost sister Emily. Haven't seen her in years. Em, this is David Ellerby, my manager. He's been taking care of things for me since Liz died."

Ellerby nodded and took Emily's hand stiffly.

"Ellie, get Em a drink. And I'll have another one, too. A family reunion, of sorts, calls for some kind of celebration." She smiled at her sister. "And please call me Ravena. I gave up being Rachel many years ago. Too many bad memories."

Emily turned her head side to side, taking in her surroundings. "Well, you certainly landed on your feet, didn't you? I'm so proud of you."

"I have an appointment this afternoon but you must stay for lunch and let me show you the house."

Michael drew a deep breath and prayed that Ravena wasn't about to show her the beach, complete with security guard huddled under the seawall. Relief washed over him when it became evident that Emily's visit was a fleeting one.

"Look, please forgive me, but I'll have to take a rain check on lunch, and the drink," she said, glancing at her watch. "Actually I have a plane to catch. I'm on my way from Dallas to the Bahamas. I have to check out some property."

"Property?"

"Yes. I'm working for a venture capital company and they want me to look at casino options in the islands."

"Wow! What happened to Mexico and the millionaire businessman?"

"Oh, he's been history for some time. We broke up a number of years ago. I'll tell you all about it when I get back. I'm sorry to cut and run, but I really am under the gun at the moment. I just had to touch base with you after I heard about Liz. The poor girl never got it together, did she? I wish I could have been there for her, but you can't change the past, can you?"

She reached out and hugged her sister. "I'll stop by again when I get back," she said. "Hopefully I'll have more time and we can catch up on things."

Slightly bewildered, Ravena pointed to Ellerby, who had paused in his trek to get drinks and was standing ten feet away watching the family reunion with a frown.

"Ellerby will show you out," said Ravena. "And Ellie, give Em my phone number. Life's too short to lose touch for another twenty years."

Michael heard the sounds of patio furniture moving and footsteps receding. He waited cautiously, then edged toward the south side of the estate. He moved quickly toward the gate and hid behind a huge clump of areca palms. He watched Ravena's sister leave in a black SUV, then wandered slowly toward the gatehouse.

Harris stepped out to meet him. "Hendrix has been trying to reach you," he said. "What's wrong with your walkie-talkie?"

"Huh?" Michael reached into his pants pocket, pulled out the instrument and examined it blankly. "Jeez," he said lamely, "I forgot about it." Then his blood ran cold. A walkie-talkie was standard equipment for the security personnel, but he really had forgotten about it. And that was a dangerous mistake. If it had been turned on it would have been scratching out noises that would have exposed him on the beach.

"Actually," he told Harris, "I'm not sure it's working properly. I need to get it checked out. Any idea what Hendrix wanted?"

"No idea, but you'd better get back to the command post right away. You don't want to screw up on your first day."

Michael nodded and headed back toward the house, but he ran into Hendrix before he got there.

"There you are!" he said. "I've been trying to reach you. You must keep that walkie-talkie on at all times."

"Yeah, I'm not sure it's working. Maybe we should test it."

"Sure. But right now I need you to take your lunch break. Miss Ventura is looking for a driver at fourteen hundred hours and you need to go home and get into a suit. Something dark and conservative. You do have a suit, don't you?"

"Yes, but . . . " Hadn't he been told there would be no uniform?

"Better get a move on. You don't have a lot of time. Be at the garage by fourteen hundred hours. And don't be late. I don't know how punctual she is but it won't hurt to be early. It will hurt to be late."

Michael nodded. At least he would now have an opportunity to touch base with Jack.

As he drove out of the gate his mind wandered back to the conversations he had overheard. It was obvious that Ravena and Ellerby weren't on the best of terms. And why did Ellerby describe himself and Ravena as an inseparable team? *Whatever happens to me happens to you, too.* That's what he'd said. What did that mean? Something wasn't right in paradise.

Michael got in line at a Wendy's drive-through on his way home, grabbed a cheeseburger and ate it as he drove.

Then he phoned Jack and breathlessly gave him a rundown on his morning and the conversation by the pool.

Iverson reacted with his usual nonchalance. "You need to hang around that pool area as much as you can," he said." It sounds like a good place to eavesdrop. Would you like a listening device and maybe a tape recorder?"

"God, no, Jack," cried Michael. "Are you serious? I'm already carrying a cell-phone, a walkie-talkie and a camera. I don't have any more pockets and I already feel like a walking Radio Shack."

"Just trying to be helpful."

"All right. But what do you make of what I overheard?"

"Not sure. It sounds as though Ravena is a bit of a coke freak, but that's not surprising. Or maybe she was just referring to Ellerby's habits. Either way she sounds like a real piece of work."

"What about that 'we're a team' business?"

"Movie stars and their managers usually are a team," said Jack, "until one of them finds a more lucrative partner. That means nothing. However, it doesn't sound as though they're a very compatible team. What you heard supports what Jane observed about them together. He's pretty new in Ventura's life and they don't seem to be hitting it off very well. That whole relationship is puzzling to me, given Ellerby's background. We're doing some more checking on him at this end."

"Any thoughts on the sudden appearance of Ravena's older sister?"

"No. I see no reason to concern ourselves with her. She disappeared years ago and is probably suddenly having pangs of guilt because Elizabeth is dead and she was never around to help her. Meanwhile, you'd better get moving. Hurry up and get into your chauffeur's suit. Have you got a little peaked cap to go with it?"

"Very funny, Jack. I didn't expect driving Miss Daisy around to be one of my duties."

"Look at it this way. It's a great opportunity to get closer to her. If there's just the two of you in the car she may actually talk to you. You know, even personal stuff. These Hollywood egomaniacs love to talk about themselves."

"I guess you're right." Michael's early fears over playing security guard had been magnified by new concerns. Now he was going to be under the close scrutiny of Ravena herself.

He arrived back at the estate with ten minutes to spare, parked the Mustang, then walked around to the front of the building, where three garage doors faced the sweeping pink driveway. He punched in the security codes and the doors slid up smoothly to expose five vehicles in a garage built for six. The three doors were matched by doors at the rear that opened to the north parking lot where security and other help left their cars.

There were three aisles for cars, with a white Lincoln limousine commandeering one of them. Lined up in the other two lanes were a green Lexus, a black Mercedes sedan, a red Corvette and a black Cadillac Escalade. Ravena certainly had eclectic tastes in wheels.

The vehicles could be driven forward out to the driveway or backed out to the rear. There was a bench along one wall that seemed to be a repository for conventional auto-maintenance equipment and cleaning supplies. Michael wondered who used any of this stuff now that Senor Cruz was gone.

Michael buzzed Henrix on the walkie-talkie. "I'm at the garage," he said, "but there are five cars in here. Which one does she want to use?"

"No idea," said Hendrix. "I'm sure she'll decide when she gets there. But they're all polished and gassed up and the keys are in them. Just remember that your job is to protect her as well as drive her."

Michael mumbled something affirmative, then wandered around the garage while he waited. He eyed the limo enviously. It might be fun to drive that.

Suddenly a door burst open on the wall by the house and Ravena Ventura stepped down into the garage. Michael stared at her. He was up-close and personal with one of the world's most famous and wealthy women. But his first reaction was more shock than awe.

Chapter 23

Despite a net worth of oodles of dollars, Ravena Ventura did not look wealthy. Nor did she look sophisticated, well-groomed or even in the best of humor. She wore a tailored pink suit that had probably cost more than the average family's weekly income, but somehow she wasn't doing it justice. Her hair was stringy, and hurriedly applied makeup didn't hide the flaws in her features. She looked strangely disheveled and Michael suspected that she wasn't exactly sober.

She looked at him glassy-eyed for an eternity, then said, "Ah, you must be Michael."

"Ms. Ventura?" he responded.

Who else?" she said. "Mr. Ellerby is unfortunately detained so I requested a driver. Did they tell you I decided to take the Mercedes?"

"No ma'am, but—"

"Don't call me ma'am," she snapped. "When men call me that it makes me feel old. You may call me Miss Ravena."

"Yes . . . uh, Miss Ravena."

Michael was suddenly hating this assignment. Her big bucks and millions of idolizing fans didn't mean much to him. He decided he didn't like Ravena Ventura. Certainly not the off-screen version. He gave the limo a longing glance as he opened the rear door of the Mercedes for her.

She nodded a thank you and Michael slid behind the wheel. "Head south," she told him. "We're going to Delray Beach. Eighth Street. The Medical Arts Center. You know it?"

"N-no, Miss Ravena," Michael stammered, "but I'm sure I'll be able to find it."

He steered the car down the pink driveway, waved to Harris as he exited the gate and turned south on the coastal highway.

Medical Arts Center? Maybe she was sick. That would explain why she looked so crappy.

He heard her fumbling around in the back seat and there was a click as she opened something. He soon found out what it was.

"Hmm," she said to no one in particular. "Not much in here." The click was followed by a clink and Michael realized she was raiding a miniature liquor cabinet.

Michael adjusted the rear-view mirror and found that by cocking his head slightly he could see her. She was grasping a small glass of amber liquid.

"Michael," she said. "Would you like a drink?"

"Oh, no thank you, Ma'am, er, Miss. Not while I'm driving. I don't think it would be a good idea."

She gave a little giggle at that and raised the glass to her lips. "I guess you're right," she said. "Maybe some other time."

"Thank you, Miss Ravena."

"Do you like driving?" she asked him.

"Oh, yes," said Michael. He turned and smiled at her. "It makes a change from guard duty."

"Have you been a security guard long?"

"Not down here," he said. "Up in, er, up north."

"Do you like Florida?"

"Yes. Life is different down here." *Especially in Manalapan. How about you? Do YOU like Florida? And why are you here?*

"Are you married?"

"No, Miss."

"Girlfriend?"

"Not at the moment. I've been too busy getting established in my new job."

"I see," she said leaning over the back of his seat and eyeing him closely. He could smell the scotch on her breath. "Well, you're a good-lookin' guy, you know. You'd be quite a catch for some young chick. Or perhaps even for some slightly older chick."

She clucked at that and raised her glass in a silent toast. Michael felt his body temperature rising with it. What was with this woman? She had everything anyone could want and could have anything she'd forgotten to get. And now she was messing with the mind of the hired help.

He inwardly breathed a sigh of relief when they passed a sign advertising the Delray Beach city limits. He turned inland onto Eighth Street and took the bridge over the Intracoastal Waterway, where the road gave way to modest apartments, consignment shops and convenience stores. The Medical Arts Center was a four-story white stucco building that dominated the skyline. It was definitely the architectural queen of this section of the city. But why would Ravena Ventura be coming here? If she needed a doctor there must be classier neighborhoods harboring prestigious practitioners more in keeping with a movie star's needs and pocketbook.

He pulled into the parking lot.

"Just wait here," she ordered and stepped out of the car before Michael could extricate himself from the driver's seat and open the door for her. She waltzed toward the building's main entrance without looking back at him. He was left feeling as useless as a space heater in July as she disappeared inside.

Michael stared at the sky. It was the same every day until the thunderstorms rolled in, a bright blue canvas with patches of white clouds floating by aimlessly. The sun was merciless and Michael was starting to feel like a dishrag. His first thought was to sit in the car and run the air conditioning, but after a few boring minutes he decided to make better use of his time and check out the building. Maybe he would discover who Ravena had come to see.

He found nothing on the first floor other than restrooms, two banks of elevators and a black and gold sign advertising the doctors' suite numbers.

The tenants were a mixture of internists, ob-gyns, dentists, one cardiac specialist and two psychologists. Maybe Ravena was visiting one of the shrinks. That would make sense. He double-checked the list, scouring it in vain for a detox connection. Ravena certainly seemed to need that.

He wandered around the small silent hallway but there was nothing to do and nothing to see. At least it was cooler in here.

After a zillion futile minutes of wishing he'd brought a crossword puzzle or a paperback book, Michael returned to the information board and scrutinized the list of doctors. He noticed that the internists and ob-gyns were on the second floor, the dentists shared the third and the cardiac doc and the shrinks were on the fourth. To kill time he started examining their names, idly looking for one that shared his initials, or wondering what the letters after their names represented. There was no one around. No one else had arrived since he and Ravena got here, and no one had left. The health care business didn't appear to be on fire.

A sudden whirring of the elevators brought him back to reality. He checked the red floor numbers above the elevator doors. One of the cars was going up. It clunked to a halt on the third floor to which it had been summoned and Michael decided to hotfoot it back to the car. It might be Ravena leaving, and he didn't want her to find him absent from his post. He was supposed to be guarding the Mercedes, whisking imagined wisps of dirt from the paintwork.

Michael reached the car and turned to see the door to the building swing open. Ravena stepped out, shielding her eyes from the sun's glare and looking vaguely in the direction of the Mercedes.

An explosive crack suddenly broke the silence. Ravena screamed as something tore into the cornice over the door. She screamed again and dropped to the ground as a small shower of cement cascaded around her. Someone was shooting at her.

Chapter 24

Michael was frozen in horror for a millisecond, then he tore across the parking lot toward Ravena. She was lying facedown on the pavement. Had she been hit? Was she dead?

He dropped to his knees beside her and she turned her head slowly.

"Miss Ravena, are you all right?"

She nodded. "What the hell was that?"

"I think someone was shooting at you. We need to get to safety. We're sitting ducks here. Let's get back into the building. When I say 'go' stay as low to the ground as you can and head for the door."

She nodded again but said nothing.

Michael looked around. It was early afternoon, siesta time in a quiet part of town. There was no traffic and no one around.

Michael tried to figure where the shot had originated. It had to have come from across the street, where a row of small businesses were struggling to survive in a section of the city waiting patiently for urban renewal. There was a vacant lot of scrub and trees between a church and a small row of storefronts, ideal cover for a gunman.

There had been no more shots, so Michael decided the perpetrator had probably fled the scene after seeing Ravena drop to the ground. He likely had a getaway vehicle parked behind the church and could easily have made his escape via a side street to the back.

Michael assured himself that the danger was over but positioned himself between Ravena and the empty lot. Then, bent double, the two of them hot-footed it into the building. Once in the foyer he breathed a sigh of relief and pulled out his cell phone.

"No, no!" Ravena cried as he started to punch in numbers. "Who are you calling?"

"Nine-one-one."

"No. Don't do that. We don't want the police involved."

"Why not? I think someone just took a shot at you. You could have been killed."

"We don't need the police. We'll just tell Hendrix when we get back."

"But there's somebody out there who tried to kill you. They may try again."

Ravena gripped his arm. "And we may be over-reacting. Don't worry about it. Just drive me home."

She opened the door to the parking lot, glanced around quickly then ordered, "C'mon, Michael. Let's go."

Michael struggled to stop his hands from shaking as he ushered Ravena into the car. Maybe Jane had been on the right track from the get-go. Perhaps Ravena was the real target of Liz's killer. Whoever it was meant business. The wooded area across the street was a few hundred feet from the medical building. The shooter must have had a rifle. And he would use it again when he learned that Ravena was still very much alive.

Ravena sat in silence until they left the Delray city limits. Michael wondered what was going through her mind. Apparently not much. She started playing with her purse and leaned toward the front of the car.

"Michael," she said, "do you like coke?"

The hair stood up on the back of Michael's head. Ravena had just escaped death by inches and she wanted to chit-chat about nothing.

"Yes, it's okay," he said. "But actually I prefer Pepsi."

"Verrry funny. I'm not talking about that kind of coke. That fucking dentist sells me this stuff. Top grade, he says, but I think it's just the price that's top grade. Plus he's charging me a fortune for my new caps." She leaned toward him with a clenched-teeth smile. "What do you think of them?"

Michael mumbled something incoherent to let her know he was paying attention. Jack Iverson had been on the money, as usual. You can learn a lot about someone from being alone in a car with them. Ravena Ventura, much-loved marquee movie star, was a mess. She'd lost her twin sister in a heinous crime, someone had just tried to put a bullet in her, and her dentist was a cocaine dealer. But all she cared about was her movie-star teeth.

Ravena lapsed into silence until he pulled the Mercedes into the garage and opened the rear door. She clambered out of the car ungraciously, clutching her purse and its precious cargo.

"Thank you, Michael," she said and disappeared indoors, back to her solitary life behind self-imposed bars.

Chapter 25

Ravena was already on the phone with the security chief by the time Michael walked into the operations room. Hendrix's color was gray and he appeared to be on the verge of barfing his lunch. His side of the conversation was limited to 'Yes, Miss Ravena," "No, Miss Ravena" and the polite equivalent of "Three bags full, Miss Ravena." Relief washed across his face when he finally hung up and turned to Michael.

"She just told me," he said quietly. "She also told me none of this must leak out. Not to the police. Not to the press. Not anywhere. Why didn't you call me?"

"She wouldn't even let me call nine-one-one. Insisted on just driving home."

"Did you see the shooter?"

"Didn't see anything. It all happened so fast. The gunman must have been stationed across the street, probably with a rifle. And I heard only one shot. The shooter may have thought he'd killed her, because I thought he had when she dropped to the ground."

"Did you notice anyone following you to the dentist's office? Any other vehicles?"

"No, but I wasn't looking for any."

Hendrix shook his head. "You should have been. You're her bodyguard as well as her chauffeur. There's a lot of crazies out there and anytime she goes out that front gate she's a target. Never forget that."

Michael nodded but said nothing. He wasn't ready for a lesson in Security 101 and was relieved when Hendrix dismissed him for the day.

* * *

Hendrix may have been in a blue funk over Ravena's brush with death, but Jack Iverson reacted as though he'd won the lottery.

"What do you mean we can't print it?" he thundered down the phone. " GUNMAN TARGETS RAVENA VENTURA. It will sell through the roof."

"It will also blow my cover and probably destroy your relationship with your brother-in-law. Right now there's only one place that story could come from—and that's me. Besides which, we have nothing to flesh it out with."

Jack began to chew his lip. "True," he said at last, "but we can't just ignore it. Give me hard copy on every detail. I'm sure we can find some other sources. I can't believe no one saw anything. There are businesses in that neighborhood. Someone must have seen something, or at least heard the shot."

"Jack, there was no one around. No one came running out. It was hot as hell out there and it was siesta time. Ravena and I could have been lying dead in that parking lot until the buzzards showed up."

"Then we would have had an even better story. Anyway, I'm going to send Jane up there to check around. We'll keep you out of it. Meanwhile, meet Jane and myself at the Beachcomber in an hour. I think it's time for more beer and brainstorming."

* * *

Michael was glad of the beer and the company. He had been reprimanded by both his supervisors and he felt like yesterday's meatloaf. He'd stumbled into the middle of a sensational story only to find his hands tied.

When he arrived at the Beachcomber Jack and Jane had already taken over a corner booth. To Michael's relief, Jack had taken a chill pill.

"Peterson and I talked with JC about the shooting," he said, "and JC nixed the story until we have considerably more information without blowing your cover."

Michael raised his eyebrows as he ordered a Heineken and slid into a seat.

"Jane drew a blank when she canvassed the neighborhood," said Jack. "No one in the medical center or the other businesses admitted to hearing or seeing anything."

"I looked around in the medics' parking lot," said Jane, "but found nothing. The stonework around the entrance was pitted in a few places, but I couldn't find any slugs. They could have ricocheted anywhere."

"Bottom line is that we're nowhere," said Jack. "As usual, JC cares more about being best with the news than being first. "He turned to Michael. "Why was Ravena so insistent on it all being brushed under the rug?"

"No idea. Maybe she didn't want the cops involved because she was carrying a purseful of cocaine. Frankly, Ravena Ventura is a fucking mess. She was pie-eyed on scotch and she seems to be doing drugs up the yin yang."

"Maybe this wasn't a deliberate attempt on her life. Could have been kids goofing off in the woods across the street with a BB gun."

Michael looked at him in amazement. "Are you kidding?"

"No. I still have the hots for the story, but we've no time to turn it into anything JC will buy for this week's issue. It looks as though we'll have to fall back on MANHUNT WIDENS IN HUNT FOR RAVENA SISTER'S KILLER."

He leaned back and looked at his reporters for a positive reaction.

"What's happened to warrant the manhunt being widened?" asked Michael.

"While you were out dodging bullets, Jane was tracking down more information on that guy Ellerby. We found that there's a beige Lincoln Continental registered in his name. And that janitor told you there was a beige Lincoln outside Elizabeth's apartment building on the night of her death."

"Yeah, but I'm sure there's more than one beige Lincoln in Palm Beach County. Probably hundreds of 'em."

"Maybe. But remember he also told you there were two similar Lexuses—or is it Lexi?—parked there that night too. One of them had to be Elizabeth's rental. That leaves the other one and— "

"And you think that was Ravena's car because she has a Lexus, too."

Jack shrugged and pulled on his beer. "She did admit that she'd visited her sister at the apartment. What if she met this Ellerby guy there?"

"What if she did?"

"On the night of the murder? C'mon. Look, maybe we can get both Ravena and her manager implicated in this in some way."

"You're suggesting that *they* killed her?"

"I wouldn't necessarily go that far. We'll have to see what the cops come up with. I don't think it'll be long before Henderson is over at the estate, looking to talk to Ventura and her multi-faceted manager. Maybe he'll be able to find out how come she's suddenly got such a scumbag on her payroll."

"Just how are we going to parlay all this into 'hunt widening'?" asked Jane.

"Easy," said Jack. "With a subhead, MYSTERY OF CARS AT MURDER SCENE. Those vehicles have got to be clues, whoever's cars they were."

Michael thought it sounded thin, but didn't want to say so. "Can't we work up something on Ravena the druggie and her dentist supplier?" he asked.

"I don't think we need to get into that just yet. But by the time we've finished with Ravena Ventura she might be begging us for mercy."

"Or begging the courts for a multi-million dollar damage judgment against The Courier," observed Jane.

"I got the impression she's thinking of firing her attorney," said Michael.

Jack smiled. "Don't worry," he said. "She'll get a new one; probably a team of 'em. She'd be stupid not to. Keep your eyes and ears open tomorrow Mikey, and keep an eye out for Henderson. We don't want him running into you at Ravena's place and blowing your cover, especially since he owes us. The only fuckin' leads he's gotten so far have come from us. I don't think these dick-head local cops have ever had to investigate a real murder before. If it isn't a domestic or a drive-by they're out of their depth."

Michael nodded. Henderson hadn't had any runs or hits so far, only errors. But he needed the detective on his side. And now he had to worry that he was going to bump into him on the Ventura estate. Was it a crime to impersonate a security guard? He got the uncanny feeling that Henderson would love to throw him in jail for it.

Chapter 26

Michael strolled around Ravena Ventura's estate, taking in the beach and ocean vistas and listening to the surf endlessly pounding the sand below the seawall. It was a postcard-picture view that would have been at home in a Corona beer commercial, but it didn't make security work any less numbingly mindless.

And despite the magnificence of the grounds, there was no one to admire them. Ravena's mansion was more like a mausoleum than a home.

The only times Michael had seen Ravena since the shooting incident were when she was lounging by the pool. This seemed to be a most favored pastime, second only perhaps to drinking. Certainly she was never without a glass in her hand. As instructed, he always gave the outside patio a wide berth if she was gracing it with her presence, but wondered if this was a mistake. A chance encounter; a little idle chit-chat. It was amazing how much you could draw out of people when they were off guard. And she seemed to like him.

He wondered if he would get any more opportunities to act as her chauffeur. Probably not. The idea of being gunned down should have turned her into even more of a homebody.

Looking out for Henderson was the only thing keeping Michael alert. He knew the detective would show up at some point to question Ravena and Ellerby about the cars. If Henderson saw him playing rent-a-cop the manure would really hit the cooling device.

So he was prepared when he spotted a car pull up at the gatehouse. It was Detective Henderson's well-traveled plain wrapper.

Michael backed behind the nearest shrubbery and started to retrace his steps to the pool. He observed through the trees that Ravena was on the scene, soaking up the sun and the liquor as usual. So he took his diversionary route down to the beach and hugged the seawall.

He stopped. He could hear Ellerby's annoying whine.

"That Detective Henderson is here," he hissed. "He's on his way up to the house."

"You let him on the grounds?" cried Ravena.

"Of course I did. He's a cop. And since he's investigating your sister's murder we can't exactly tell him to fuck off."

Ravena sighed and sat up. "I guess you're right. You'd better go meet him. Bring him out here. We can offer him a drink. Maybe relax him a little."

"He won't want a drink. He'll be on duty. I'm sure he isn't here for your autograph."

"Whatever. But don't just stand there. Go get him. And bring me another drink back with you."

Ellerby curled his lip. "It's time you got yourself a new maid."

"I told you to hire somebody."

"I'm working on it," he snarled and stormed away.

Michael decided to stay in the shadow of the seawall. Jack was right. It was a good place to eavesdrop. The only problem would be if Henderson got the urge to stroll on the beach.

He hugged the seawall, knowing he was invisible from the pool area, and cocked an ear when he heard Henderson's voice above him.

"Miss Ventura, Mr. Ellerby," he said. "I'm sorry to impose on your privacy but I do have a few questions."

"Of course," said Ravena. "Have a seat . . . there's some shade over there. I guess you haven't found my poor sister's killer yet?"

"No ma'am, but we're working hard on it. However, I think you and Mr. Ellerby here may have been two of the last people to see her alive." He flipped open a small notebook and looked at it studiously.

"Miss Ventura, you told me you had visited her apartment on one occasion. I believe it may have been on the night she died."

Ravena sprang up, startled. "What? Really? How can you ascertain that? That would be terrible."

Henderson focused intently on his notes. Did Ravena think it was terrible to be the last to see her sister alive, or was it terrible that such a fact would be revealed?

"I'm afraid it appears so," he said. "The ME's office indicated that Miss Thomas had been in the water about forty-eight hours," he said, "and we estimate the time of death at a few hours before that. You do own a light-green Lexus, Florida tag number I28BEK?"

"Not sure about the tag number detective, but a green Lexus, yes."

Henderson wasn't sure about the tag either. DMV had given him the plate number of Ravena's Lexus but he had no tag number for any of the vehicles the super had spotted outside Elizabeth's apartment.

"A light-green Lexus was observed outside Miss Thomas's apartment the night she died," he said. "We surmised it might have been yours."

"Well, I guess it could have. But there must be lots of light-green Lexuses around. And Elizabeth was driving a Lexus, too."

"Yeah, her car was parked there at the same time. But the interesting thing is there was a third car there; a beige Lincoln Continental." Henderson swiveled in his seat to face Ellerby. "I believe you own a beige Continental, Mr. Ellerby. Were you there also on the night in question?"

The color in Ellerby's face drained visibly in the sunlight. He opened his mouth and his lower lip quivered for two nano-seconds before he spoke. "Miss Ventura called me when she went to see her sister and I met her over there," he said slowly. "Miss Ventura, as you know, is a very compassionate person and she wanted me to meet her sister in the hopes that I could help get her life on track. Obviously we were too little, too late."

Henderson turned back to Ravena, who was now sitting on the edge of her lounge chair, making a failing effort to look composed.

"Why didn't you tell us that the one time you went to see your sister was right before she died?" he asked.

Ellerby cut in quickly. "To be honest, Detective, we were hoping to keep that confidential. Not because we have anything to hide but for security purposes. If the murderer learned that we had been there on the night she died, Ravena herself might be in danger."

Henderson nodded. "I understand, but you should have told us. The information would have remained confidential. By the way, Miss Ventura, do you own a gun by any chance?"

Ravena turned ashen. Henderson had changed gears without a pause.

"Well, uh, yes. A revolver, a .38 Special. Or at least I did own it. I haven't seen it around anywhere in ages. My ex-husband bought it for me. He thought it would be good protection, though I don't know why." She smiled weakly. "I've always had plenty of strong men around me for that."

"Perhaps you could find it for us," said Henderson.

"Well, of course, but I really don't know where to look. It may even have been stolen. I had to let some of my help go, and one of them may have lifted it. Or it may still be in L.A. I haven't seen it in a long time. I really don't like guns."

"I see," said Henderson. "The theft of a gun should be reported, you know. A couple of shots had been fired in Miss Thomas's apartment, perhaps on the night she died. We're just trying to tie up loose ends." He looked up at her with raised eyebrows. "Maybe your sister got hold of your gun without your knowledge."

"I don't think that's likely, but I guess it's possible. But I was told she didn't die from a gunshot wound."

"No, she didn't. But there may be some connection between the gunshots and her death. What shape was she in when you last saw her? Happy? Depressed? Worried? Anything like that?"

"She appeared to be her normal self—which was usually high on something. I was always telling her off about that."

"And about what time did you leave Miss Thomas?"

"About ten o'clock. We weren't there too long. She wasn't exactly in a social frame of mind. I loved her to death but she wasn't always the most pleasant soul when she was on a toot. She just wanted money, not serious help, so we left."

"That's interesting," said Henderson slowly. "The medical examiner found only minor traces of alcohol and cocaine in Miss Thomas's system."

Without waiting for that to sink in, he turned to Ellerby. "Just how long have you been Miss Ventura's manager?" he asked.

"Oh, only a few weeks. Why?"

"Just wondered how you met. You don't seem to be very well-known in show business circles, at least not in Miss Ventura's circles."

Ellerby looked glassy-eyed. "Really?" he said.

"We met at a party," said Ravena curtly. "And I really don't know what any of that has to do with my sister's murder."

"Quite correct, ma'am," said Henderson. "Just curious." He got up, stretched, and made a futile attempt to straighten out the wrinkles in his suit. "I'm sorry to have bothered you. We'll keep you informed of any developments. I can see myself out."

He shook hands and headed back toward the house.

"See him out," snapped Ravena as soon as the detective was out of earshot. "Make sure he leaves and doesn't start snooping around in the house."

"Quit whining," said Ellerby. "We've got more important things to worry about. What exactly did you do with the gun?"

"It's in the drawer by my bed."

"We've got to get rid of it. Henderson is likely to be back with a search warrant and he'll tear the place apart looking for it."

"Just get him out of here. Then we can dump it in the ocean and no one will ever find it."

Michael pressed himself into the seawall until the cement blocks were grinding into his back. He didn't dare risk any noise. One crunch of his shoes on the sand and he'd be a dead duck.

He could hear movement on the patio, but he had no idea who was moving where. He hoped everyone was going into the house.

Ravena Ventura definitely had something to hide. And Ellerby was panicking about the gun. The two of them knew a lot more about Elizabeth's final hours than they were willing to divulge. Maybe Jack had been right. Perhaps they had killed her.

After a few heart-stopping minutes Michael edged to the north side of the patio, and then tried to blend into the landscaping between the beach and the house. Somehow he had to find a way to get inside that building.

Chapter 27

While getting into the house was a challenge, facing his security chief was Michael's immediate problem. Hendrix was probably wondering where Michael was and why his walkie-talkie was inoperative again. *Sorry sir, but it interferes with my eavesdropping.*

He poked his nose around the door to the security office, but Hendrix merely looked up at him and asked, "Know anything about boats?"

Michael grinned. "Sure. A boat is something you sink all your money into until you drown in debt."

"Ha, ha! If you want to be a comedian around here you'd better work on it. And you don't have time for that right now. Miss Ventura is asking for you. She wants to see 'that nice young man who drove me to the dentist.' She wants you to wait for her down by the gate and see her safely to the dock. She's taking the boat out someplace."

"She wants me to drive the boat now, too?"

"No. I suggested security should accompany her on her little cruise but she said it wouldn't be necessary. That Ellerby was going with her. I talked her into having one of us meet her at the gate, escort her across the highway and secure the dock for her departure and return." He looked at his watch. "Better get moving. And keep your eyes peeled. We don't want another shooting incident."

"Aye, aye, cap'n," said Michael and retreated out the door as Hendrix threw a wad of paper at him. "And turn that goddamn walkie-talkie on," Hendrix yelled after him.

Michael walked down the driveway and spent five minutes in idle conversation with Harris at the gatehouse before he spied Ravena and Ellerby skimming toward them in a golf cart. They screeched to a stop and Harris opened the gate.

"Hello, Michael," said Ravena with a smile. Ellerby merely scowled as the two of them abandoned the cart in the middle of the driveway. Michael raised his right hand in a salute and then led the way across the highway.

Ravena was wearing miniscule pink shorts and a white T-shirt, and was hauling a huge overstuffed tote bag. Ellerby was maintaining his usual well-oiled look in a black polo shirt and well-pressed tan slacks.

Michael unlocked the gate in a wall that protected the dock from public access. Beyond it loomed Ravena's yacht, sleek, white and resplendent in the glare of the afternoon sun.

"Great day for a sail," said Michael, eyeing the sky as Ellerby and Ravena stepped up a narrow gangplank onto the deck. "Do you need help with anything?"

"No thank you," sniffed Ellerby. "I can manage this quite well."

"He says he's had a lot of experience with boats," confided Ravena with the hint of a sneer. "I guess we'll find out. Perhaps you could untie us when we're ready to go. I don't think we'll be more than an hour. I haven't been out on this boat in…ages. Lost my sea-legs, I bet."

"I'll give you a blast on the horn when we're back and ready to dock." said Ellerby as he headed forward. You can help secure the boat."

Ellerby disappeared onto the bridge and there was a rumble, a throaty roar and churning water as the engines displayed their power from the bowels of the vessel.

Ravena clutched her tote bag as though her life depended on it, smiled weakly and disappeared below deck. Michael untied the ropes from the dock and tossed them onto the yacht. Then he stepped back, waited and watched as the vessel pulled away into the Intracoastal, made a wide sweeping turn and headed south to the Boynton Inlet and the open sea.

Michael was pumped. The house was now empty except for a part-time cook who would be busy in the kitchen. If he could avoid Hendrix he'd have time to do a little reconnoitering.

He headed quickly back up to the security command center where Hendrix was bogged down in paperwork. He nodded absent-mindedly when Michael told him the boat had left the dock.

Michael slowly wandered out of sight of the office then quickly made his way over to the pool area. The doors to the lanai were wide open, welcoming him into the house with open arms. This was going to be easier than he'd thought.

Michael didn't know what he was going to find. He didn't even know what he was looking for. At least he wouldn't bother looking for the gun. That would be in Ravena's tote bag, on its way to a watery grave.

The lanai led Michael to the huge hallway, facing the main entrance at the other end of a vast expanse of marble. This was one huge room, broken near the half-way point by the staircases that curved gracefully up to the second floor. Michael had a map in his mind's eye of the ground floor layout, thanks to Jane's impromptu tour. But the upstairs was a mystery. Ravena obviously hadn't wanted to take Jane up there. She had dismissed that section of the house as just bathrooms and bedrooms. But people kept their most valuable possessions and their most guarded secrets in their bedrooms.

Michael checked his watch. He figured he had about forty-five minutes before the yacht was expected back so he decided to take a peek behind the door under the stairs. This, according to Jane, was Ravena's study, a room that might have secrets to reveal.

He feared the door might be locked but it opened to his touch and he carefully closed it behind him as his feet sank into a plush burgundy carpet.

The study was just as Jane had described it, dark but homey, with a warm woody feeling that somehow seemed out of place in South Florida. French doors in one wall led to an atrium where areca and adonidia palms wafted silently in an invisible breeze. The sun's fragmented glare cascaded through the doors, creating eerie strips of light and shadow across the room. Shelves lined with books reached from floor to ceiling. Catty-corner from them was a huge mahogany desk. A small computer monitor was perched precariously on one end, standing guard over papers piled haphazardly in the middle of the work area. A vase of wilting white and yellow flowers, forlorn, forgotten and bowing their heads as they awaited their death, sat on the other end of the desk.

Michael glanced at the untidy heap of papers. They looked like junk mail, or bills. Probably both.

He tried the desk drawers to no avail. They were all locked. But there had to be a key handy. He ran his fingers under the lip of the desk and probed the desktop carefully around the office flotsam and jetsam. He came up empty.

He transferred his attention to the bookcases. What kind of stuff would a movie star read? He ran his gaze over the volumes that were at eye level, an odd mixture, from Shakespeare and Dickens to Stephen King and spiritual guru Deepak Chopra. The top shelf contained a mini law library, conveniently out of easy reach, and Michael also spotted a number of pop psychology works, some of which were familiar to him.

Then he noticed a small wicker wastepaper basket by the side of the desk. Dumpster diving! That's what enterprising reporters were noted for. He knelt down to look at the few crumpled papers in the bottom of the basket when he was startled by the blast of a distant foghorn.

Ravena and Ellerby were back already. He had to get out of there!

Chapter 28

Ravena and Ellerby were approaching the dock, looking for Michael. Frantically he grabbed a crumpled sheet of paper from the wastebasket, pushed it deep into the back pocket of his pants, and rushed to the door. He opened it a few inches, peered out to make sure there was no one to see him then ran for the front entrance and down the driveway.

He arrived to find Ravena at the rail of the yacht, looking anxiously at the dock as Ellerby struggled to bring the boat alongside.

After helping secure the vessel Michael was given the privilege of driving the golf cart up to the house then was left to resume his surveillance duties, religiously looking for ninjas on the rooftop or invading by dinghy from the sea. If he were to spot such intruders, he had no idea what he would do. He was not armed (thank God!) and he wasn't exactly built like the Incredible Hulk. He figured he'd just call Hendrix for help. After all, saving Ravena from whatever might be lurking out there was not his primary objective. Been there, done that. He was supposed to be digging up dirt on her and solving her sister's murder.

Michael checked out with Hendrix at the stroke of five, and headed home. On the way he called Jack at the office, but he'd left for the day. He had his home number and his cell but decided that the daily debriefing could wait. Besides, he needed time to think about Ravena's gun. Since it was now likely to be at the bottom of the ocean somewhere, it was no longer useful evidence. What Michael knew and what he could prove were vastly different things. The bullets in the wall at Elizabeth's apartment most likely came from that gun, since Ravena was going to great lengths to keep the weapon out of police hands. But did this mean she had killed her sister? The cops were emphatic that Elizabeth had no gunshot wounds.

Once in his apartment, Michael changed into shorts and a T-shirt. He cracked open a Heineken, picked up his discarded clothing and felt the tiny wad of paper in his back pocket. It was probably nothing, but it was a trophy of sorts.

He sat on the edge of his bed and unfolded it, trying to smooth out the creases. He stared at it in disbelief. It was full of meaningless doodles and numbers interspersed with Ravena Ventura signatures, apparently scribbled hastily in pen again and again. It was surely an autograph hunter's gold mine, but it provided Michael with no story ideas or headlines that would make his editor happy.

Nevertheless, he folded it carefully and put it on his nightstand under his cell phone. Knowing Jack he'd probably want to have it analyzed by one of those shrinks who evaluated doodles.

After another Heineken and a dinner concocted from the lean offerings in his freezer, Michael lay on his bed and contemplated tomorrow's debriefing with Iverson. Commonsense soon gave way to wacky headlines:

MOVIE QUEEN'S SHOCKING SECRETS... WHAT RAVENA'S DOODLES REVEAL ABOUT HER...EXPERT BREAKS RAVENA'S SECRET CODE.

They were ridiculous. But Jack would probably be excited about them, until he tried to get them past the lawyers. Michael drifted off to a disturbed sleep punctuated by dreams of hieroglyphics and Ravena's face morphing from that of a screen siren to the image of a sorry addict.

* * *

Michael woke before sunrise anxious to get into the office, where the day began amiably with coffee and doughnuts grudgingly provided by his editor. Then Jack, Jane and Michael adjourned to the conference room where Michael filled his colleagues in on the conversation he had overheard and Ravena's sudden desire to take a short cruise.

"Couldn't you have tried to stop her from getting rid of the gun?" asked Jack.

Michael stared at him blankly. "How? She'd probably have used it on me. I'm more concerned about alerting the police. Shouldn't we be telling them that the gun has gone to a watery grave?"

"Let me worry about that," said Jack. "We don't know for sure that she did dump the gun in the ocean. And I certainly don't want to blow your cover. We knew Henderson was on his way up there to talk to Ventura. I tried to warn you but your cell kept forwarding me to voice mail. Why don't you leave the fucking thing on?"

Michael shook his head. "You're starting to sound like Hendrix," he said.

"Who?"

"Never mind." It was a drag having two supervisors.

"Anyway," said Jack, "getting that Q and A between Ravena and Henderson was a good break. Just don't get caught eavesdropping."

"Can we use it?"

Jack shrugged. "Don't see why not. It's the truth, isn't it? All Henderson is likely to tell us is that he and Ravena had a 'useful' conversation. He's not going to give us shit unless he thinks he has to."

"Won't he wonder how we got our information?"

"Who cares? He can piss and moan all he likes. For all he'll know Ravena Ventura told us about it herself."

"And then *she'll* be pissed off! What about the agreement we have with her?"

"Forget that, it didn't last more than one week. Don't think she even expected it to. I think she used us to get the biggest headlines she could about her reward money. Thanks to us she came across as a brave trouper, a guardian angel and a caring human being. None of which she is."

Jane laughed. "She's already pissed at us. She's trying to figure out where we got the stuff about 'Mystery Cars at Crime Scene.'

Probably thinks we've got her place bugged. You know, maybe we could plant a few bugs in her home, and even in her cars."

Jack shook his head slowly. "Risky, and not too legal. They'd throw the book at us if we did that."

"What's this *we* shit?" said Michael. "I'm the one sticking his neck out. Incidentally, I did get inside the house for a quick look-see."

"You did?" said Jane. "Find anything interesting?"

Michael pulled the crumpled sheet of doodles out of his pants pocket. "Well, not really," he said, "but I seized the opportunity when they took the boat out. I had a look around Ravena's study while the house was empty."

"And? Find anything interesting?" asked Jack.

"Not a lot. Discovered she has a wide-ranging taste in books."

"Oh yeah; I wonder who reads them to her? Is that all you turned up?"

"Well, I did find this." Michael opened the sheet of doodles. "I dug this out of the waste-paper basket by the desk."

Iverson grabbed it, stared at it then turned it over in a futile search for more on the blank side. "So?" he said. "What are we looking at here?"

"Your guess is as good as mine. Ravena was probably doodling or something when she was on the phone. Lots of people do that. "

"Well, it's mostly her name, written over and over again, and a higgledy-piggledy bunch of numbers. Do we know that this is her artwork?"

"No," said Michael, "but I'm willing to bet it is. That room seems to be her private sanctuary. I guess Ellerby could have been in there. But that arrogant little prick would be more likely to doodle his own name than hers."

Jack waved the paper in the air. "Reminds me of a story we did a while ago from a doodle expert, one of those trained-seal shrinks that has you look at inkblots then tells you what a dirty mind you've got. I know what he'd say about this. 'The writer is egotistical but secretly unsure of herself and loves the power of money.'"

"That could be a large segment of the human race," muttered Jane.

"My point exactly," said Jack. "I'm not sure this is going to help us much but kudos for getting it, Michael. I just hope Ravena doesn't miss it."

"I doubt it. It was in her waste bin, after all. And I thought digging around in people's trash was one the things good reporters do."

"Sure," said Jack, "but only when the trash is outside on public property. "You can't go rummaging around inside their houses and walking off with whatever takes your fancy. That's known as *stealing*!"

He folded the paper quickly and handed it back to Michael as though it had suddenly caught fire. "Hang on to it," he said, "but don't take it back to the estate."

"Because it's hot merchandise that could land me in jail?"

"Don't worry about it. Look, I think you've really come up with something on Henderson's visit to Ravena. It'll give us a great headline this week."

He paused, waiting for a response, but all he got were blank looks, so he pressed on. "How about RAVENA MET WITH SISTER ON NIGHT SHE DIED? Then a deck, SHE MIGHT HAVE BEEN LAST PERSON TO SEE HER ALIVE."

"Except for the killer," ventured Jane.

"Of course, unless she *is* the killer!"

"Why would she kill her own sister?" asked Jane. "She had everything to lose and nothing to gain by doing so. Elizabeth seemed to be a bit of a slut, a deadbeat and a druggie, but Ravena had managed to distance herself from her and Elizabeth never really hurt her career. In fact if Ravena had played it right it may have helped her. Knowing that Ravena Ventura had such a family cross to bear could have invoked sympathy from her fans. It would have made her appear more human, more fragile, and more…vulnerable."

"Bring on the violins," said Jack. "You're probably right. But JC has already decided she might have done it and wants to pursue angles that lean in that direction. Peterson doesn't necessarily agree. Ravena Ventura does have deep pockets and we could all wind up working for her if she decides to sue."

Such talk made Michael nervous. He was anxious to change the subject. "Okay," he said. "But what about the gun?" "We'll press Henderson for something after we tell him what we overheard about the gun, but I'm sure we'll get diddly out of him. There might be a headline down the road like MYSTERY OF RAVENA'S MISSING GUN."

Michael smiled. "How about COPS DRAIN ATLANTIC IN SEARCH FOR RAVENA'S GUN?"

Luckily a phone call averted Jack's response and the meeting broke up.
Michael left the conference room with mixed feelings. He knew he was walking a tightrope between right and wrong, truth and fiction. Life in the investigative news business was a unique roller-coaster where you seemed to go up and down at the same time. It wasn't a business for queasy stomachs, or for people who couldn't cover their tracks . . . or their rear ends.

Chapter 29

Michael bent Jane's ear as they walked back to the newsroom.

"You know," he said, "I've never met JC but he seems to have good gut instincts and Ravena certainly isn't the person her fans think she is. Maybe she really does have something to do with her sister's death. It's tough to believe that she murdered her but, as Jack says, she may know who did. Perhaps that's why someone tried to kill her, too. And that guy Ellerby bothers me. Why is he always hanging around? He's even living on the estate with her."

Jane raised her eyebrows. "Is he sleeping with her?"

"I've no idea, but somehow I don't think so. They barely tolerate each other. But why would Ravena need to tolerate him at all, unless he's got something on her? What was it I overheard him say to her? 'We're an inseparable team. What happens to me happens to you.'"

Jane laughed. "Was that before or after she told him to go fuck himself?"

"Can't remember, but it sure sounded sinister to me. This disreputable guy suddenly shows up as her manager? And it's like he and Ravena are super-glued at the hip."

Jane bit her lip. "Be careful when you go back to Ventura's place. I don't know about Ravena but Ellerby is a nasty piece of work. If your cover is blown you might lose much more than your security job."

"Thanks for caring about my welfare, which is more than I can say for Jack, but let's not get melodramatic. I've got a lot more digging to do. And I haven't taken any pictures yet. I'm surprised Jack hasn't reamed me about that."

"Don't stick your neck out to get photos. Besides, it'll be tough to be able to use them. There are laws about taking photos on other people's property without their permission.

"Anyway," she added as they reached their desks, "I've got to get on the horn to Henderson and somehow tell him what we heard about the gun. I wonder why he seems so interested in it since Elizabeth wasn't shot."

"He certainly wasn't interested in it until I pointed out possible bullet holes in the wall. And why would Ravena and Ellerby apparently rush to dispose of the gun if it wasn't involved in the crime? I've been mulling over what we know and what we think we know, and I reckon it's time to do some research into what we don't know. Some old-fashioned book learning."

He headed across the office to where Maria Versailles, head of The Courier Research Library, sat behind a small PC and an enormous pile of books and papers that made Jack Iverson look like a neat freak.

Michael left the office that night with a sheaf of computer printouts and a hard-cover book from The Courier library that Maria warned would cost him a broken arm, if not his job, if he didn't return it.

It was another night for a frozen dinner and a beer then he stretched out on the bed and started to go through the documents that Maria had pulled up for him. Finally he opened the book and began reading fervently. The next thing he knew he was waking up at three o'clock the next morning, still fully dressed. He'd fallen asleep at page fifty-two.

He looked hard and long at his bedside clock and watched it roll over four more minutes. It was far too late, or too early, to call anyone. He couldn't sleep, and he couldn't wait to get into the office in the morning. Time was hardly moving. He lay back down to think, then reached for the book and picked up reading where sleep had cut him off.

When daybreak finally came, Michael had a quick shower, decided to skip breakfast, and was one of the first in the newsroom for once. He grabbed a coffee from the break room and pored through the morning newspapers while he waited for Jack and Jane to show up.

Lack of sleep and too much coffee had him fighting off a headache when Jack finally breezed in.

"What's up, Mikey?" he asked. "Insomnia?"

"You can say that again, Jack. Did Jane ever get to talk with Henderson yesterday?"

"Oh, yeah, and then some. Henderson was steaming, yelling, threatening, going on about interfering with a police investigation."

"And?"

"And nothing. He was just blowing smoke. Jane started spouting about the First Amendment then reminded him that it was *us* who'd led *him* to the bullet holes and the possibility that Ravena and Ellerby had visited Elizabeth on the night she died. Jane's pretty tough in the trenches. She gave him both barrels."

"Do we know if the sheriff's department has released Elizabeth's body yet?"

"Good question. If they did they haven't told us about it."

"I think I'll get on to Henderson about that. I've got some thoughts I want to check out with him."

"Like?"

"I'll tell you later. They may be stupid. But if they're not we could have our hands on one hell of a story."

Iverson stared at his reporter and shook his head. "All right," he said, "but we've got to keep the pot boiling. JC has zero patience and he's looking for a major Ravena headline every week now. He thinks it should be a snap when we've got a man on the inside."

"We've been doing okay so far. Isn't he ever satisfied?"

"Rarely. You do a good job, he wants a better job. You do a better job, he wants the best job. I don't want to worry you, boy-o, but we're all in the hot seat here. If we don't keep producing we're gonna be pulled off the story. Perhaps off The Courier payroll, too and I don't know about you, but at my age I don't want to be going back to covering council meetings and charity balls for the Podunk Press."

"Let me talk to Henderson," said Michael.

It took an hour and four fruitless calls before he could hook up with the detective.

"Well, well, hotshot," he said. "I thought you'd died and gone to that newsbeat in the sky, or at that place in the other direction. Not that I missed you. I'd rather talk to that firecracker girlfriend of yours anyway."

Michael ignored him. "How are things going on the case?"

"They're going."

"I was wondering about the body. Has it been released to Miss Ventura yet?"

"Miss Thomas's remains were sent to the funeral home last night and Miss Ventura has been informed."

"Which funeral home?"

"What difference does it make? Brickell and Sons in Lake Worth. That was at Miss Ventura's instructions. They will take care of the cremation and Miss Ventura will get the ashes as requested."

Michael paused for a second. "Exactly how did you identify the body, detective?"

He could sense Henderson stiffening in his seat.

"How do you think? The usual ways. Besides, Miss Ventura herself saw the body and made a positive ID."

"What about fingerprints? Dental records? DNA?"

"What about 'em? We found the victim at the wheel of a car she had rented at the airport. The rental papers were in the glove compartment–soggy but still legible. She had a California driver's license in her purse with her picture on it. The clerk at the rental agency ID'd her from it. Her teeth were in good shape but we never saw any need to trace dental records. Some of the prints found in her apartment matched the body, and so did a couple of partials in the trunk of the car. Okay? Satisfied? Why the dumb questions?"

"Just checking, detective. It's a reporter's job to be thorough. Thanks for your help."

Michael put down the phone, rummaged around in his desk drawer and grabbed a roll of Scotch tape. Then he turned to Jack.

"I may be crazy," he said, "but I need to get to the funeral home before Elizabeth Thomas is reduced to a pile of ashes."

"Wha–?"

Michael was already heading out of the newsroom, leaving his editor open-mouthed. Jack smiled to himself. Michael was acting like a hound dog after a rabbit and he liked that in his reporters.

* * *

Michael had no trouble finding Brickell and Sons on Lake Worth Road, just west of the town's business district. It was a magnificent edifice, a stucco and faux brick monument to the dead that would have made any city proud and surely caused plenty of citizens to be satisfied that they had expired in Lake Worth.

Michael pulled up the Mustang sharply behind a gleaming black hearse stationed in front of highly polished double doors. He rushed into the building, headlong into an atmosphere of reverence and tranquility that only undertakers could create. He was in a small vestibule with knee-deep carpeting, wood and brass ornaments and piped-in organ music that wafted through the carefully perfumed air as though calling all comers to meet their maker.

The route to whatever sanctums lay beyond was almost instantly blocked by a somber authoritative figure in a double-breasted black suit.

"May I help you sir?" asked the Man in Black. His tone suggested that the most help was likely to be assistance in leaving the premises.

"Uh, yes," said Michael. "I hope so. I came to see Miss Thomas."

"I see," said Mr. Black gravely. "And you are . . .?"

"I'm her cousin. I just got in from California."

"Oh. Well, I'm sorry sir, but Miss Thomas's remains have already been dispatched to Miss Ventura at her request." He sounded more relieved than sorry.

"You mean she's already been cremated?"

"Yes, sir. And at Miss Ventura's request we selected a beautiful urn for her."

Michael looked crestfallen.

"Actually sir, you probably wouldn't have wanted to see her. You know, under the circumstances."

"Circumstances?"

"Yes, sir. You know, considering the autopsy that was required. And with cremation and no viewing services the cosmetic work was deemed unnecessary. If you understand, sir."

"I see." Michael wondered if Mr. Black ever had nightmares about his job.

"Miss Ventura has indicated that she intends to have a private service and scatter the ashes at sea," the undertaker continued. "Of course as her cousin you probably know that."

From his tone Mr. Black had apparently figured that Michael was no cousin, probably just another nosy reporter.

Michael mumbled his thanks, fumbled his way through the double doors and squinted in the sunlight. Another dead end, in more ways than one.

He arrived back at the office to find Jack with the phone glued to his ear, barking orders to some luckless underling. He hung up when he saw Michael and peered at him over his glasses with a silent "well?"

"Too late," said Michael. "When I got there they'd already shipped the ashes to Ravena." He slumped in his chair.

"I know," said Jack. "We just got a news flash from that Usher woman announcing that Ravena would be scattering the ashes in the ocean from her boat tomorrow."

"Yeah? Are we going to be on board with her?"

"Are you kidding? She won't give us the time of day now. I think Usher faxed us a release just to warn us to stay away. I don't think they want a media circus, but they'll probably get one. Photo and I have arranged for a boat to be standing by to follow Ravena's yacht. We'll have a photog out there with long lenses and I don't think it'll be difficult to get some shots of Miss Movie Star emptying her womb-mate into the Atlantic. Ravena might invite some of the regular press aboard her boat, probably the local papers, but I can guarantee there won't be room for us."

Jack laughed. "You'll probably be on patrol tomorrow working hard at keeping us out! Anyway, what were you babbling about when you ran off to the funeral home?"

"Doesn't really matter now. It's just made it more difficult for us to blow this whole thing wide open."

Chapter 30

Jack Iverson stared, swallowed hard enough to alarm his Adam's apple, then opened his mouth and tried in vain to say something. He was too late. Michael had already left his desk for the Research Department, where Maria Versailles was defending her station against an irate photo editor.

"Bring the book back?" she asked Michael, snapping gum sharply.

"No, sorry. I'm still in the throes of it."

The research chief rolled her eyes. "If I don't get it back I'll have your balls for breakfast."

"That hungry, huh?" Michael knew Maria's reputation for her bark, but he wasn't sure about her bite. "Actually I was wondering if you had any DVDs or tapes of Ravena Ventura's movies. Anything she might have made in her career."

Maria's eyes widened. "Waddya think this is? Do we look like Netflix over here? The only tapes we keep are those we make ourselves and porn stuff that a few big stars try to pretend they never made."

"Any of those?"

"Plenty, but not with Ravena Ventura in them. And if you really want her movies I can recommend Netflix. They've probably got all of them."

Michael thanked her and returned to his editor's desk.

"Jack," he said, "if you've got nothing special you want me to do I'd like to go out and work on some research. I'll check in with you later."

Iverson nodded. "Get outta here," he said. "You need an afternoon off. Go stroll on the beach or swim in your pool or something. I'll talk to you later."

Michael nodded and left. There was the promise of a sunny dry winter day in the air, the type of weather that would soon create an influx of humanity from the northern states. The beach and the pool sounded enticing, but the funeral home had left him too frustrated and hungry for answers.

He took Maria's advice and rented four Ravena Ventura movies. It looked like another stay-at-home evening, this one sitting in front of the TV.

After two movies Michael decided he was not a Ravena Ventura fan. He'd seen *The Gray Rain* before he left Detroit. In that movie Ravena played a scheming mistress who blackmailed her married lovers then dumped them in rapid succession. But the handful of other offerings he'd picked up seemed to be chick flicks, sappy love stories with vague plots wrapped around them.

After watching *The Vixen* and *A Woman Scorned* he decided that Ravena was too melodramatic and didn't change her personality from one character to another. Not that any of the roles she played reflected her real-life personality. On-screen she was a sensual sex siren, not the hardened potty-mouthed drunken bitch he'd seen in real life. That transformation could make a Courier story in itself, but that wasn't what Michael was looking for. And he was certainly no movie critic. He was trying to focus on Ravena's body language and personal little idiosyncrasies that might come through beyond her artificial screen persona.

He'd just flipped to movie number three, *Reckless Heart* (ugh!) when his cell phone trilled. To his amazement and joy, it was Jane. It was seven o'clock. What could she possibly want?

"Hi, Michael," she said. "Sorry to bother you, but I wondered how the 'research' was going."

"Nauseating," said Michael. "It would be a more pleasant experience if I could find whatever it is I'm looking for."

"What *are* you looking for?"

"I'm not really sure. I won't know until I find it, if I ever do."

"Well, frankly, I called you because Jack is having a fit. He's starting to worry about you. And he usually doesn't worry about anybody but himself."

"What the hell is he worried about?"

"He thinks you may be going off the rails a little. What's the infatuation with Elizabeth's body, or the fact that it's been cremated?"

"I'm concerned about it because there's no hundred percent solid evidence that the body in that car was Elizabeth Thomas. The cops treated the ID of the body as routine, but the situation was far from routine and they certainly weren't thorough."

"Didn't they check everything they could?"

"They checked everything that appeared to be obvious. But I'm sure they were careful not to make too many waves around a famous movie star who has power and money.

"So just what are you researching?"

"I'm trying to learn something about identical twins. Seems that even identical twins aren't totally identical, though it's not always easy to tell them apart. Research loaned me a fascinating book on the subject. Identical twins look the same, sound the same, have the same DNA, share thoughts and even medical problems, but the fact remains they are two separate, individual people. Identical twins have very similar, but not identical, fingerprints. The same thing with their teeth. And their handwriting is usually different."

"Your mind has been working overtime, hasn't it?"

"Yes, and I was afraid Jack would steer me in another direction. That's why I rushed up to the funeral home. I wanted to try to get a fingerprint from the body somehow. I thought maybe I could sneak one onto a piece of Scotch tape, but I was too late."

"But the cops fingerprinted the body, didn't they?"

"Of course. But they were pretty sloppy about it. All they compared them with were prints they found in the car and at Elizabeth's apartment. And you know they aren't going to give us a set. If I could have gotten fingerprints off the body, then found a way to get the other sister's fingerprints, maybe I would have been able to have someone compare them. But that didn't happen."

"So now what?"

"Not sure yet, but there's got to be something. There's the teeth. Henderson told me no one had bothered to trace Elizabeth's dental records. I took Ravena to a dentist in Delray, remember? But I haven't figured out how to make use of that. One thing I am sure of. Either Ravena is involved in Elizabeth's death, or Elizabeth is involved in Ravena's. And I'm leaning toward the latter."

"Why?"

"Remember when the cops fingerprinted Elizabeth's apartment? They said they found prints in the living room, which is where they found the blood and presumably where she died. But they found no useable prints in any other rooms. The rest of the place had apparently been wiped clean. Why?"

"I have a feeling you're going to tell me."

"I'm pretty sure my prints are all over my apartment, and yours are all over yours. So if you wanted to give the impression that one of your visitors lived there, and
not you, you'd get rid of your fingerprints in all areas of your home where no one but you is likely to have been. Right?"

"Yeeees, I guess so." Jane didn't sound so sure.

"Right," said Michael triumphantly. "We know Ravena was at the apartment that night. Suppose Elizabeth killed her for some reason and decided to switch identities with her. She wouldn't want her own prints on everything in the apartment so she wiped every room clean except the one where the murder took place. That would leave one twin's prints left to create a match with the dead body and the other's to help identify a visitor to the apartment."

Jane's head was swimming. "Why haven't you told Jack any of this?"

"Because I've been slowly trying to get the puzzle pieces to fit; except they don't. I've only just arrived at where I'm at and I can't prove any of this. I can't afford to go to the mat with it and be wrong."

"Michael, you can't afford to keep this to yourself. Jack knows you've got a bug up your ass about something and he'll wheedle it out of you anyway. He'll be a lot less pissed if you're upfront with him."

Michael sighed. "I know. You're right. I'd just like to get my ducks in line first. I don't want him to pull me off the story because he's thinks I've gone loopy."

"He won't do that. He's much more likely to pull you off if he thinks you're not a team player. Besides, he's no slouch. He may have some ideas that could help."

"Okay," he sighed. "I'll give him a call at home. If I tell him over the phone I won't have to watch the ugly faces he's going to pull while he's deciding whether to send for guys with white coats and butterfly nets."

Jane laughed. "So what exactly have you been doing tonight?" she asked.

"Watching movies. Ravena Ventura movies. And they aren't very exciting. They make me understand why someone might want to kill her. She may be a good actress but her genre isn't to my taste."

"No. I'm sure it's not. Her pictures are designed to make bored and lonely housewives cry. I'm not bored, lonely or a housewife, but if you could use some company . . ."

Michael pounced on her words. "That would be great," he said. "I don't have any wine but I have some beer. And I have tissues in case Ravena makes you cry."

Jane responded with a giggle that made him buckle at the knees. He quickly gave her directions to his apartment. "I'm gonna call Jack right now," he said. "I'll see you in a few."

Michael glanced around his apartment. It looked like the typical mess a bachelor would live in. But he didn't have time to tidy it up. He had to call Jack before Jane arrived.

Surprisingly, Iverson said nothing while his reporter bombarded him with rhetorical questions.

"Why wipe out only *some* of the fingerprints in the apartment? Why is this scumbag Ellerby suddenly in the picture? Why is Ravena suddenly getting rid of all the staff that knows her? Why does one of the world's most beautiful women suddenly need her teeth capped? Why was Elizabeth's body almost drug and booze-free when we know what her lifestyle was like?"
"So where are you going with this?"

"Think about it, Jack. Let's play 'what if'—as in, what if Elizabeth is still alive and Ravena is dead?"

Jack made a grumbling noise in his throat. "This is fascinating, but where you're going is all conjecture. Two and two don't make five. Besides, why did Elizabeth have to kill Ravena? The two of them look alike. She could have passed herself off as her sister anytime she liked."

"She'd already tried that, remember? The L.A. bureau dug up information that Elizabeth once tried to charge stuff to Ravena's account at a fancy store on Rodeo Drive. She came unstuck when the store called Ravena's people about it because she was known to be filming in Thailand at the time. That was just one of the messes Ravena had to sort out on her sister's behalf."

"Point taken. But we still have nothing we can prove."

"No. But if you have any ideas . . ."

"Let me sleep on it. And keep your ideas to yourself. Don't go blabbing around in the local bars, or holding tête-à-têtes with other people in the office."

Michael told him that Jane was on her way over.

"All right," said Jack. "But stay sober, stick to business—and don't go banging her. She's a nice girl and a good reporter. And I need her to stay focused on business."

The doorbell rang just as Michael hung up. It was Jane, standing there, smiling expectantly and waving a bottle of merlot. It promised not to be a nauseating evening after all.

Chapter 31

It was a good day for a funeral at sea.

It dawned in typical South Florida fashion with a purple-black sky melting away into tinges of yellow that sent shimmers across a placid Atlantic.

Michael wondered if he would be invited aboard Ravena's yacht when her sister made her final journey to somewhere in the endless ocean. He doubted it. Probably just Ravena, Ellerby, hopefully a minister, plus a couple of reporters from the local daily papers. Elizabeth Thomas's final send-off would be nothing more than a publicity op for Hollywood's premier goddess.

He showered, dressed and looked around his modest apartment, drinking in the detritus of the previous evening and the evidence of Jane's visit. He picked up the wine bottle and wiggled it to make tiny waves in what little remained of the merlot. They had had a good time. Good rapport. They had joked, laughed, and torn a couple of Ravena's movies to shreds. And they had behaved. *No, Jack, I didn't bang her!* In fact Michael hadn't even kissed her, if you don't count the peck on the cheek when she left shortly after midnight.

Yes, they had enjoyed each other's company, but the evening brought them no closer to a solid story line. As far as investigative journalism went it wasn't a night to remember.

Michael was halfway out the door when he decided to call Jack before his cell-phone use would be restricted at Ravena's estate.

Did your movie reviewing reveal any clues?" Jack asked sarcastically.

"No," said Michael, "but I'm going to watch more tonight. I know there's got to be something."

"It may be a moot point. I called Peterson last night to discuss what you told me and— "

"What! You asked me to keep it to myself and you're blabbing it to the executive editor. I'm going to be the laughing stock of the office."

"Nah. It is fascinating, after all. And I thought he might have some ideas about it."

"And did he?"

There was an uneasy silence. "Not exactly," Jack said at last. "But he didn't laugh it off. However, Peterson told me JC is getting antsy about you being undercover at Ventura's place. After the shooting incident he's decided you may be in harm's way and that we're not getting enough information to make it worthwhile."

Michael was deflated. "I thought I was doing okay."

"You have been. But like I told you, JC always wants more and always wants better. Peterson said he'd been complaining about paying someone just to be a security guard for a Hollywood floozy."

"Oh, great!"

"It's all right. Peterson talked him into giving you a few more weeks. Told him it was like a massive work in progress, that no one was trying to kill *you* and that it made sense to have people inside on a story of this magnitude. Just think, Mikey, if you could prove any of those stories running around in your head it'd be like the Second Coming for us."

"Yeah, sure, except I'm nowhere. Maybe we should confide in Henderson. The cops have more resources than I do."

"God, no! I'd rather we crack this than have to give credit to the cops. Besides, I think they've jumped on Ravena's bandwagon. They seem to have decided that Elizabeth's death was a drug-related killing by some out-of-town scumbag who'll never be found. It makes their life easier and they'll be happy to let the case slide out of the spotlight. We have to do all we can to prevent that from happening. JC still wants to hit this story hard, every week. We have to come up with good front-page headlines on a regular basis."

"I wish we could resurrect the attempt on Ravena's life at the medical center."

"With what? All we have is your first-person account of one gunshot—an unsubstantiated two-graf story that Ravena will probably deny and which will get you kicked off the estate. Like I said before, it may have been nothing more than a juvenile prank that got out of hand. Stray bullets aren't that unusual in urban America."

"Fine Jack. But we seem to have a little role reversal here. You're the one who taught me to think of a headline then dig for the story. And that's where I'm coming from now. A bullet whistling over Ravena's head is only one of many unexplained oddities in her life. I just—"

"You just don't have any facts yet, boy-o. JC won't buy a story that's ninety percent speculation. I'll talk to you later."

The phone went dead.

Michael rubbed his chin and contemplated his options. If his days at Ravena's estate were numbered he had to make the most of his time there. Hurriedly he hunted around for his phone book and looked up the Cruzes' number. Mrs. Cruz knew Ravena's mansion like the back of her hand. She could help him.

After five minutes on the phone with her he scooped up his car keys and developed a game plan as he drove. Buoyed by his thoughts, he bounced into the security office to greet Hendrix.

"Morning chief," he said. "Today's the funeral, huh? I guess there's no chance of me getting a slot on the boat with them?"

Hendrix shook his head. "Sorry," he said, "but you're too late. Willis and Seward both asked me for that assignment and Miss Ventura wants just one bodyguard to accompany them and a second to be on duty at the dock. They're going to toss for which one of them gets to go on the boat. I've assigned you to the pool area. Samuelson is going to be outside guarding the front entrance, but we don't want any wayward press sneaking around the back."

"Okay. Sounds like a plan." *A plan that would dovetail perfectly with his own.*
Michael would now have another golden opportunity to sneak a peek at Ravena's private confines.

He couldn't wait for two o'clock to roll around, when Ravena, Ellerby and their chosen members of the Fourth Estate would set sail for the final chapter in Elizabeth Thomas's short and pathetic life.

He moved into action as soon as the funeral party was safely on board the yacht.

He slipped into the lanai, walked swiftly to the entrance hall and glanced around. There was no one in the house to be seen and no one to see him. No members of the mainstream press were loose on the grounds, all the other security guards were at their posts and Hendrix was probably holed up in his quarters.

Michael stepped back out onto the outside patio and looked around again to make sure he could not be seen. Then he zeroed in on his target, an empty martini glass on a small table by the pool. Ravena had left it there after toning up her blood alcohol level while she worked on her suntan.

He carefully pulled a paper towel out of his pocket, circled the rim of the glass with it then picked it up with his fingertips. He was careful not to touch the bowl or the stem any more than necessary. He paused, glanced around again, and took it to his car. Quickly, he opened the trunk, pushed the glass into a Ziploc bag then hid the bag under a towel.

He closed the trunk quietly, retraced his steps through the lanai to the hall and checked his watch. The yacht had pulled out with the funeral party about five minutes ago. That should leave him plenty of time. He wandered slowly down to the stairway then bounded up the right-hand staircase two steps at a time.

He found a corridor stretching the length of the house, with two smaller corridors running off it. He needed Ravena's private suite, but where would it be? There were rooms everywhere. Mrs. Cruz said it was overlooking the ocean, so he turned right and peered through the first open door on the southeast side of the house.

It was a sizeable bedroom, tidy but obviously lived in. The daily maid service had done its work that morning, but there was a crumpled towel left on an easy chair near the bed and the door to an oversize walk-in closet was ajar.

Michael slipped around the half-open doorway, slid into the closet and froze. This was not Ravena's room. The closet contained half a dozen expensive suits, charcoal gray, navy blue and even one in a nauseating beige color. The owner had to be that little creep Ellerby. So this was his pad.

He looked around the room and glanced under the bed like a small boy looking for boogey monsters. Nothing there. Not even a lonely dust bunny.

He opened the top drawer of a walnut night table. Pay dirt! A gun was nestled among an untidy collection of odds and ends. So Ravena hadn't disposed of her weapon after all. Then he realized it wasn't Ravena's gun. Michael knew very little about guns but this was not a revolver. Must be Ellerby's gun. *So the little shit has an equalizer, too.*

Michael checked his watch again. He was wasting time. Thirty-five minutes had now gone by since the yacht had left on its funeral voyage. He needed to get moving. He edged out of the room, praying that it looked just as it had when he entered it. He stealthily stepped across the atrium balcony to the northeast wing of the house.

Once there he decided to take the first ocean-side door he encountered. It too was ajar.

This had to be Ravena's suite. It was twice the size of Ellerby's. In fact it was three or four times the size of Michael's entire apartment. The room was ornately decorated with a professional, fussy, feminine touch. A flowery blue and white sofa dominated a sitting area, but the centerpiece of the room was a king-size four-poster bed with silk sheets and an enormous comforter that complemented the couch.

One wall featured double French doors that led out to a deck overlooking the pool. The deck ran the width of the room and was framed by a three-foot-high white metal railing. Michael stepped outside and looked down cautiously. There was no one around. He looked out to sea. Nothing there either. So far so good.

He returned to the room and studied it carefully. He found the bathroom and an adjoining dressing room then zeroed in on double pocket doors set in one wall.

He carefully slid open one of the doors with his fingernails and found himself in yet another room, a wardrobe wonderland the size of a basketball court. A guy could get lost in here. It was just as Mrs. Cruz had described.

Michael wandered around, drinking in the diverse marvels of Ravena's wardrobe. He thumbed through a wall of expensive gowns and thought he recognized one from last year's Oscars. Funny, he'd always had the impression those fancy clothes were merely loaned to the stars.

But clothes weren't what Michael was here for. He found a light switch and moved on, around a corner and past an area devoted to daywear, short-skirted dresses that any woman might wear to the mall or out to lunch, except these had undoubtedly cost a small fortune.

Now Michael was in the bowels of Ravena's wardrobe, beyond seemingly endless racks of shoes and built-in drawers that kept swimwear, underwear and nightwear in obsessive-compulsive order.

He came to the back wall and was confronted with lines of shelves, all piled high with storage boxes. This was what Mrs. Cruz had told him about. Personal items stashed away for posterity.

Michael grabbed the nearest box and pulled it down. It was full of old greeting cards and invitations to long-forgotten Hollywood social functions. He moved to the next box. Nothing but press clippings and promotional material for Ravena's movies.

Then he found what he was looking for—a box of photographs. He thumbed through them carefully until he found Ravena smiling up at him from a wedding photo in a small gold frame. The picture had obviously been thrown in this container of forgotten dreams after the divorce. He carefully lifted it out and replaced the box on the shelf.

He took another quick glance at his watch. He had to be almost out of time. Then he froze.

He heard voices, a man and a woman trying to talk each other down. They were too far away for him to make out what was being said but it was easy to put names to the voices. Ravena and Ellerby were back. They were downstairs. In the house. And he was standing in her bedroom with her wedding photo in his hand. He was trapped.

Chapter 32

Michael edged slowly to the door. The voices were coming from somewhere below him, strident tones enhanced by the acoustics of the vast atrium. Ravena and Ellerby were bickering as usual. And they were getting closer.

Escaping down the stairs was out of the question. But how else could he get out of there unnoticed? If Ravena was about to venture upstairs she would surely head for her private suite.

He looked around wildly. Quickly, he stuffed the photo frame inside his shirt and made a beeline for the French doors. Cautiously, he eased his way out onto the deck. He carefully closed the doors behind him and peered over the railing to the pool area below. There was no one in sight.

If Ravena and Ellerby came out to the pool he could perhaps head back down the stairs. He waited, trying to strain evidence of their presence through the sound of the surf hitting the beach. But he saw and heard nothing.

If Ravena and Ellerby were staying indoors Michael's best escape route had to be straight down. He made his way to the north corner of the balcony, carefully edged his way to the rail and looked down. It seemed to be a long drop to the patio, but hell, it was only one story, eight feet, maybe ten at the outside? He was five-foot-ten and he quickly computed a drop of no more than four feet from the soles of his shoes to the pink slabs below. Surely that would be a piece of cake.

He climbed over the rail at the corner, balanced by his toes on the four-inch rim of the deck then dropped down until he was hanging by his fingers. He dangled precariously for a few seconds then his feet kicked the corner pillar immediately to his right. He tried to wrap his legs around it, but it was too wide and would only hamper his fall.

To hell with it! He had to take a chance on being seen, or on being injured if he landed awkwardly.

Michael pushed himself away from the pillar and let his fingers slide off the edge of the overhang. He fell and rolled, then stood up, somewhat surprised that he appeared to be in one piece and hadn't attracted any attention.

Eat your heart out, Jackie Chan!

Quickly he hot-footed it around the corner to the staff parking lot, then tried to turn his gait into a stroll as he made his way to his car. He fumbled for the photo frame, pulled it out of his shirt and threw it in the trunk. At least he'd escaped without shards of glass imbedded in his torso.

His heart was still thumping as he checked in with Hendrix to get confirmation that the ashes had been disposed of successfully and that the priest and the press contingent had left.

He wondered how Jack would react to what he had done. Heck, he was pulling out all the stops to get a killer story, wasn't he? The good news, at least, was that Ravena and Ellerby hadn't seen him or heard him. Whatever scuffling noises Michael may have made in his amateurish escape had been shut out by their never-ending war of words.

* * *

The raucous voices that had alerted Michael were muffled as Ellerby hustled Ravena into the lounge where she had talked with Jane.

He closed the door behind them.

"Thank God that's over," he said. "Let's hope that's the end of these 'Meet the Press' situations. News people are the last breed we need around here."

"Oh, give it up, Ellie. I'm a big movie star, remember? Publicity is very important, especially when you're not actually making any movies. It keeps the fans interested. I can't sit around here forever, hiding behind the rock you crawled out from under."

"Look!" Ellerby started pacing around the room. "Just sit down. There's something we have to talk about."

"You know, Ellie," said Ravena, "I get sick of talking to you. You're around my neck morning, noon and night. I need a life—and I don't need you in it twenty-four/seven."

"Well you'd better listen up good right now. We've got problems. Dr. Drew wants more money."

"Whaddya mean, more money? I paid him for the dental work. And the coke."

"He's threatening to drop the dime. He wants a hundred thousand dollars, in cash, to keep his mouth shut."

Ravena turned beet-red. She was fueled by anger and more than a little panicked. "You idiot!" she screamed. "You brought him into this. What did you tell him?"

"Nothing. I've known him a long time. I told him you urgently needed dental work, that we could use a steady supply of good blow and that I knew he could provide both."

"You asshole! Just how much does he know?"

"He ain't stupid. He did some checking and figured a few things out for himself. He's starting to look like serious trouble."

"Checking into what?"

"He started sniffing around in Hollywood and found out who was responsible for that big white Ravena Ventura smile. Then he had a little 'professional' chat with
the guy, who was shocked to learn that all his good work had come undone. Then Doctor Drew began badgering me about it."

"He wants a hundred thousand dollars, just like that?"

"Yes, just like that. He says he isn't greedy."

"Yeah, sure. You know there'll be more. That's how blackmailers work. Well, he's your boy. So you do something about him."

"Like what? You gonna write me a check for him?"

"Fuck no. I'm not talking about paying him. I'm talking about convincing him to keep his mouth shut."

"You mean—"

"I mean you figure something out. Don't act so goddam dense. I'm not going to let some slimy little drug-pushing dentist fuck everything up. This guy is your buddy, so get your miserable little hide out there and help make things happen the way they're supposed to."

Ellerby studied the carpet. "I'm going to need a lot more money," he said.

"I told you I wasn't going to give him a dime. If you want to pay him you can do it out of your so-called salary. And when he comes back for more we'll be in the same position we are now. And then you can pay him again if you can't keep him quiet."

Ellerby sat down resignedly.

"All right," he said quietly. "I'll deal with him. But I need a bigger cut. You're worth almost a quarter of a billion dollars and I deserve a much bigger slice of it."

Ravena stood up. "We'll talk about that later," she snapped. "Right now I'm going to take a long, hot shower. You make me feel dirty."

She swept out of the room leaving Ellerby alone with his thoughts. He knew what he had to do.

Chapter 33

Jack was apoplectic.

His face turned red, his eyes bulged, his hair, what there was of it, seemed to stand on end as if electrified.

"You did what?" It was a scream but it came out as a hoarse whisper.

Michael looked around the newsroom nervously. Everyone was used to Jack Iverson's stand-up routines of feigned horror and largely ignored them. This one had the makings of the real McCoy, but either no one noticed or no one cared.

Michael wasn't sure what to say, so he said nothing. Jack stared him down then quietly ordered him, "Find Jane and meet me in the conference room." Then he stood up stiffly, grabbed a legal pad and stormed down the hall.

Michael noticed with relief that at least he wasn't going to drag Peterson into this.
Thankfully this was going to be a private little screamfest with only Jane to witness the reaming of his new butt-hole.

Michael found Jane at the coffee machine. "Jack wants us in the conference room," he said. "I think he wants you to watch while he tears me limb from limb. Or fires my ass."

Jane's mouth dropped and she hurriedly put down her coffee cup. "What in hell have you been doing?" she asked.

"You'll find out when we get in there. It's very embarrassing."

Jane picked up her coffee and followed him down the hallway. Jack stood at the open conference door like a guard inviting a condemned prisoner into the execution chamber. The two reporters shuffled in and Jack slammed the door behind them and sat down with a thud at the head of the table.

"All right," he said wearily. "Let's take it from the top. You stole a glass and a picture frame from Ravena Ventura and you want to get them checked for fingerprints."

Jane's eyes grew saucer-like and her mouth fell open again. She knew better than to say anything.

"I didn't exactly steal them," said Michael. "I only borrowed them."

"Without permission."

"Well, yeah. She wasn't likely to give me permission, was she? But I planned to put them back after we got the prints off them. No one would be any the wiser, except us."

"And how are we going to get prints off them? This isn't the goddam police department and we don't have our own forensics lab."

"I thought you might know some way we could have them checked out. You know a lot of people."

Jack pounced on him.

"The police don't exactly jump through hoops to help the press, especially The Courier, find clues in a murder case," he said. "And I don't have any dusting powder in my back pocket, or the knowledge to tell a whorl from a whatnot, even if I could pull up prints."

Michael was crestfallen. "I'm sorry, Jack," he said. He felt ashamed and embarrassed, and Jane's presence wasn't helping. That was probably why Jack had invited her to watch this demeaning spectacle.

"Being sorry doesn't eradicate what you've done. Courier reporters don't steal. It's one thing to take a sheet of paper someone threw away, but you could get into serious trouble for this. We get a bad enough rap as it is without your mug shot being on the six o'clock news. Don't you have any fucking commonsense at all?"

"Do you want my resignation?"

"Shit no! We're up to our asses in alligators here but so far no one outside this room knows anything about this. I just want you to realize you fucked up big time and trust there won't be a repeat. Just because you're working for The Courier doesn't mean you shouldn't have any ethics. The laws of the country still apply to us, you know. And sometimes they're applied even more stringently. We are always under a microscope. We expose people and the things they do, and they fear us and hate us for it. And the rest of the media fear us and hate us because we're so much better at it than they are."

Michael felt like a mouse in a cage with a python. "What would you like me to do?" he asked.

"Is there any chance Ventura is going to miss the photo and the glass?"

"Doubt it very much. She leaves glasses around all the time. She relies on Ellerby or the maid service to pick them up and take them to the kitchen. And she may even have forgotten the existence of the photo. Mrs. Cruz said she had a lot of photos put away of her and the ex. They came with all her other stuff when she moved from L.A. Mrs. Cruz said she just had it all stored in boxes and never looked at any of it. It was all yesterday's news to her."

"Then it's your choice. Return these things if you can do it without getting caught. Or just get rid of them."

Michael was puzzled, and relieved. Jack wanted to brush it under the rug. "Can't we somehow get them checked for prints before I unload them?"

"Whatever. But I don't know how. And the fewer people who know of their existence the better."

He stood up. "That's all," he said, eyeing his reporters up and down. "What goes on in this room stays in this room. Understood?"

They both murmured "yes" and Iverson left them sitting alone.

The silence was deafening until Jane suddenly let out a "Wow!"

"Wow is right," said Michael. "I guess I was pretty stupid. I just got carried away."

Jane nodded. "You're lucky Jack didn't get someone to carry you away. I've never seen him so pissed."

"I seem to have that effect on the people I work with. But the photo frame and the glass could be very useful if we could get prints off them. Obviously any prints on the glass would belong to Ravena. But what if prints on the photo frame don't match? After all, she must have handled it at some point in the past."

"I know that," said Jane. "But what good would it do? You can't go running to the police with this stuff."

"Yes, but *we* would know and perhaps somehow we could get the police interested in checking it out for themselves. Imagine how clever Henderson would feel if he could get the credit for uncovering something like that. Not that it matters. I don't have a clue where to go to get fingerprints checked out."

"I think I do," said Jane. And she proceeded to tell him.

Chapter 34

Michael phoned Hendrix the next morning to call in sick. He mumbled hoarsely and vaguely about cold or flu symptoms but the security chief didn't seem to care much. The job was largely a do-nothing precaution to satisfy the client and there was a good chance one security guard's absence wouldn't be noticed even if Hendrix didn't bring in a substitute.

Then Michael made a second phone call, set up an appointment for ten o'clock and tooled into downtown Delray. He took the main east-west artery, Atlantic Avenue, to the intersection at Swinton Avenue, the crossroads that divided the city into four quadrants. Swinton began life to the north in an upscale residential district, turned into a mix of boutiques and restaurants downtown then ran south parallel to the railroad tracks into an ethnic neighborhood that old-time residents still referred to as Blacktown.

African-Americans still dominated this area but they now shared it with Hispanics, Haitians and a growing number of whites. South Swinton was lined with a collection of rickety old frame homes that had been transformed into respectable mom-and-pop businesses.

One of these homes was Michael's destination, and it wasn't too difficult to find. A modest wooden sign proclaiming "Edna Schiel, Private Investigations" stood by a small wooden gate set in a chain-link fence. The fence cut off a small clapboard house from its look-alike neighbors. The building had been painted off-white in the not-too-distant past but the shingle roof appeared to be one good thunderstorm away from extinction. Weeds were winning the battle with a tiny lawn in the front yard but window boxes overflowing with red flowers were working hard to create some curb appeal.

This was not Michael's mental picture of a private investigator's office. He'd never been in one before, but he'd seen enough movies to know that they were usually bare-bone cubicles on the upper floors of rundown office buildings; and the gumshoes themselves were always men.

However, Jane had insisted that Edna was the crème de la crème in local PIs and he'd googled her to find out that this appeared to be true. Certainly she was a pretty high-profile character, a self-driven activist who enjoyed banging heads with local politicians. Perhaps she was too high-profile for the task at hand. But she was honest, forthright and trustworthy, according to Jane. And she had a lot of connections, a lot of fans, and a high success rate on her case load.

Michael pushed open the gate, stepped gingerly up the creaky wooden stairway to the front porch and rang the bell.

He heard it resonate inside the house and waited hesitantly, tightly clutching a plastic grocery bag. There was no immediate response and he was overcome by a sudden sense of relief. Perhaps Ms. Schiel had had to leave in an emergency. Perhaps he should forget the whole thing.

He was trying to decide whether to try the bell again or to walk away when the door opened and he faced a sixty-something woman who might have been somebody's grandmother and would never have been confused with Sam Spade. She had a kind face devoid of makeup and wore a black and beige plaid skirt and a copper-colored blouse that struggled to confine her ample chest.

Michael stared at her.

"Good morning." Her voice was low and raspy. It seemed to match her image. "Mr. Hanlon?"

"Yes, Ms. Schiel. Please call me Michael."

"Come in," she said. It was an order and Michael snapped to attention as she disappeared back into the darkness. He followed her into the house to be enveloped by a strangely comforting odor that reminded him of old buildings, old furniture and old people.

The front door opened directly into what had once been a small living room. Now it was an office of sorts. Consignment-shop furniture shared space with a Victorian roll-top desk that might have been a genuine antique. A small computer sat on a tiny fold-down table in one corner. The room was cluttered with souvenirs from a storied past—some Caribbean chic, some Florida cheap. Reading matter was everywhere: books, well-thumbed magazines, old newspapers, local and out of town. Edna Schiel was obviously an avid reader and not much of a housekeeper.

Michael began to panic. He wished he hadn't come. But now he was in the house with this strange woman and the front door was closed behind him.

"Have a seat," she said. "And call me Edna. Everyone does, except when they're calling me things I don't want to hear." She cackled at that and Michael's heart sank even lower. Now he was sure this had been a mistake.

He perched on the edge of a well-worn sofa and tried to swallow the lump that was forming in his throat.

"Ms, uh, Edna," he said, "I'm a newspaper reporter and a colleague suggested that you might be able to help me. But I am concerned about confidentiality." He was hoping she would say there was no client privilege in the private-eye business so he could leave gracefully. But he was disappointed.

"No problem, Michael. What we discuss here is strictly between us. I have a good working relationship with the police, if not the city bureaucracy, and we try not to bother each other. They do their thing and I do mine. But I hope you aren't in any trouble." She leaned forward and peered at him.

"No, nothing like that." *Merely wobbling on the edge of it.* "It's just that I'm working on this story and I need to keep it under wraps."

"Very well, tell me how I can help you." She sat down opposite him and clasped her hands in her lap. Now she was starting to remind Michael of his first-grade teacher.

"Can you take fingerprints?" he asked nervously as he emptied the contents of his grocery bag onto his lap. He held up the Ziploc bag containing the martini glass.

Edna Schiel laughed. "Of course I can. Anyone can. All it takes is some powder, a brush and Scotch tape."

Michael nodded. At least he'd been on the money when he'd taken Scotch tape to the funeral home.

Edna eyed the glass cautiously. "Taking fingerprints isn't the difficult part. Problems only occur when you try to identify them. I assume that's what you're after."

"Yes, sort of," said Michael, pulling the photo frame out of a large brown-paper lunch bag that had been a belated attempt to protect it. "What I really need to know is whether fingerprints on this glass match any prints on this photo frame."

Edna handled both pieces carefully, placed them on her lap and studied them.

"This woman looks familiar," she said, contemplating the photograph. "She's very beautiful." She looked quizzically at Michael.

"Yes," he said. He realized he had to come clean with this odd woman. "It's Ravena Ventura, the actress. Wedding-day photo from a few years ago. My guess is you'll find her fingerprints on it, perhaps along with a few others. I need to know if they match any prints on the glass."

There. It was out. Could he trust this old lady?

"And if they don't? Do you have a way to identify Miss Ventura's fingerprints?"

"No. But if there are no matches between the prints on the glass and the prints on the photo frame it will tell me that the person who'd held the glass wasn't Ravena, wouldn't it?"

Edna Schiel cackled again. This young man was amusing her. "Maybe," she said, "maybe not. You're assuming that Miss Ventura's prints are on the photo frame but I sense you can't prove that they are."

Michael said nothing.

"Let me see," she said. "You think this actress's prints are on the photo. But you think someone else's are on the glass?"

"Maybe."

"Do you have a clue as to whose prints might be on the glass?"

"If they're not Ravena's I'm pretty sure they'll be her sister's."

"Ah, yes. The twin sister who was murdered?"

"Yes."

The rotund investigator sat up and smiled at him. "You're trying to get to the bottom of the murder mystery, huh?"

Michael wriggled uncomfortably and nodded.

"Then let's see what we can do. I may be able to help you. But I don't work for free. I usually charge a hundred dollars an hour plus expenses with a $500 retainer. For this little job I'll settle for just the retainer."

Michael shrugged. Perhaps he could write off her charges on his expense account. More likely Jack would suggest he chalk it up to experience. He nodded agreement.

"You know," she said brightly. "I read somewhere that Miss Ventura's sister had been in trouble with the law back in Los Angeles. Maybe the police there would have her prints on file. Perhaps we could cut a few corners here and find out if the prints on the martini glass match hers."

"How can we do that?" Michael asked.

"Shouldn't be too difficult. I have a good friend in forensics in Miami. And he knows people in Los Angeles. I may be able to persuade him to get a comparison between prints on this glass and prints of the sister that the police are sure to have on file. I'll tell him a

Ravena fan bought the glass on eBay but isn't sure it's hers now he's read about her twin sister."

Michael's heart jumped a mile. He didn't need prints off the photo frame if he could get access to Elizabeth Thomas's police records. If the prints on the glass matched those in law-enforcement files he would have her dead to rights.

Chapter 35

Edna Schiel had promised Michael a response in a day or so. That was a long time to be on tenterhooks. He was anxious to get the glass and the framed photo back where they came from. He speculated on what could be hanging over his head. Things like charges of stealing, burglary, breaking and entering, impersonating a security officer, trespassing. . . The list seemed endless and he wanted it to go away. He had been impetuous and stupid, and he wasn't sure he'd done the right thing by drawing Edna Schiel into it. Could he really rely on her? Despite her track record as a feisty hero of the little guy she looked less like a private eye than anyone he had ever met.

Michael decided to spend the afternoon watching two more movies, the only Ravena Ventura flicks he hadn't seen. But after four frustrating and boring hours in front of the TV he decided to drop by The Courier, even though conventional office hours were over. As expected, the newsroom was all but deserted. No Jack, no Jane, just a few stragglers making calls to the West Coast, where it was still mid-afternoon.

But there was a warm body at the photo desk. He went over to where a lone young assistant was shutting down her Macintosh and rummaging through her purse for car keys.

"Sorry to bother you," he said, extending his hand and introducing himself. The girl swept back long dark locks with one hand and looked up at him with doe-like eyes. She gave him a limp-wristed handshake and a shy smile.

"Hi," she said. "I'm Maggie. Maggie Mulcahey. I've seen you around. Can I help you with something?"

"Actually, yes," said Michael. "I wanted to look at photos of Ravena Ventura. Do you have a file I could look through?"

Maggie Mulcahey smiled again. "We digitized the entire photo library a few years ago. Good job we did. We must have more than three thousand photos of Ravena Ventura on file. Anything specific you want to see? Movie roles or real life? It could take you forever unless you can narrow your search."

"Sorry," he said. "It's not going to be that simple. And I see you're about to leave."

"That's okay. I can leave you to look to your heart is content."

"I'm not sure that's a good idea. It's not safe to leave me alone with technology."

Maggie laughed. "Don't worry about it." She hit a button to reboot her computer. "It's simple. Look!"

Fingers flashing, she entered a password, hit a couple of keys then typed "Ravena Ventura" into a box that appeared onscreen. Thirty small photos of the actress immediately unfolded on the monitor, starting with one of Ravena fighting back tears as she scattered ashes into the ocean from her yacht.

Maggie scrolled down to more shots, including long-lens images of Ravena at a restaurant with Gordon Meriwether.

"These are all in order by date," explained Maggie. "Most recent pictures first. You can re-arrange them any way you like. You can move photos from two years ago to the top if you like."

Michael pointed to the screen. "You say you have thousands more than these?"

"Oh yes." Maggie Mulcahey was in her element. "All we have to do is scroll down. The log says we have 3,247 photos in this file—all featuring Ravena Ventura." She looked up at him, seeking admiration. She wasn't disappointed.

"That's great," said Michael. "Can we make any of them bigger?"

"Sure. Just double-click on one and it will fill the screen. To make it small again just hit the top right button on the photo. "She stood up. "Want to sit down and try it?"

"Sure," said Michael and slid into her chair.

Maggie picked up her purse. "Sorry," she said, "but I have to go. My mom and dad are visiting from Jersey and they're taking me out to dinner. If you want to print anything, just blow the pictures up and hit the print button. They'll come out in that printer over there. When you're finished hit 'File' then 'Close' and shut it down. Knock yourself out!"

Maggie scooped up her purse, turned to leave then hesitated. "I'll give you my cell number," she said, "just in case you get into computer hell." She scribbled it on a legal pad on her desk then she was gone. Michael was alone with a comprehensive pictorial history of Ravena Ventura.

He stared for a long time at the first row of photos. They all featured Ravena leaning over the side of her yacht, cascading her sister's ashes into the water. They had obviously been taken from another boat nearby.

Michael selected one of the photos and blew it up. There was something unsettling about it. It wasn't the subject matter. Human ashes were often dumped into oceans. But something didn't look right.

He printed it out, then returned to the screen and studied the other tiny photos. He paused at a close-up presumably taken by a local press photographer on Ravena's yacht. She was holding up the small metal urn containing the ashes while she tried to wipe away tears with her other hand. *Hey, she was an actress, wasn't she?*

Michael printed that picture as well.

There were a dozen similar photos of the funeral at sea, nothing very exciting. Michael scrolled down to rows of shots taken before the murder. Half a dozen pictures of her having dinner with her attorney. They weren't very good quality—grainy, cloudy and distorted by reflections through the restaurant window. "Newsy" is how the Courier staff would describe them because they gave readers the feeling they were looking at something they weren't supposed to see.

Despite this Michael didn't find them very interesting, but he blew up the best-quality photo from the set and sent it to the printer. Then he shuffled the pictures he had printed and stared at them intently. There had to be *something* here!

He went back to the screen and scrolled down again. Photos of Ravena in slinky gowns at a myriad of Hollywood awards shows. Holding awards aloft in three of them, including an Oscar. Apparently the industry thought highly of her acting skills. Michael wondered what they thought of her drinking and drug habits, her short fuse and her penchant for profanity. They probably didn't care.

The pictures rolled by, back to her earlier years, her marriage, hanging on the arms of various boyfriends and leading men, then back to shots from her fledgling and short-lived TV career as a child. He paused at one showing a young Ravena with her family: Liz, her parents and an older girl who was presumably Emily, the twins' big sister. He sent that to the printer as well.

Then Michael scrolled back up to the awards shows and settled on a bosomy shot of a triumphant Ravena brandishing one of her Oscars. He printed that then shut down the computer. He scooped up his print-outs, stuffed them into a manila file folder and headed home.

* * *

The phone on his kitchen wall was ringing when he walked through the door. Maybe it was Jane, he thought hopefully. No such luck.

"How was your day?" Iverson asked, but he didn't wait for a reply before barking, "Do you know the name of Ravena Ventura's dentist?"

"Huh?"

"You said you took her to see a dentist in Delray. Do you remember his name?"

"I never knew it. Why do you ask?

"Because a dentist at that Medical Arts building has just been found dead in his office. Shot. Just wondered if it was Ventura's dentist.

"When did this happen?"

"No idea, but his body has just been discovered. We got a tip from one of our editorial assistants who's married to a Delray cop. The police are on the scene as we speak."

"Are we looking at murder here?"

"Don't know yet. The guy could have shot himself. Only reason I'm interested is because his office is in the same building where you took Ravena. His name's Wetherby. Dr. Drew Wetherby. Ring any bells?"

"No. No reason it should. There were four or five dentists in that building. Don't recall any of their names. They all had offices on the third floor."

"How many times did you take Ravena there?"

"Just the once. I only got to drive her because Ellerby wasn't available for some reason."
Iverson sighed. "I'm sure the cops will go through the doc's records and check on his patients, though I imagine Ravena Ventura would have used some other name. And there's nothing for us in this unless she's connected. I'll let you know what we find out."

He hung up, leaving Michael to ponder the situation. If Wetherby had been Ravena's dentist he'd also been her drug dealer. His demise could have been a drug deal gone wrong. Perhaps the elusive Eighth Street gunman had finally put a bullet in someone. Or maybe it was merely a case of a dentist caught bonking some guy's wife while he had her in the chair.

Michael tried to call Jack back, but the line was busy. Then he dialed Jane's number, but that was busy, too. The two of them were probably talking to each other.

To hell with it. He picked up his car keys and headed out the door.

Chapter 36

The Medical Arts Center in north Delray was only five minutes away. As soon as he rounded the corner onto Eighth Street he could see evidence of police activity ahead— flashing blue, yellow and red lights emanating from half a dozen police cars parked in a semicircle in the medical building parking lot.

Michael found a place to park a few feet from the action, got out of his car and looked around. There were cops everywhere but the frenetic flashing of the lights disguised a lack of activity. Michael looked for a familiar if not friendly face, like Detective Henderson, but these were Delray Beach city cops, not sheriff's deputies. Different turf, different group of ball-busters.

He strode over to the nearest uniformed officer and flashed his press pass.

"Sorry," said the patrolman, "no one but law enforcement and the medical examiner allowed past this point." He jerked a thumb toward a cluster of people to his right. "Your news buddies are over there. Detectives will answer your questions after we get the body out of here. The ME is up there now."

That was no help to Michael. He didn't want to see any of his questions answered in the local paper tomorrow morning. And he didn't want to share any of his information with the regular press. It wouldn't be good for the dailies to find out that the dead dentist might have a link to Ravena Ventura. They'd be all over that like sprinkles on ice cream long before The Courier could get on the newsstands.

There was a sudden flurry of activity and the uniforms guarding the parking lot moved in formation closer to the main entrance of the building. A carefully bagged body was being trundled out on a gurney and loaded into an ambulance.

The operation was being choreographed by two or three plain-clothed detectives. Michael had to get to them first.

The knot of reporters surged closer to the action in tune with the police net. Michael moved to the other side of the cordon-offed officers and saw his chance.

He was by the corner of the building now and largely being ignored. Everyone's eyes were riveted on the removal of the body. Hugging the wall, Michael slipped in front of the line of officers. Then he made a beeline for the nearest detective as the cops changed positions to create a path for the departing ambulance.

"Sir! Officer! Detective!" Michael brandished his press pass.

"I'm sorry, sir," said the detective, "but this area is off limits. I'll talk to the press shortly."

"I understand that," said Michael, "but there's something I need to discuss with you privately."

The detective eyed him quizzically. "Something to do with what?"

"Something to do with this, uh…situation. I was wondering if the victim might have been Ravena Ventura's dentist."

"Ravena Ventura?" The cop looked puzzled. "You mean the actress?"

"Yes."

"I've no idea. Why do you ask?"

Michael tried to choose his words carefully. "I know she had some work done by a dentist in this building. It might not be this guy, of course, but it could be. And if there did turn out be a connection, that would link Ravena to two mysterious deaths, wouldn't it?"

He paused, watching the wheels turn, waiting for something to sink in.

The detective tried to find his face in his shoeshine, then said, "I've no idea who's connected to what yet, but you sound as though you know something you're not telling me."

"I don't know anything for sure. I'm just trying to cover all the bases."

"Obviously we're going to check on everyone who knew the deceased; family, friends…patients." The detective was eyeing Michael warily. "We have people going through his records now. I'm sure if Miss Ventura is a patient she'll be on file in his office. We'll check it out."

"Would you let me know?"

"Sure." It was a noncommittal dismissal.

"I'll call you," offered Michael. "Do you have a card?"

The detective sighed, dug in his pocket and came out with a business card.

Michael glanced at it quickly and read the contents out loud as though looking for confirmation. "Detective Harry Christopher, Delray Beach Police Department."

"Thanks, detective," he said and smiled as he pushed one of his own cards into the cop's hand. "Remember, if what I asked you turns out to be affirmative, you heard it here first!"

Detective Christopher looked askance at Michael's card and grimaced.

"National Courier, huh? Should've known. Get outta here!"

Michael took his cue and left. He prayed that if a Ravena connection did turn up in this case, he'd learn about it before the mainstream press. Heck, he might even wind up being a witness. Wouldn't that be a trip? Jolly Jack Iverson would have a seizure!

Michael returned to the solitude of his apartment. He uncapped a beer and decided to sit down and replay one of his Ravena movies. Maybe it would help him relax. Heck, it would probably put him to sleep.

After twenty minutes of wrestling with the thought that the beautiful woman onscreen seemed very unlike the Ravena Ventura he knew, he drifted into more garbled dreams of a blonde sex siren that kept dissolving into a rough diamond with a short fuse, a sharp tongue and an ugly disposition.

* * *

Michael awoke on the sofa the next morning with a headache and a stiff neck. He could have used a couple of hours in a real bed, but he was running late. Hurriedly he showered, dressed and headed for the Courier offices.

He filled Jack in on his impulsive trip to the previous night's crime scene, wondering whether he'd get praise or yet another penance to pay.

Surprisingly, Jack's emotions remained firmly in check. "Have you read the paper this morning?" he asked.

"No, not yet," said Michael. "Anything surprising?"

"Not really. Evidence suggests it *was* a murder. The cleaning crew found the dentist shot in his office about an hour after he'd closed for the day. No suspects yet. Probably somebody he knew or it might have been a burglary gone bad."

"Why would anyone break into a dentist's office?"

"Who knows? Maybe somebody with a hankering for gold teeth."

"No mention of Ravena Ventura?"

"Not a whistle. But that's not something the cops would release to the world anyway."

"I'm hoping I've got the inside track on that. Detective Christopher thinks I may know something. I'm hoping he's got me on one of those lists of 'people of interest.'"
Iverson grunted. "Don't get too excited. Those folks usually wind up getting charged with the crime. In any event, if Ventura isn't

connected to this dentist in any way, The Courier won't be interested. If we did in-depth stories on every murder in America we'd denude the world's forests and sell no papers. Meanwhile, need I remind you we need a Ravena story to sit up and beg for?"

"I'm waiting to hear word back on something. And I have a few things to check on."

He was anxious to hear from Edna Schiel and Detective Christopher. The waiting was unbearable. He stared at his cell phone and the landline on his desk, willing one of them to ring. But they didn't. No one was trying to reach him. Not even his creditors.

In desperation, he decided to call Edna.

"Hello, Mr. Hanlon," she said brightly. She sounded younger and more exuberant than Michael's memory of her. "I was just about to call you."

"Any luck?" he asked.

"If you'd like to stop by I can return your glass and photo frame. I have a report for you. Good news . . . and not-so-good."

"What did you discover?" Michael wasn't in the mood for good news-bad news games.

"Why don't you drop by when you have the time?" said Edna. "I'll be home all day."

He told her he'd be right over and pocketed the phone.

* * *

Edna was waiting for him when he pulled up outside her house. She opened the door before he could reach it and ushered him inside.

The glass and the photo frame were also waiting for him, neatly packaged in clear plastic on the small coffee table in the front room.

Edna nodded toward them. "I sent them to my friend," she said. "He got a few prints off the glass, plus a few smudges. The photo frame wasn't so good. A ton of people had handled it so there were just a lot of old, blurred latents, a confusing jumble of both left-hand and right-hand prints."

"So you can't tell if any of them match the prints on the glass?"

"Not with any certainty. The best they could do was a five-point match. In some jurisdictions that would almost be enough to say they probably belong to the same person. But it would be tough to get a conviction for any serious crime with less than a ten-point match."

Michael was crestfallen. Was this the good news or the bad?

"Were you able to get a comparison between the prints on the glass and anything in police files?" he asked.

Edna smiled. "My friend asked the Los Angeles police for a check against Elizabeth Thomas." Then she added triumphantly, "You have a more definitive match there."

Michael's eyes widened and his jaw dropped. Edna eyed him with amusement.

"Don't get too excited," she told him. "They gave you a twelve-point match between prints on the glass and the prints they have on file for Elizabeth Thomas. That sounds pretty good until you realize that you're dealing with identical twins."

Michael looked at her skeptically. "What do you mean? I know that identical twins have different fingerprints."

Edna nodded. "Yes, they do, but they're usually not as different as yours and mine are likely to be. No one really knows why, but fingerprints are believed to be molded by movements of the fetus in the womb, and even identical fetuses don't move in unison like the Rockettes. So twins' prints aren't identical, but they do share many of the same nuances."

"So what are you telling me?"

"That we have nothing conclusive. The problem is we don't have any established Ravena Ventura prints to go on. The prints on either your glass or your photo frame could be those of either twin. So that's where we are. Good news and bad news. Enough evidence to raise serious thoughts, but like I said, no slam dunk. Sorry."

Michael was shattered. A dead end. A waste of time and five hundred bucks down the drain!

"Well, thanks anyway," he mumbled. He picked up his two pieces of carefully wrapped "evidence" and looked at them disdainfully. "I'd better get these back to where they belong."

Edna Schiel folded her hands on her lap, cocked her head to one side and eyed Michael intently. "You're a very astute and determined young man," she said. "I've been reading up on Ravena Ventura and her sister. You may not have anything to take to the bank, but there's enough to make it worthwhile to keep digging. I've often been pleasantly surprised by my gut instincts."

Michael responded with a weak smile. The old lady was trying to make him feel better. He'd put himself at risk getting hold of this martini glass and the photo frame. Now he had to find some way of returning them without getting caught.

Chapter 37

Michael drove slowly back to the office to find Jack Iverson in unusual good humor. At least that would make it easier for Michael to tell him his tale of woe. He wasted no time explaining his wild goose chase for fingerprints.

"Inconclusive," he said, with finality.

Jack put an elbow on his desk and rubbed a stubbled chin thoughtfully. "You know," he said at last, "the fingerprints don't prove you wrong. They're just not quite enough to prove you're right."

He leaned over to where Michael was sitting in a metal chair next to Jack's desk. Jane was eyeing them intently from her own work station and Michael felt very uncomfortable. "Peterson and I had a chat with JC," said Jack. "He wanted to know how you were doing. We didn't really have much to offer so we filled him in on your nutty theory."

"What?" Michael jumped to his feet. "Why'd 'ya do that? He must think I'm crazy. What did he say?"

Jack leaned back with a sly smile. "He laughed," he said. "Laughed his socks off!"

"He laughed at me?"

"No, Mikey, He didn't laugh *at* you. Your idea just made him laugh. And it takes a lot to make JC laugh."

"All right then, what did he actually say?"

"He said what a great story that would be. Then he wanted a little meeting to discuss avenues to explore that could nail it down."

"Did you tell him I was trying to have fingerprints checked?"

"Yes, but I didn't tell him that you'd stolen some. He didn't realize that twins didn't have identical fingerprints. After we told him he wanted to know other ways in which identical twins were different. You should have been there. You've learned more about this stuff than we have. We did tell him about teeth possibly being different. That was all we could think of. He sent us away to research it and put more people on it if we have to."

"Didn't you guys come up with any fresh ideas?"

"Only one, and it's pretty obvious, when you think about it. If we could find someone who knows Ravena Ventura well we could maybe arrange a meeting between the two of them. Someone very close to Ravena, like Meriwether, for example, might notice if something was amiss."

"Nice twenty-twenty hindsight, Jack. But it's not very practical. Since her sister's death, Ravena seems to have been deliberately avoiding contact with everyone who knows her. She's been holed up in that mansion alone, except for Ellerby. She's fired almost everybody who was around her. She started with the Cruzes and all her security cops until the only long-standing person still on her payroll seems to be Usher. And I think most of her contact with Ravena is done by phone or the Internet."

Jack sniffed. "Okay. You got any ideas, then?"

"Yes, one. It concerns something the private eye said and a thought came to mind when you mentioned people who knew her. I've been looking at file photos of Ravena and there's something puzzling me. Someone who was close to her might be able to solve my problem without us having to arrange a meeting."

"And that is . . . ?"

"Tell you later, Jack. First I'd like to bounce something else off the Cruzes."

"Don't keep bugging 'em too much. They're waiting for us to give them more money, even though we've fed them another thousand for providing background on our murder stories."

"Don't worry. If they can help me out here they may be worth a bonus."

Michael marched over to the photo library, which was now being manned by half a dozen female assistants poring over large-screen Macs. He knew none of them by name except Maggie, so he singled her out for help.

She gave him a warm smile. "Did you find what you were looking for the other night?"

"I found some things that might be of interest. But I need more. Would you have time to look in Ravena Ventura's file for pictures of her doing something with her hands, like signing autographs, writing something, even just holding a drink?"

Maggie looked at him quizzically but knew better than to ask questions. This job was nothing like her previous one in an insurance office. Courier editors and reporters were always looking for something wacky and the product of her labors usually found its way into the paper, sometimes in ways that boggled her mind.

"Sure," she said. "Give me a little while. I'll see what we've got. Only a few thousand pictures to wade through, remember?"

Michael nodded his appreciation. Maggie was cute and flirtatious. But he needed to get to work. At his desk he called the Cruzes' apartment. "Sorry to bother you again, Mrs. Cruz," he said, "but I wondered if you or your husband know whether Ravena is right-handed or left-handed."

The question was met with heavy silence. Michael could hear Marguerita Cruz breathing into the phone. Then, finally, "Do not know, senor. Never think about it. She must be right-handed. Think most people are."

"How about your husband?"

"Oh, he is right-handed. I'm sure he is. Si, he is."

Michael winced. "Okay, but does he perhaps know if Ravena is right or left handed?"

"Do not know, senor, and he is not here now. He has new job. With landscape company," she added proudly.

"And in the last few days before Miss Ventura let you go you don't recall seeing her using her left hand?"

"No, senor. But I not look for things like that," she added defensively. "After sister die, Miss Ravena was not herself and I stay out of her way as much as possible."

Michael gave up. He thanked the housekeeper profusely, even though she had been less than helpful.

"What was that all about?" asked Jane.

Michael looked at her. Would she think he was mad? She seemed to have acquired more respect for him since he went undercover and he had no desire to change that.

He filled her in on the fingerprint fiasco.

"I'm looking for differences in Ravena now and Ravena before her sister was murdered. Twin sisters simply aren't total carbon copies of each other and Mrs. Cruz said Ravena had changed after her sister died. Then there's something that Edna said, something about right hands and left hands. Makes me wonder if one of the sisters was right-handed and the other was a lefty."

"And what have you come up with so far?"

"Nothing yet. I need to look back over Ravena's movies but I don't recall spotting anything that will tell me whether she's right or left-handed. I've also been looking at still photographs of her, but so far I haven't found any clues there either."

"What about the twins' teeth? Wouldn't they be different?"

"Sure, but that's an even more difficult line to pursue. Talking about teeth, I still haven't heard back from Detective Christopher about that dentist's client list."

Michael dug out the detective's card and picked up the phone again. He'd been a reporter long enough to know that if you're waiting for a callback *you* had to phone *them*.

Christopher was less cutting than Henderson, and left Michael staring into space as he put the phone down. He looked up at Jack's desk, but the editor had disappeared.

"Well?" asked Jane. "Get anything?"

"Maybe. Detective Christopher told me the murdered dentist had no files on anyone named Ravena Ventura. Which isn't too surprising. I'm sure she wouldn't use her professional name. I asked him about Rachel Thomas and Elizabeth Thomas and no bells rang. Of course she could have used the name Fannie Fidget for all anyone would know. But Christopher let it drop that they had found cocaine and other illegal drugs in the dentist's office. That clinches it for me. Wetherby had to have been her dentist."

He sighed. "But it's not going to help us get into Ravena's mouth, is it? She could be any one of hundreds of women in his files. And how am I going to find earlier impressions of Ravena's teeth to match whatever this Wetherby guy may have on file?"

"You probably can't," said Jane, "so stop obsessing about it. But at least we now have connected Ravena Ventura to two murders."

"We need to tell the police that Ravena's dentist was her drug dealer."

"Why? It may not be relevant. And we don't want to open a can of worms by suddenly accusing Ravena of being a druggie."

"But if the police think the dentist's murder is drug related they may never link Ravena to him."

"True. But we know something else the cops don't—that there's more to Ravena than meets the eye. We need to talk to Jack. Where the hell is he?"

"Don't know," said Michael. "Probably in of those interminable editorial meetings where I bet—"

He was cut off in mid-sentence by the sight of Maggie, the photo assistant, heading across the newsroom toward him, waving half a dozen photographs.
"Couldn't find much," she said breathlessly. "We can sort celeb photos lots of different ways, but not by 'use of their hands.' I didn't get too far before they pulled me off to dig out some pix of Brad Pitt. Don't know if any of these will help."

She fanned them out on the desk and stepped back for Michael to examine them. Jane slid over to look over his shoulder.

Michael shuffled them around on the desk. He noticed a couple of Oscar shots that he had copied earlier, but nothing else jumped out at him. There was one shot of Ravena at an amusement park, being mobbed for autographs. But she had neither pen nor paper in either hand. Another one showed her schmoozing at a nightclub with unidentified people. Her table was overflowing with drinks but her hands were busy gesticulating as she talked excitedly with her friends.

"We just don't know," said Jane. "Face it, Michael, she's probably right-handed. Most people are, you know."

"Thanks a lot. That's exactly what Mrs. Cruz said. I think one twin was left-handed and the other one right-handed. See!" He pulled out the photos he'd printed earlier showing the actress scattering her sister's ashes into the ocean. "She's holding the urn in her right hand. Now look at these shots of Ravena at the Oscars. She's holding her Oscar in her left hand."

"So what? Maybe her right arm was tired. Or perhaps she wanted to save it for more hugs and handshakes."

Maggie picked up the last photo in the pile she'd brought over. "What about this one?" she said. It showed an intense younger-looking Ravena Ventura, in T-shirt and jeans, swinging a baseball bat at an invisible ball.

Michael studied it and frowned. "When was this taken?" he asked.

"About fifteen years ago," said Maggie, "when she wasn't as famous or as reclusive as she is now. Celebrity charity softball game in L.A."

"Thanks, Maggie. This is very interesting. Look how she's swinging the bat. She *is* a lefty!"

"Sure looks like it," said Maggie. "Hope it's useful to you."

"Absolutely," said Michael as Jack Iverson reappeared at his desk.

"Hey, Jack," he called. "Come look at this."

Iverson glanced at the photo, then at Michael. "Yeah. So? Ravena used to play softball. Lots of Hollywood stars do that. Good exercise. And good for their image, you know."

"I know, but look. She's a lefty!"

Iverson looked puzzled. "So what? Lots of people are. Righties and lefties. That's life—and baseball. And don't forget switch-hitters."

"Switch-hitters? This is charity softball, not the World Series."

"What's the difference? Some right-handed people would bat left anyway. Some folks are weird like that."

Michael shook his head and stared at the photo. "Jack, you're incorrigible," he said. "You know what I've got to do? Somehow I've got to get Ravena to give me her autograph."

Chapter 38

Michael saw it before he heard it: a glint of light flashing from the tip of the peninsula across the water from Ravena's estate.

He had just turned the southeast corner of the house to find Ravena at her usual spot, reclining in front of the pool in a white bikini, drink in hand; suntan lotion on a table by her lounge chair. He was wondering how to broach the subject of an autograph when he heard the first crack, then another.

Gunfire!

Someone was turning the patio into a shooting gallery. Ravena screamed and jumped to her feet. Her glass dropped to the patio and shattered into a thousand pieces as a bullet clanged into the poolside furniture and ricocheted off in a clatter of metal on metal.

"Miss Ravena, get down! Get down!"

Michael screamed at her as he dropped to his haunches. She was momentarily paralyzed in bewilderment. Something immediate and violent was invading her space and she suddenly realized she was in danger. She began to run toward the house as another bullet crashed into the shrubbery that fringed the patio.

"Get down!" Michael yelled again. "Someone is shooting at you. Drop flat on the ground and try to stay under cover."

Michael was now lying on his stomach, thankful for the large assortment of patio furniture that surrounded the pool. He hoped it would be enough to provide cover.

Two more bullets cut across the patio, one perilously close to Ravena as she lay prone, trying to conceal her body in a network of outdoor tables and chairs. One bullet skidded across the cement and hit the wall of the house below the windows. Chips of dark blue tile flew like shrapnel as another hit the edge of the pool then dropped into the water.

The shooter didn't appear to be much of a marksman, but spraying the pool area with bullets would be enough for one to find its target. Michael was fumbling for his walkie-talkie when he spotted Hendrix.

"What the hell?" screamed the crew chief as he appeared around the corner on the far side of the patio.

"Get down, sir!" yelled Michael. "Someone is shooting at us from Prince's Point."
"Okay. We're on it. Stay down and take care of Miss Ventura. We can block off the entrance to the point and trap this asshole." Hendrix began barking orders into his walkie-talkie and disappeared around the corner.

Take care of Miss Ventura? How was Michael going to do that without exposing himself to a bullet from this whack job? Then he realized that the gunfire had stopped. He slowly got to his knees and glanced across the water. No more flashes in the sunlight. No sign of movement in the trees and sparse scrub on the headland. Had the shooter gotten out of Dodge?

"Miss Ravena, are you all right?" he asked.

"Yes, Michael. But what the hell is going on?"

"I don't know, but we'll find out. Hopefully Hendrix will catch this guy. Someone is out to kill you? Any idea who it might be?"

Ravena laughed mirthlessly. "I'm sure there are plenty of nuts out there who'd get a kick out of killing me."

"Whoever he is, I think he's gone. I'm going to crawl over to you then we should stay low and head for the house."

They reached the lanai without incident, where Ravena stood up and sighed. "Thank you, Michael," she said.

Michael wasn't sure what to say. "Just doing my job, Miss Ravena. There wasn't really much I could do, under the circumstances. I'd better get back out there in case this guy has a boat and shows up on the beach."

Ravena nodded and took off into the bowels of the house leaving Michael wondering what he would do if a crazed assassin did show up on the beach. He was unarmed and his experience in martial arts was limited to watching it on TV. He just hoped Hendrix and his posse would corral the guy on Prince's Point.

Someone certainly wanted Ravena dead. But who? And why? If Ravena knew, she wasn't saying, but now Michael knew that for once Jack had been wrong. The incident at the medical center hadn't been kids with BB guns.

He walked down to the beach gingerly, but there were no boats in sight, no assassins wading ashore. He looked across to the point. A car was creating a mini sandstorm as it barreled towards two others parked between two palm trees. That would be Hendrix and his crew. Had they nailed the guy? Michael couldn't tell what was going on and wished he had binoculars.

He had an urge to take his car over to the point and join them, but he knew his responsibility was to stay on the estate and guard Ravena. She was inside the house now and reasonably safe. But where the hell was Ellerby?

* * *

Hendrix and his crew were back after twenty minutes and Michael was summoned into the office.

"Did you get him?" he asked.

"No. The shooter had left by the time we got there. That property is supposed to be closed off with a chain-link fence until the developers do something with it, but there was a whole section missing and someone had driven a vehicle in there. We went up to the edge of the point and found some casings. I called the Manalapan police, filled them in and left them to sort it all out. I told them about the earlier attack, too, though it was out of their jurisdiction. Don't think they've ever had to deal with anything like this before.

"I've spoken to Miss Ventura, who's shaken a little but okay. She wanted to keep everything under wraps, of course, but I felt we had no choice but to notify the police. I've also talked with Richard."

"Richard?"

"Blackwell. Our employer! He agrees we did the right thing under the circumstances, though he thinks we should have called the police before we drove over to the point. Not that it makes any difference. Whoever was trying to kill Miss Ventura would have been gone before anyone got there. But the cops will make sure Prince's Point is secured and off limits to all unauthorized persons. What we have to do is make sure Miss Ventura stays safe. No one on our staff must say anything to anyone about this situation, except to the local police, who by their very nature will keep everything under wraps as much as possible."

"What about Ellerby? Have you seen him?"

"No. He went out this morning and hasn't returned yet."

"Lucky guy," said Michael, but he wondered just how lucky. Ellerby had also been out of the loop when the shooter had tried to kill Ravena at the medical center. How fortunate. Or convenient.

Chapter 39

"Great stuff, Mikey!"

Jack Iverson was beside himself. He held up his hands, palms facing each other. There was another headline coming. "GUNMAN ATTACKS RAVENA," he announced proudly. "STAR ESCAPES AS HE SPRAYS HER HOME WITH BULLETS . . . COURIER WORLD EXCLUSIVE."

Michael gave him a broad smile. How could JC nix this one? There was just one problem. "Won't it blow my cover?" he asked.

"Not with the Manalapan police on the case. If they release anything at all to the mainstream press it will probably be a couple of grafs on the Police Blotter to suggest that they had investigated gunshots in the something-or-other block of Ocean Avenue. That would be enough to wind up The Courier's rubber band without your input. I only hope the other tabs overlook it, but if they don't they aren't going to get the details we have. And now we can bring in the earlier gunshots at the medical center. The shooter has to be someone with a rifle, just like last time. A handgun certainly wouldn't be much use across the water from Prince's Point."

"What about Ellerby? He could be involved in this. He wasn't around at the time of either shooting."

"Yeah. I know it looks suspicious, but why would Ellerby want Ravena dead? He's got to feel like he won the lottery with her being in his back pocket. He's obviously getting a good stipend for being her manager and maybe a little nookie on the side, too. You don't kill the goose that lays the golden eggs."

"Guess you're right. It's just that the guy gives me the creeps. I get the feeling he's a real psychopath. He could be guilty of anything. In any event, I'm sure the shit's going to hit the fan when Ravena sees our next headline."

* * *

Storm clouds were roiling over the Atlantic, black and gray powerhouses plowing toward the coast ominous and dangerous, but no more so than the dark clouds forming in Ravena Ventura's drawing room.

She paced back and forth until it seemed a path would be embedded in the Persian carpet. The latest Courier headlines had taken her to boiling point, but the detailed story of her brush with death was playing second fiddle to the demise of Dr. Drew.

She paused, her face inches from her manager.

"You're a fucking idiot, Ellie."

The diminutive man jerked his head sideways as she spat the words at him. He stepped away from her to dodge any physical traces of her venom.

"You told me to take care of him," he said, "and that's what I did."

"I didn't suggest you kill him!"

"Sure sounded like it to me. Anyway, how else would you expect me to deal with him? He knew too much and he was asking for too much. He would have bled us dry."

"He was a major drug dealer. You could have played the blackmail card, too. It would have been a Mexican stand-off. You had enough on him to put him away for years. You should have known better than to have hooked up with him in the first place. There are a million dentists around and you pick the biggest scumbag in town."

Ellerby sat down defensively on the edge of an overstuffed chair. "I picked him because I knew him," he said. "Besides, he had first-class Colombian stuff. No problems with it. All we could handle, and then some."

"You can buy coke anywhere."

"Well, it's done. At least he won't bother us again."

"No? His ghost may come back to haunt us. Now the cops have another murder to solve that has links to us. We could be in some serious shit. And now we've got this crap going on with some lunatic armed with a rifle. Do you have something to do with that, too?"

"Don't be ridiculous."

"Are you taking potshots at me then feeding information to The Courier? Where did they get all that shit? I hear they pay their sources pretty well."

Ellerby glared at Ravena. "You know, I've put everything on the line for us. I'm not stupid enough to talk to The Courier. You're the one who did that, remember? But I do need a bigger cut. I'm worth it and you know it."

Ravena looked at him with derision. "We've had this conversation before. You keep saying we're a team but you need me more than I need you. I control the money, remember? Where's your gun, by the way?"

"Upstairs by the bed where I always keep it."

"You'd better let me have it. I'm going to have to get rid of it, like I did the other one."

"I can get rid of it myself."

"Except you won't. I want to make sure that gun disappears. Any connection to you means an instant connection to me and I'm tired of you trying to call all the shots."

"Well, I am your manager."

A chuckle erupted in Ravena's throat. "You couldn't manage a flea circus. Now that I have a new housekeeper and a part-time secretary starting next week I don't need you around to be a gopher. I think it's time we put a little space between us for a while. Now go get me that gun and don't forget the ammunition. I don't want a trace of evidence left around here. If those cops come by with a search warrant we'll be toast."

Ellerby got to his feet resignedly and left the room. Ravena continued to pace, muttering under her breath. Her life was not supposed to be like this. She wanted the fun and the freedom that money was supposed to bring. And here she was, stuck in the walls of this mansion like a prisoner. But not for much longer.

Ellerby returned and handed her a 9-mm Glock and two clips wrapped in an old T-shirt. He'd given up the gun fairly easily. Ravena suspected that he had another weapon stashed away somewhere.

"Do you want to take the boat out again?" he asked her.

"No. I'll see to this later. In the meantime I think you ought to move out for a while. Why don't you go up to your place in the boonies for a week or so and keep a low profile?"

"You need me here Ravena," insisted Ellerby.

"Quit whining. You make me wanna puke."

"We need to cover each other's tracks. It looks better, more professional, if I'm around during this crisis period in your life."

"Don't worry, honey, I can take care of myself. And I'm sure you've built up enough survival instincts over the years that you can take of yourself. And you being here all the time does *not* look good. I'm sure everyone thinks Ravena Ventura is screwing her manager. What is it, Ellie? You want to be in the gossip columns too?"

Ellerby gave in. He had to be careful how he handled his meal ticket. When they first met he knew she had a wild streak but she'd turned into a frustrating hard-nosed witch.

"All right," he sighed. "I'll pack a bag and move up to the Acreage for a couple of weeks. There are things I need to attend to up there, anyway."

"Good. Just try to stay under the radar. With everything that's going on I need to start acting more like a movie star and less like Howard Hughes."

"What do you mean?"

"I need to get out more. Show the world that Ravena Ventura is still alive. Shit, I may even announce I'm going to do a movie."

"Come on. You know that's not a good idea right now."

"You're one to talk about good ideas. From here on out I'll decide what's a good idea and what isn't."

She caressed the gun, then walked over to a bureau and pushed it into the back of a drawer. "Anyway, I'm only jerking your chain. Just get out of here."

Ellerby's lips tightened. He didn't like the direction things were going. But his hands were tied as long as she had control of the money. He had to find a way to get more of Ravena Ventura's loot into his life. Then she would be expendable.

"I'm going to pack," he said quietly. "You know where I'll be. Just don't leave that gun lying around."

Chapter 40

Michael was stunned by the news when he clocked in for his next shift at Ravena's estate. Ellerby had left unexpectedly on a business trip and Ravena had hired a new part-time secretary and a full-time Hispanic housekeeper/cook. The latter had moved into the Cruz's former digs, a modest apartment tucked away on the ground floor, well hidden from any residents or visitors who were higher on the social scale.

Ellerby's disappearance was good news. He'd been forever prowling around and now he would be one less person to worry about if Michael got a chance to return the framed photo to the closet upstairs. Right now it was wrapped in a towel and tucked in the trunk of his car. As for the martini glass, Michael figured it would be more noticeable if he returned it than if he didn't. No one seemed to have missed it from the patio table, so he'd left it at his apartment. Its next stop would probably be the trash.

Michael's day was getting off to a slow start. He was still in the security office, attacking the coffee maker for the second time, when a woman he'd never seen before stepped through the connecting door from the house.

She was about thirty, with lank brown hair tied back severely, horn-rimmed glasses that would mean business in any office, and a mustard colored suit that trussed up what might have been an interesting figure if given the chance. Michael decided she would probably merit a six or seven on the Bo Derek scale if she didn't wrap herself up like a mummy.

The glasses slipped down her nose as she looked over them, nodding at Michael like a chicken wolfing down corn.

"I'm looking for Mr. Hanlon," she said, "Michael Hanlon." She made it sound like a call to jury duty.

"That would be me," said Michael. He thought better of offering his hand when he realized she had no intention of making any physical contact with him.

"That's good," she said, as though she had discovered buried treasure. "I'm Wendy Spooner, Ms. Ventura's personal secretary. She asked me to find you and tell you to have the limo ready for eight o'clock Saturday night. She wants you to drive her to South Beach. I've booked a table for six for her at the Tsunami."

"Oh! Okay." Michael feigned disinterest. "Will her guests be traveling with her?"

Spooner stared at him. It was outrageous that some sniveling little security guard would dare to ask for personal information about someone above his station.
"She will be meeting her guests at South Beach," she said stiffly. "Some of Miss Usher's Hollywood clients. Once there, you are to remain with the car until she is ready to be transported home."

Michael's initial reaction was to tell her, expletive not deleted, what to do with her orders and to get that stick out of her ass. Luckily commonsense held sway.

So he was to drive Ravena to Miami, which meant he would have at least an hour alone in the limo with her. This might be his best chance, perhaps his last chance, to break down her barriers.

* * *

Michael was feeling smug and he couldn't hide it from his editor.

"Jack," he said, "I've got a story lead for you. A Ravena Ventura lead."

Jack Iverson looked up, scowled then broke out in a grin.

"Sorry, Jack. Don't get too excited. I haven't solved the murder. But if you want to let the dogs out I can tell you that Ravena will be making a rare public appearance Saturday night at Tsunami in South Beach. She's meeting some of that Usher woman's clients from California. Don't know who they are but this will be Ravena's first venture out into the limelight since her sister died."

"How do you know all this?"

"You're looking at her limo driver, remember? Her little soiree may not do much for our investigation but you might get a good photo spread out of it."

Iverson opened a desk drawer, pulled out a lead sheet and began to scribble on it.

"Great," he said. "Don't forget about your day job, Mr. Chauffeur. Maybe you could provide words to go with the photos."

"Love to, Jack. I'll do what I can but I'm already under orders to stay with the limo at all times."

"That guy Ellerby going with her?"

"Don't think so. And that's an interesting thing. Ellerby has dropped out of the picture. Umnexpected business trip, according to scuttlebutt. And Ravena is suddenly replacing the help she got rid of. A new live-in housekeeper started Monday and Ravena has a new part-time secretary. It's like she's suddenly coming out of her shell."

Jack stroked his stubble. "Hmm; that's interesting. I'll try to find out who Ravena is meeting at Tsunami. Stay on top of things."

* * *

Michael spent most of Saturday baby-sitting the limo. He took it to the car wash, filled up the gas tank and had the oil and tire pressures checked. He was becoming delusional about the vehicle. If only he owned it. Then he wouldn't have to be the chauffeur. He could hire his own driver and whisk Jane down to South Beach in style. They could shop, dine, and hit a couple of nightspots. Then maybe they could make out in the back of the limo on the way home. It had worked for Ravena and that Bobo guy.

Michael's walkie-talkie brought the curtain down on his daydream. Hendrix wanted to see him.

At the office, Michael found Hendrix looking like he had the world's woes on his shoulders.

"Ravena's new secretary tells me you're driving Ravena to South Beach tonight."

"Yeah. That's not a problem, is it?"

"I sure hope not. After what happened I'd like her to stay put. But suddenly Miss Go Nowhere decides to go nightclubbing. There's obviously someone out there who wants her dead. I suggested that if she was determined to go she should take four or five security guards with her. But she refused, insisted on you, and only you, accompanying her. I think she's got the hots for you."

"So what do we do?"

"We don't have much choice. She pays the freight around here. But you've got to be very careful. She could be in grave danger when she leaves the property."

"Maybe, but she was in grave danger on her own patio, too. And the fact that she's going to South Beach hasn't had any publicity. Anyone wanting to kill her would have to be watching her night and day. There's no evidence that they are."

"And no evidence that they aren't."

"Don't worry," Michael said quietly. "I'll take care of her."

Michael knew he'd be worrying enough for both of them. Driving Ravena to a nightclub had suddenly lost its appeal. What if the killer really was out there, watching and waiting?

Chapter 41

Ravena was ten minutes behind schedule, but it was worth the wait. She tripped into the garage on four-inch heels, her body contours exaggerated by a figure-hugging blue dress that left little to the imagination. A slit up-to-there revealed ample flashes of thigh and her breasts were straining to expose themselves to the world.

She was a little glassy-eyed but ready to fly.

"Hello, Michael," she said, rolling the words around her tongue. Michael thought he detected a wink. It promised to be an interesting evening.

"Evening, Miss Ravena," he replied stiffly as he opened the rear door for her. "I'm told we're going to South Beach?"

"Yes," she said as she slid into the back seat. "It's time I got out into the world. My press secretary, Usher, is meeting us at Tsunami with a few of her clients who just flew in from the west coast. Do you know it?"

"The west coast, ma'am, or Tsunami? Actually, neither, but— "

Ravena giggled. "Oh, you are funny. I meant Tsunami, of course. I don't think I've ever been there before. But perhaps I have. I can't remember where I've been and where I haven't. It's all a blur."

Yeah. Blurs are very convenient. "I've never been to the west coast," said Michael, "or to Tsunami, but I had the foresight to find out where it is. Tsunami, that is. Still not sure about the west coast."

She giggled again. Ravena had definitely geared herself up for a party.

They left Manalapan and headed to the Interstate, then turned south toward Miami. Once on the highway Michael observed through careful squinting in the rear-view mirror that Ravena had been able to unearth a supply of nose candy from the bowels of her purse and was busy giving herself a jolt.

She seemed to be in an unusually upbeat mood, so Michael decided to risk more conversation. "No Mr. Ellerby tonight?" he asked.

"No, he's working out of town. He has things to attend to." She leaned forward. He could feel her breath on the side of his neck. Her voice was suddenly reduced to a whisper. "Besides, who needs him? I've got you to take care of me. Right, Michael?"

Michael fought to concentrate on the road ahead. "Don't worry, Miss Ravena," he said. "You'll be safe with me."

He wasn't sure that was true but it seemed to satisfy her. She sighed and leaned back in her seat.

No Ellerby! He'd been around since Day One after Elizabeth's death, hanging around like a leech in a swamp, except when someone was taking potshots at Ravena. Now he had vanished again and Ravena Ventura seemed more relaxed without his ubiquitous presence.

No Ellerby! The thought was bouncing around in Michael's mind like roof tiles in a hurricane. What was he missing? What was his brain trying to tell him? Maybe Ellerby was the key to the story he was looking for.

Ravena and Ellerby had never seemed to be hitting it off. So why had she hired him in the first place? Where did he suddenly come from? Why had he moved into her home? And why was he conveniently out of sight when the mystery gunman showed up? The same old nagging questions. And now there were new ones. Like, where has he gone? And why has he gone there?

Michael fidgeted in his seat, figuring out his options. Ellerby knew something, something about Ravena, something about her sister's death. If only he could find Ellerby and spend five minutes alone with him.

A wisp of warm sweet breath at the back of his neck brought him back to reality.

"You're very quiet, Michael."

"I just thought you'd like your privacy, Miss Ravena."

"Well, you're not much company. Usually my fans like to talk my ear off. But perhaps you're not one of my fans?"

"Oh yes. I've seen just about all of your movies." *And hated most of them.* "Actually I was wondering how to broach the subject of asking for your autograph without sounding like an idiot."

He could sense Ravena smiling smugly behind him. "I'd be happy to give you an autograph," she said. "If you wanted one you'd only be an idiot for not asking."

Shit! He had no paper, no pen and no pencil. And heavy fast-moving traffic was demanding his attention.

"Sorry, Miss Ravena," he said, "but I don't have anything for you to sign. Do you by any chance?"

"I'm not in the habit of carrying pencil and paper around with me. I leave that to those morons in the media. But don't worry I'll give you an autograph."

Michael found himself wriggling in his seat, trying to find a position where he could observe his passenger in the back of the limo. But she was making no move to sign anything.

"I'll sign a napkin or something for you when we get to South Beach," she promised. "Is it for you, or your girlfriend, perhaps?"

There was that question again about his love life. "Oh, just for me. I haven't found a girlfriend yet."

Michael's enthusiasm for an autograph faded with the realization that any signature he might get would be useless to him. He didn't care about the autograph. He just wanted to watch Ravena write it. And now the whole opportunity had been blown out of the water because he hadn't been properly prepared.

"Maybe I can find something you can write on while I'm waiting with the car," he suggested in desperation.

"Don't worry," she said. "I won't forget about it, you know. Now tell me why you don't have a girlfriend. Are you gay?"

She was leaning close to him again. He could smell her perfume, feel the warmth of her body, and sense her eyes boring into the back of his head.

"No, I'm not gay. Just too busy, I guess," he said. "I haven't been down here long and I'm busy trying to make ends meet."

"Not a very good answer, Michael," said Ravena. "We'll have to see what we can do about that."

Suddenly satisfied with the conversation, she sank back into her seat and stared at the traffic through the heavily tinted windows with a faraway look in her eyes.

An uneasy silence settled inside the limo, broken only by bedlam when Michael was waved into a convenient parking spot at the entrance to the Tsunami nightclub in Miami Beach.

Passersby stopped to see what important figure might be emerging from the limo and the paparazzi, in a flurry of cameras and flying arms, materialized from nowhere and hurled themselves into position to cordon off the vehicle. They didn't know who was arriving. They didn't care. A limo was enough to start their motors.

Michael stepped out of the vehicle and two Tsunami bouncers were at his side before he could open the door for Ravena.

"Who we got here?" asked one.

"Ravena Ventura," said Michael. "The actress," he added unnecessarily. "She's alone."

"That's okay," said the minder. "We'll take care of her." He and his partner, equally equipped with Samson-like attributes on a two-fifty-pound frame, maneuvered Michael out of their way and opened the rear door of the limo. Then they cleared a path through the surging humanity for the movie queen's grand entrance. They'd done this before, many times. The arrival of Ravena Ventura was great publicity for their club, as long as they were able to keep the crowd under control.

Michael tried to help them carve a walkway for Ravena from the curb to the door. *How ironic. If the photographers only knew they were being impeded by a reporter.*

Ravena sprang to life. She seemed to relish the attention. She waved, she smiled, and she fluttered her eyelashes for a couple of dozen digital moments. When they reached the entrance she winked at Michael and disappeared inside.

"Park out back," growled one of the bouncers. "Down the street, first right, then right again."

Anxious to get out of the melee, he did what he was told. He wanted to be inside the club to find out who was attending Ravena's little soiree but he knew that would never happen. The chances of a chauffeur getting past the door were somewhat less than zero. He remembered what he'd been told about his job: You sit or stand around for hours, nothing to drink, nothing to eat, then you put up with crap from the wasted big shots you drive home.

The back of Tsunami was no seedy alleyway. The club backed onto a private well-lit parking lot guarded by a chain-link fence and a buff young surfer with a walkie-talkie. The attendant waved Michael through nonchalantly and he found a parking spot next to three or four other limos.

There were no signs of life. The other drivers were either playing Sudoku behind their tinted windows or had found somewhere better to be. That was fine with Michael. He had no desire to engage in shop talk with real chauffeurs.

He had his orders to stay with his vehicle and await further instructions. He had nothing to do to pass the time but think, a pursuit that often took him into unknown and dangerous territory.

He was learning a lot about Ravena. She was very chameleon-like. He'd seen the nasty, bitchy side of her. He'd also seen a soft, warm, vulnerable woman who appeared to want to open up to him. He tried to think of new ways to find out more about her. Maybe even to answer some of those questions constantly gnawing at his brain. Different scenarios began to spin around in Michael's mind like a kaleidoscope on steroids, faster and faster, then slower and slower. Finally he dozed off and lapsed yet again into the world of bad dreams.

A half-naked Ravena Ventura was trying to lure him into her bed when he was jerked awake by an urgent intermittent buzzing sound. It took him a few seconds to realize where it was coming from and what it was. The phone in the limo.

Gingerly he picked it up.

"This is Harriet Usher, Miss Ventura's press secretary," announced a grave voice. "Miss Ventura is leaving now and will need assistance. Are you parked in the rear lot?"

"Yes, ma'am."

"Good. Is there anyone else around? Any paparazzi?"

Michael surveyed the parking lot. "No, the place is deserted. I guess all the photographers are out front."

"Let's hope it stays that way. I'll bring Miss Ventura out the back door. Please meet us there."

Usher hung up without waiting for a response. Michael frowned. She had made it sound as though Ravena was handicapped and in a wheelchair. He circled the parking lot and pulled up outside a door marked "No admittance. Exit only."

He soon discovered that his mental image of a handicapped Ravena wasn't far from the truth. She wasn't in a wheelchair, but one would have helped. Instead she was clinging grimly to Harriet Usher, who had one arm behind her in a losing attempt to prevent

Ravena's knees from buckling. Whatever it was movie stars did in nightclubs, Ravena Ventura had done it to excess.

"Help me get her in the car," snapped Usher. "Quickly, before any of those assholes from the press show up."

Michael fought off an urge to tell her she was already talking to an asshole from the press and helped steer Ravena into the limo. The two of them bundled her into the back, where she collapsed in an untidy heap.

"Take her straight home," said Usher. "I have to get back inside. I have other clients who need me."

Michael nodded sympathetically. It must have been quite a party.

He glanced into the back seat as he slid behind the wheel. "Are you okay, Miss Ravena?" he asked, but there was no response.

He crossed the causeway into Miami and headed north up Interstate 95 in a silence punctuated only by the sound effects of Ravena's uneasy sleep. She was twisting and turning in her seat and snoring spasmodically.

It was two in the morning and the highway was unnaturally empty when he crossed the Palm Beach County line.

With no vehicles in sight, Michael sat in the center lane and maintained a steady sixty-five. Then a set of headlights suddenly brushed his rear-view mirror. Someone was coming up fast behind him, swinging into the left-hand lane. Michael moved over to the right lane and glanced over to see a large SUV draw alongside him.

Suddenly Michael heard a pop and an explosion as glass shattered in the back of the limo. Ravena woke with a start.

"What the hell . . . ?" she yelled, instantly a lot more sober.

Two more pops and then a loud bang. Michael's heart was in his mouth. The gunman was back—and using them for target practice. Suddenly he felt a tremor in the steering wheel and the limo began to slide out of control. The car's rear window was gone and now the shooter had hit a tire.

"Stay down, Miss Ravena," he yelled as he struggled to regain control of the car. "Some idiot is shooting at us."

He heard moaning from the back seat as he fought to drive into the skid. The car was bumping badly at the rear, zig-zagging across the freeway. Slowing down now, Michael managed to steer toward the shoulder and sighed with relief as he brought the limo to a halt.

He looked around gingerly but the SUV had gone. He was again alone on the road. Then he remembered what Hendrix had told him: Check to see if you're being followed. Obviously someone had been tracking him, but he'd been too preoccupied to notice.

Michael leaned over and looked into the back seat. "Miss Ravena, are you all right?"

"Yes, I think so; sitting in a sea of glass, but otherwise okay. I'm getting tired of this. What the fucking hell is going on?"

"Only wish I knew. Just stay where you are. Don't move."

Michael got out, opened the rear door and carefully helped Ravena out of the vehicle. He looked at what remained of the left rear tire. It was going to be a long night.

Chapter 42

Once again, at Ravena's insistence Michael did not call the police. She seemed more afraid of the publicity it would generate than the thought that a killer was out there gunning for her. Someone wanted her dead, but she appeared to be more concerned about her image than her safety.

arned that Hendrix had quietly arranged for a security car to follow them at a discreet distance. A traffic tie-up on the causeway had left them miles behind but they would be there shortly.

Michael waited in trepidation. He hoped the killer wouldn't decide to come back for another shot. Dodging bullets on I-95 was way above a reporter's pay grade, even at The Courier's rates. Ravena sat with him in the front of the limo, tight-lipped and uncommunicative. She looked worried, more than a little scared, and she was now more hung over than pie-eyed.

After bundling her safely into the backup vehicle, Michael changed the tire himself and drove slowly back to Manalapan. His head was thumping, his hands were dirty and he was desperate for sleep. He knew he'd have to discuss the incident with Hendrix, and he was duty bound to report it to Jack, of course. But they would both have to wait until morning.

* * *

It was almost noon when Michael crawled out of bed. He still felt like crap but he had work to do.

He called Hendrix, who told Michael he wanted a detailed written report, and he wanted it fast. He didn't ask about Michael's welfare. Not that Michael cared. His priority was to touch base with Jack and Jane.

Unfortunately both seemed to be out of the loop. Neither of them was answering the phone. They were probably out to Sunday brunch, or at the beach, hopefully not together. The beach sounded inviting, but no sea breeze was going to get Ravena Ventura out of Michael's head.

He was up to his armpits in the middle of a big story and was slowly but surely being suffocated by it. He decided to see if Detective Christopher pulled a shift on Sundays.

Michael's call did nothing to make Christopher happier about pulling a Sunday shift.

"I told everyone that the news media would be informed when we had something," he said. "Right now, we've nothing new to report."

"Ravena Ventura's name didn't show up anywhere as one of Dr. Wetherby's patients?"

"I already told you that. No. You keep asking the same questions in the hopes that the answers are going to change. But they aren't."

"Okay. I'm sorry. But I have another question. Did you by any chance find a name like Ellerby on the doctor's patient list?"

"I can't give out information like that," snapped Christopher. "I'm not about to divulge a whole list of patient names so the press can harass them at will."

"I understand that. But if there's a David Ellerby on that list it will mean something. Actually the name may not be Ellerby. It could be David Ellerman. Or David Elfman, Desmond Emerson or even Derek Edmunds. They're all the same guy."

Christopher's voice tightened. "What do you know about him?"

Michael's heart missed a beat. "Do you mean one of those names is on the list?"

"Just a minute."

It was a long minute, but Michael could hear papers rustling.

Finally Christopher resurfaced. "There's an Emerson here," he announced. "What about him? We're routinely checking on all the doctor's patients, but we haven't been able to locate them all yet."

"Like I told you, Ellerby, Elfman, Ellerman and Emerson are all the same person. I've no idea which is his real name."

"Do you know this guy?"

"Well, sort of."

"Do you know where he is?"

"No."

"How did you come to know him?"

Michael wasn't comfortable playing games with the police. "His name first came up when we were investigating the death of Ravena Ventura's sister."

He didn't want to say more, but he remembered Jack's penchant for headlines. And he realized that he had the makings of a good one.

"You'll find that he's connected to Ravena under the name Ellerby. He's her manager. Maybe she knows where he is."

"Okay," grunted Christopher. "We'll check it out."

Michael put down the phone and smiled to himself. Yes, RAVENA QUESTIONED IN DENTIST'S MURDER would be an intriguing headline. It paled a little alongside GUNMAN ATTACKS RAVENA AGAIN but, as Jack had told him, it was good to have headlines in the bank.

Now he was ready for the beach. Check out the bikinis, treat himself to dinner overlooking the ocean. Life was looking up.

* * *

The sun was starting to sink when Michael returned to his apartment and called Jack, who, true to form, wasted no time in changing his reporter's mood.

"Glad you called," he said. "I was about to phone you. You'd better come into the office early tomorrow. JC wants a meeting on Ravena Ventura and he wants you at it."

That was scary news. Michael had yet to meet the mysterious God-like editor and CEO of The Courier, who was rarely seen but was always present, forever poking invisible fingers into every corner of the organization.

"Sure," said Michael, trying to sound as though he didn't care, then told him about the incident on the freeway.

"Good God," said Jack. "What the fuck? Whoever wants Ravena dead is getting bolder. Jeez Louise! Are you sure it wasn't just some crazy road-rager you'd cut off?"

Michael rolled his eyes. "Yes, Jack, I'm sure. It wasn't kids with a BB gun either. And I wasn't hurt, thanks for asking."

"Sorry. We'll talk about it tomorrow. If we can figure out *why* someone wants Ravena dead that might lead us to *who*. See ya at eight-thirty."

There was a click and Jack was gone. He hadn't waited to hear any of the details. He didn't even wait for Michael's headlines. Oh well, they would save. Michael would see what the Great Man himself thought about it all in the morning.

Chapter 43

The morning came too soon. Michael was terrified of his first face-to-face meeting with JC, even though he told himself it was an irrational feeling. After all, what could the man do to him? Fire him? Humiliate him in front of his supervisors? He wasn't likely to parade him naked through the newsroom and push toothpicks down his fingernails. And surely he wouldn't intimidate him any more than he intimidated everyone else in his employ. So what was there to worry about?

Despite all this rational thinking, his armpits were soaked and he felt himself visibly trembling when the call came to assemble in JC's office.

"Jack," he whispered as they marched down the hall. "What do I call him? JC, or what?"

"Call him Sir," Jack huffed. "Or Mr. Calloway. Definitely not JC. And not Jason. No one is allowed to use his first name."

Michael tiptoed into Calloway's office behind Peterson, Iverson and Jane as the final piece in Team Ravena.

Unlike the cluttered newsroom, Calloway's lair was spacious and well-appointed, with plush pale green carpeting, paneled walls of knotty pine and windows from floor to ceiling. From his ornate raised desk JC had a picture postcard view of palm trees swaying amid flowering hibiscus and bougainvillea.

A sofa lined one wall facing the desk, but the editors ignored it, pulled up leather chairs and positioned them in a semi-circle around JC. Michael took their lead and dragged one to the end of the row.

Calloway got to his feet and stretched out his hand to Michael. He was nothing like Michael had imagined. JC towered over everyone in the room at six-foot-three but he was too overweight for his height to be imposing. He wore a pale blue button-down shirt open at the neck and gray slacks, both of which bore signs of having been laundered too many times. No power suits here. And the fearful JC was disarmingly charming.

"Hello, Michael," he said. "Welcome to The Courier."

Michael decided not to remind him that he'd been at The Courier for almost a month. He smiled, mumbled "pleased to meet you, sir" and was greeted with a shark-like grin devoid of human emotion.

"I've heard a lot about you, Michael," said Calloway as he flopped back down behind his desk. "We've had good stories on the Ravena case, but we need to get better focused. That's why we're here today. We don't want to let the story disappear from the public psyche and there are still a lot of unanswered questions out there that the police seem to be ignoring. We've got to get a new approach, investigate new leads. I'm looking for ideas."

He stared with steel-gray eyes at his semicircle of editorial minions, and started washing his hands in anticipation of a positive response. His audience looked
uncomfortable. Each one of them was hoping that one of their colleagues would say something sensible to break the ice.

Michael realized that JC hadn't been told about the latest attack on Ravena's life. Should he bring it up, or would protocol dictate that he not steal his editor's thunder? But Jack was showing no signs of saying anything.

Peterson finally broke the awkward silence. "We're covering all the bases, Mr. Calloway. Jane is on the cops' case every day but I fear they've given up on solving the crime. They're tending to believe Ravena's theory that the killer was some small-time drug dealer who may never be found. Meanwhile, Michael is still operating undercover at Ravena's estate."

Calloway turned to face Michael at the end of the row of prisoners.

"Yes," he said. "I wanted to talk about that." The bonhomie had evaporated. A glassy-eyed stare told Michael that his welcome to the paper was already a microscopic footnote in history. Michael had to defend himself. And he realized he was alone. His colleagues weren't prepared to bat for him until his mettle had been tested. This could be a Courier hazing ceremony.

"Well sir," Michael stammered, "I've been there almost four weeks now but it's difficult to get close to anyone. Actually there is hardly anyone to get close to except Ravena herself, and she and the interior of the house are off limits."

Calloway raised his eyebrows. "So this is a waste of time?" he snapped.

"No, sir. I chauffeured Ravena to a nightclub in South Beach last night and we were attacked by a gunman again on the way home. No one was hurt, luckily, but her limo was damaged. Someone is definitely trying to kill her. This was their third attempt."

Calloway stared at Michael with hypnotic eyes.

A deathly silence was finally broken when Jack Iverson found an ounce of courage and cleared his throat.

"We haven't had time to analyze this latest development," he said, "but Michael has come up with good headline material since he's been onsite and he's had a couple of one-on-ones with Ravena when he's been acting as her chauffeur."

"And a couple of brushes with death," said Calloway dryly. "I don't want my reporters in physical danger." He glared at Iverson and Peterson. Putting a Courier reporter in harm's way was not in the cards.

Michael broke in quickly. "I guess I was in the right place at the wrong time, but the shooter wasn't aiming at me. And I may be on to something. I've overheard a few strange and strained conversations between Ravena and her manager, Ellerby. He's been staying at the estate, but he's suddenly left. Ravena says he's on a business trip. But he's been noticeably absent during all three attacks on Ravena's life and they've never gotten along as far as I can tell. It's a mystery how he showed up in her life in the first place but he and Ravena were with Elizabeth Thomas on the night she died. I've now learned that Ellerby was a patient of that Dr.

Wetherby who was found murdered in Delray. I'm pretty sure Wetherby was the dentist Ravena saw when I drove her down there. I'd like to try to find Ellerby and approach the story from his angle."

Jaws dropped along the line of embattled journalists.

"The police investigating the dentist's murder haven't been able to find Ellerby yet," Michael continued, "but I told them Ravena knows him. I'm sure they'll be questioning her as to his whereabouts and that in itself could give us a good story."

He paused then threw out his headline, RAVENA QUESTIONED IN DENTIST'S DEATH. . . STAR LINKED TO SECOND MURDER.

It was met with stony silence then Peterson and Iverson started scribbling crazily on their yellow legal pads.

"We could do this story before we, or the cops, even find Ellerby," said Michael.

More silence. Then Calloway nodded. "Okay," he said slowly, then turned to his two senior editors. "Go for it."

There was more fervent scribbling, accompanied by frenetic nodding of heads.

"Now," said Calloway, "There's one other point I want to touch on." He turned back to Michael and the shark-like grin reappeared.

"I'm told you've been boning up on identical twins and have an interesting theory on Ravena and her sister. Why don't you fill us in?"

"When the story first broke I was fascinated with them being identical twins," Michael explained, "so I found a book on the subject. I learned a lot about twins. For example, identical twins aren't identical, and the scientific community doesn't even use that expression for them. Yes, they do look alike and they share the same DNA, but there are subtle differences."

"So?" Calloway's right foot began to tap in agitation.

"So I've been looking for differences between the Ravena every moviegoer knows and the Ravena who's currently living at her mansion."

"And?"

"And I'm afraid I haven't come up with anything yet. Twins' teeth are different but I have no way of comparing Ravena's with her sister's. Fingerprints are different and I thought I was on to something there, but that's tricky because the differences in twins' fingerprints can be subtle. Now I'm in the middle of comparing photographs."

"Yes?"

"Nothing to date. It's possible one of the twins was right-handed and the other left. I haven't nailed that down yet, but I've been watching Ravena's movies and every time I see her in real life I sense that there's something different about her. It's nothing I can put my finger on, but — "

"All right, all right." Calloway cut him off. "If you want to keep pursuing this, that's up to you. But in the meantime we have a paper to get out. And we have a lot of ground to cover. Let's work on Ravena's link to this dentist before events overtake us. And we need to focus on the third attack on Ravena and track down this Ellerby guy."

He stood, indicating the meeting was over, and the quartet headed hurriedly for the door. As they filed out Calloway boomed, "David, Jack, could you hang on a minute?"

They shuffled back in. After Jane and Michael closed the door behind them, Calloway turned to his editors.

"Just one thing," he said. "This Michael Hanlon seems a go-to guy. But is he playing with a full deck?"

Chapter 44

Once freed from JC's office, a spring materialized in Michael's step as he and Jane walked back to the newsroom. It was like miraculously surviving a train wreck.

"That wasn't too bad," he said.

Jane gave him an impish grin. "Don't get too excited. The three of them are still in there, probably discussing your future." Then she laughed and grabbed his arm reassuringly. "Don't worry, you're new enough around here to warrant a honeymoon period. JC will be quizzing Jack and Peterson about you. You know, your background, your personality, your work ethic."

"He didn't know any of that when he hired me?"

"No. Remember that he didn't hire you. Jack did. JC never hires anyone as lowly as a reporter. That way, if they don't work out he can never be blamed for having bad judgment. He doesn't hire, he just fires. And he usually gets someone to do that for him too."

Michael nodded glumly as they reached their desks. "Not much wiggle room for making mistakes around here, is there?" he said then turned as he heard his name called.

It was Jack, hurrying toward his desk, a pencil in his ear, a legal pad waving wildly in his hand and a worried look on his face.

"I need to talk to you," he said. "The meeting went okay, but now JC is concerned about your safety. Every time Ravena has been shot at you've been in the line of fire. He insists on pulling you off the security guard gig. He begrudgingly agreed to keep you available for chauffeuring work, though, since it gets you up-close and personal with Ravena. Just stay away from trigger-happy people."

"Wish I could. When does this take effect?"

"With JC, everything takes effect immediately. I'll talk to Blackwell. He can tell Ravena that you've found another position but might still be available if she needed a part-time driver."

"If you say so," said Michael. "But I need another day. Now I have an excuse to talk face-to-face with Ravena to tell her that I'm leaving. It may be profitable."

"In that case go back tomorrow. We can tell JC you have to tie up loose ends. If you do see Ravena just tell her you've found another job, which won't be a lie anyway. Hey, if she likes you maybe she'll offer you more money than you're getting at The Courier."

"Very funny, Jack. That's not likely. And I wouldn't want it, anyway. I'd miss you too much." *But not half as much as I'd miss Jane.*

Iverson guffawed and threw his legal pad down on his desk. "Make yourself useful then," he said. "Give me your copy on Ravena and the dentist and the latest shooting. Then you can help Jane track down Ellerby."

* * *

Michael and Jane manned phones and the Internet in a vain attempt to find Ellerby's whereabouts. All the possible contact numbers on their list had been disconnected or elicited no response, so they turned to the paper's overburdened Research Department in an attempt to uncover new leads.

For Michael there was nothing but frustration at every turn. And the subject of the twins was needling him. Jane seemed to be humoring him and Jack and JC thought he was crazy. He needed to talk to someone.

He decided to test the waters with Detective Henderson. As Peterson had said, the sheriff's detectives seemed to be losing interest in the case. Maybe Henderson would be happy to have a new avenue to explore.

No such luck. As usual, Henderson didn't sound pleased to hear Michael's voice.

"Oh it's you, hotshot," he said. "I was hoping you'd dropped out of my life. Solved the Thomas case for us yet?"

"Not quite. I just have a dumb question for you," he said. "Have you wondered at all whether Elizabeth Thomas could have killed her sister and taken her place?"

He was met with a customary silence from the other end of the phone, then a sudden gale of uproarious laughter.

"Been reading The National Courier again? Seriously, I hope you aren't planning to run a story like that!"

"Not yet, but I'm working on it. I just need a little evidence."

"I'd suggest you get positive proof before you put that in your paper. Anyway, how would you go about telling identical twins apart?"

"I think you know the answer to that question. And it would be easier for you than for me. I'm sure you're aware that twins' fingerprints and teeth are different. And sometimes one twin can be right-handed and the other left. I'm pretty sure from photographs that the real Ravena is left-handed."

There was more silence from the detective's end of the line, but no more laughter.

"Look, kid," he said at last. "There have been seventy-one murders in our jurisdiction so far this year, and twenty-eight of them are still unsolved. We don't sit on our asses here making up stories. We leave that to folks like you. Thanks for sharing your thoughts with me, but I've got work to do. Call me back when you've cracked the case."

Henderson hung up, leaving Michael holding the phone impotently. He should have known the detective would blow him off. What a waste of time that was. He'd hoped to at least plant a seed but Henderson's mind appeared to be infertile. He turned to Jane.

"You know," he said, "neither Ravena's movies or still photos tell us anything definitive, but there must be someone in L.A. who can confirm if Ravena Ventura is, or was, left-handed. Her ex-husband, or that attorney boyfriend."

"You're right, but are you ready to open that can of worms? You don't even know whether Elizabeth Thomas was left or right-handed. Ravena's associates in California aren't likely to answer any of our questions and they'll probably be on the phone to the cops complaining that The Courier is harassing them. Then all hell will break loose."

"Yeah, I guess you're right."

Once again the wind had been taken out of his sails. He had only one card left to play on the subject of cross-over twins. He had to talk to Ravena face-to-face.

* * *

Hendrix corralled Michael as soon as he arrived at the estate the next morning. "I hear you're leaving us in the lurch," he said. "Promotion?"

"Not exactly, just got another job."

"Well, good luck. Hope it pays better than this one. Maybe I'll see you around. Blackwell told me to make sure I had your cell number. He told me you might still be available to drive Ravena."

Michael gave him the number then went out onto the patio, figuring he was likely to stumble across Ravena by the pool. But she was a no-show. He dawdled around the back of the house as long as he could but she never emerged.

The morning slowly evaporated and after lunch Michael decided to take the bull by the horns and break the house rules.

He went into the building through the lanai, and wandered through the hallway until he reached the staircase. That reminded him that he still had the photo frame in the trunk of his car. Too bad. It would have to stay there. He wasn't going to risk trying to return it now. Chances were its disappearance would never be noticed anyway.

The huge house was eerily silent and he wondered what it would feel like to be rattling around alone all day in such a sterile environment.

Ravena had to be around somewhere. He called her name, but not too loudly, and there was no response. He wasn't sure where to go. There was a new housekeeper now, probably tucked away in the kitchens somewhere preparing the evening meal. She might know where he could find Ravena but he wasn't sure where to find the kitchens and he didn't want to be caught wandering all over the place.

He began to retrace his steps toward the back of the house when he heard Ravena's voice. She was in her office, yelling at someone in a torrent of foul language. He paused by the door and tried to pick up the conversation but all he could make out were the four-letter words. He couldn't hear any other voices. Suddenly she screamed "Fuck you!" followed by a crash. Then silence.

Had the argument turned physical? Was she in trouble? Michael gingerly rapped on the office door. "Miss Ravena," he called, "Miss Ravena, are you all right?"

The door was flung open and she stood before him. Her mouth was curled up in anger and flecks of spittle edged the corners. Her blue eyes were wide and ice-cold.

She stood for a second staring at Michael then suddenly dissolved into the movie queen he had last seen on the drive to South Beach.

"Oh, it's you, Michael," she said simply.

"Sorry, Miss Ravena, but I was looking for you and I heard um . . . noises. Are you okay?"

"Yes, of course. I was just on the phone giving a moron a piece of my mind." She laughed nervously. "It was nothing. I didn't think anyone would be able to hear me."

"Well, I was walking by," Michael explained quickly. "I was trying to find you. I just wanted to let you know that I wasn't going to be here anymore and—"

"I heard. Hendrix told me."

"I have a new job, but I could make myself available to chauffeur you any time you needed it. Mr. Blackwell said it would be okay if it was okay with you. And I, uh, would enjoy doing that . . . if you'd like me to, of course."

Michael felt very servile. If he'd had a cap he would have been wringing it in his hands by now.

Ravena smiled at his obvious discomfort. "Of course, Michael," she said. "I'm very grateful for the way you took care of me last night. Hendrix told me to ask for you if I ever needed you."

"Thank you, ma'am." Then, "There's one little thing, one favor I would like to ask of you, Miss Ravena."

She raised an eyebrow, but said nothing.

"When we were going to South Beach you promised me an autograph," he said. "I wondered if you could sign this for me."

He pulled out a photo of her, a two-year old studio shot copied from Courier files.

"Of course," she said, took it from him and stepped back into the office.

Michael paused at the door then followed her in at a discreet distance. He couldn't afford to let her out of his sight. He watched as she went to her desk, fumbled around for a pen and scribbled on the picture.

Then she turned, smiled and handed it back to him with a flourish. "There you go, Michael," she said. "Sorry I forgot. I always try to do right by my fans."

Michael mumbled his thanks, stopped himself in the middle of touching his forelock, backed out of the room and headed down the hallway to the patio.

Once outside he examined the picture to see what she had written.

"Best wishes to Michael, my favorite driver. Love, Ravena Ventura"

How sweet, thought Michael. How really sweet. Sweet because Ravena, supposedly a lefty, had written it with her right hand.

Chapter 45

Ravena was livid, and getting edgier by the minute. She paced back and forth in her study. She eyed the phone on the desk, picked it up, put it back down, and picked it up again. She cradled it to her bosom like a baby then stared blankly at it.

Finally she carefully put it back on the hook, opened a desk drawer and pulled out a cell phone.

She was very much alone, and felt it, but she glanced nervously around the room. This was supposed to be a refuge, warm wooden walls and shelf after shelf of books like silent soldiers on guard, except it wasn't working. The friendly confines were closing in on her. All thanks to that damned Ellerby. What an irresponsible, self-important jackass. He was loathsome. Ironically he was both her lifeline and her one-way ticket to perdition.

She was starting to shake visibly. She took a deep and determined breath, tightened her grasp on the phone and punched in a number.

It rang. And rang. She was about to hurl the phone at the wall when a familiar voice answered.

"Ellerby?" she asked cautiously, "Is that you?"

"Of course. No one but you knows this number, sweetheart."

Inexplicably, hearing his voice gave her confidence.

"Don't be too sure of that," she snapped. "Guess who just called me. The cops."

"What did they want?" Ellerby didn't sound too alarmed. Not alarmed enough. "I thought Detective Henderson had given up on the case," he said. "I read in yesterday's *Post* that he'd moved on to an investigation into some real-estate broker's murder in West Palm."

Ravena flicked her hair out of her eyes.

"I don't know anything about that nor do I care. It wasn't Henderson who phoned me. I got a call from a Detective Christopher, Delray Beach Police Department.
Apparently they've connected you to Dr. Drew somehow and—"

"How did they do that?"

"How the fuck would I know? I'm not a cop."

"For Christ's sake calm down. Tell me exactly what he said."

"He said they were trying to contact everyone who knew Dr.Wetherby, including his patients, and the name Desmond Emerson came up. Somehow they had gotten the idea that I knew Desmond Emerson."

"But you don't, do you?"

"Oh, yes I do. And I know it's you. This is the computer age, Ellie. You can't hide much from anybody anymore. It didn't take me long to find out that Emerson and you are one and the same person. I'm not a stupid little slut like those whores you deal with in your movies."

"All right, all right already. So what did you tell this detective?"

"Obviously I told him that I'd never heard of any Desmond Emerson."

"Clever girl. Then you're off the hook."

"Like hell, Ellie. I told you these cops aren't dumb. Somehow they know that Desmond Emerson is one of your fancy pseudonyms. Why else would they call me? So then Christopher mentioned the name David Ellerby and if I knew him. What was I supposed to say to that? Then he asked me if you were around, that he'd like to talk with you. Just routine, he said. Routine my ass. They always say that."

"Then what? For God's sake, baby, tell me everything that was said."

Ravena jerked the phone from her ear.

"Don't call me 'baby.' I'm not your baby. I told him you weren't here, that you'd gone out of town on business, that I didn't know where you were or when you'd be back. Then he asked if I had a phone number for you. I gave him the number of that cell you said you lost. Then he asked again where you might be, like what city you'd gone to on business. Told him again I didn't know, that you had other business dealings to take care of besides my career. Ain't that the truth! But he didn't like that answer much so then he asked me if you had an address in Palm Beach County. I told him I thought you still had an office somewhere but you'd been staying here since my sister died."

"That all sounds good."

"Then I asked him why he wanted to speak with you. He reassured me that it was just standard procedure that they were checking on Dr. Wetherby's patient list and wanted to talk with everyone on it. I hope I'm not on that list in some form or another."

"No, of course not. I told Dr. Drew yours was a one-shot cash deal with no connections back to you. That's why I arranged for you to see him in the first place. Dr. Drew and I had done business together for years. He understood."

"Yeah, he sure did. He understood enough to know that he could put the squeeze on both of us."

"Yes, well, I took care of that problem, didn't I? At your suggestion."

"We've already been through this. I didn't tell you to fucking shoot him. I hope neither he nor you left anything lying around at his place that could connect him to me."

"Of course not," scoffed Ellerby. "We have nothing to worry about. I'm just one of his occasional patients. He did a root canal once and cleaned my teeth twice."

"Don't get too overconfident. The cops will find you. Where the hell are you right now, anyway?"

"Up in the Acreage."

"Oh yeah. The Palace of Porn."

Ellerby sniffed. "I like to think of my movies as art films. You know they're a legitimate venture. Anyway, you know I'm looking to get into the mainstream movie business."

"Fat chance."

"There is if you'd stop being an asshole about it. You remember what we talked about. Eventually the cops will move on to other things and no one will remember your sister. Or if they do it will only be with sadness and sympathy for you."

"I'm not going to make any movies with you, Ellie. So forget it."

Ellerby's voice tightened. "I told you before, we are a team, whether you like it or not. We've got an unbreakable bond. At some point it will be time for you to start looking at those scripts that agent keeps trying to push onto you. Pick one, insist on having me on board in some capacity, and we'll take it from there."

"Bullshit. It's not going to happen. No studio would ever go for it. And neither would I. And I'm not going to make any indie movies. Besides, I don't need your help to make a movie."

'Yes you do. And you need to launch your own production company."

"With you at the helm? Don't make me laugh. I can see the headlines now: 'Ravena Teams Up With Porn King.'"

"It won't be like that. David Ellerby is a legitimate name with no ties to anything you couldn't be proud of."

Ravena laughed. "Is that why David Ellerby is currently hanging out at David Elfman's porn studio? You know it's only a matter of time before the cops put it all together and your mug materializes in their databases."

"What the hell? I've shit-canned the porno business anyway. I told all my girls I've closed shop and I've even gotten rid of my minders."

Ravena's eyes widened. "You're up there alone?"

"Yeah. They weren't doing anything anyway, while I was in Manalapan with you. And now we can take care of each other. As soon as the cops lose interest in me I'm coming back down there, we'll pick a script and go back to L.A. together."

"In your dreams, Ellie-boy! If you're so sure of yourself with the police why are you hiding away in the boondocks?"

"It was your idea, remember? You wanted some breathing room and I have eight months left on the rent here. It's private, quiet and secure up here. No one bothers anybody. God knows what my neighbors are up to. Homes are probably full of meth labs, or worse."

"Don't be ridiculous. Anyway, the cops probably already have the address of your little hideaway. Since they've connected Emerson to Ellerby I'm sure it won't be long before the name David Elfman of Elfman Productions pops up on their computer screens. Plus you already have a record for dealing. That will connect you to Dr. Drew."

"I keep telling you I'm not worried. Did you get rid of the gun?"

Ravena paused. "Not yet," she said slowly, "but I have plans for it." She smiled. "That's something you won't have to worry about."

"Look, Ravena. I take care of you and you take care of me. That's the deal, remember? That way neither of us will have to worry about anything. Just don't do or say anything stupid. And don't call me. I'll call you on the cell."

Ravena clicked off, threw the phone back in the desk drawer, then thought better of it. Her new secretary, that snotty Wendy Spooner who Ellerby had found, would be arriving soon to set up shop at her desk. What the hell for she didn't know. Ellerby had probably hired the bitch to spy on her while he wasn't around.

She took the phone with her and went upstairs to her bedroom. She fumbled in a jewelry case, pulled out a couple of keys and went into the dressing room. There she pushed a couple of floor-sweeper gowns aside and pressed a button set in the paneled wall. One small panel slid open to reveal a safe. She fiddled with one key, then the other and the door swung open to reveal Ellerby's Glock, now carefully swaddled in cloth like a newborn baby. She placed the cell phone beside it and re-locked the safe.

She'd had enough of Ellerby, and his gun. And she had plans for both of them.

Chapter 46

Michael was spent. His mind was numb, his eyelids were heavy, every part of his body was crying out for relief. Hours of pent-up energy had been expended on futility. He and Jane had spent the day combing the county, trying to track down Ellerby under any of his various names. And they'd drawn nothing but blanks.

The Courier's Research Department had armed them with detailed contact lists on him, including phone numbers and addresses that went with his string of aliases.

All were in Palm Beach County—and all were dead ends. All the phone numbers had been disconnected, which probably meant that Ellerby was no longer at any of the addresses on their list. But the addresses represented the only trail they had. Michael's only hope was that the neighbors would cough up some useful information.

He and Jane split the county in half. Jane took the south, Michael the north. It was after six o'clock by the time he'd fought rush-hour traffic back from the county line to the Beachcomber in Delray, where he'd agreed to meet Jane at the end of the day.

She was perched at the bar when he walked in, surrounded by a gaggle of Courier newsroom girls. She slid off her stool when he walked in, picked up her wineglass and nodded to an empty booth.

"How did you make out?" she asked.

"I didn't. Zilch."

"Me neither," she said, kicking off her shoes. "So we know where he's been, but we have no idea where he is. Of course he may have left town, but I'll bet he still has a base of operations here somewhere."

"Of all the places I went to he'd been a renter at all but one. That was a small condo in North Palm Beach that he'd sold eighteen months ago. The new owner didn't have a clue about him, and didn't want to know."

"I found the same thing. A couple of apartments where he hadn't lived in some time and a few small homes that he'd rented. I found a few neighbors who remembered him by one name or another, but no leads. He was pretty transient and he kept a low profile. I didn't find anyone who really knew him, or would admit to it."

Michael waved a waitress over and ordered a beer. "I'm sure Ravena knows where he is," he said.

"But there's no way she'd tell us, even if we got the opportunity to ask her."

"Unless I got her good and drunk and took advantage of her."

"In your dreams, loverboy."

Michael smiled. "Yeah. Besides, she's too old for me. And I don't like her personality. I don't think we'd be very compatible."

Jane shrugged. "You could be compatible with her money."

"Probably wouldn't be worth the hassle. And I—that's it! The money! The old expression, 'follow the money.' That's the avenue that could lead us to Ellerby."

"How? It's Ravena who has the money, remember?"

Yes, but Ellerby follows money whenever he stumbles across it. We know from his background and phony names that he's the type who's always looking for a fast buck. He materialized out of nowhere around the time Ravena's sister was murdered. Somehow he managed to sink his hooks into her. We need to follow his tracks back from her. Think. What money-making enterprises was he in before Ravena came into his sights? We know he pushed drugs and as Elfman he was connected to the porn business. Maybe someone in the skin trade knows him, and where to find him."

Jane stiffened. "Well I don't know anyone in that business. Nor do I want to. And I'm not volunteering to scour all the adult bookstores and sex shops in the county on a wild goose chase."

"Don't worry, I'll do it."

Jane finished off her wine, and twirled the empty glass in her fingers. "Don't let me twist your arm." "Look, we know he made X-rated movies, with real porn stars. It might be a questionable business but it's a real business."

"Yes, but the only address we have for Elfman Productions is a defunct post office box. That's not going to help us."

"But he obviously had a place somewhere where he shot those films. Maybe he rented a warehouse or something under some name we haven't come across. His stuff wasn't just amateurish motel-room crap featuring two-bit hookers."

"Oh? And how do you know that?"

"The porn industry takes itself seriously, and Elfman Productions is a serious player in it. He won two AVN awards."

"AVN? What's that?"

"Stands for Adult Video News. It's the trade magazine of the porn industry. They offer movie awards every year, like the Oscars."

"How do you know all this? Is this your secret hobby?"

"Hardly. The magic of the Internet will reveal all to anyone who's interested. It took me less than five minutes to find out that Elfman is no slouch in the skin biz. He takes pride in his work, and his girls would be good-looking professionals. I bet some of them would know where he is."

"Ah, yes. And if we only knew where they were."

"Porn stars don't stay out of the limelight anymore. In fact, driving down here tonight I passed one of those 'gentlemen's clubs' advertising a couple of triple-X rated movie stars as the premiere attraction."

"You mean the Keyhole Club in Boynton?"

"See, you know more about that business than you care to admit. Anyway, I could stop by that place tonight and see if anyone there knows Elfman. It's certainly better than wasting gas and coming up empty. Wanna tag along?"

Jane gave him an icy stare. "No thanks, Sir Galahad. Only certain kinds of women frequent places like that and I'm not one of them."

"I was only kidding," Michael said hurriedly. "But if I hit pay dirt I'll buy you dinner. Best place in town."

"And if you catch some incurable disease or get thrown out on your ear I'll visit you in the hospital. Not."

She stood up and wriggled into her shoes under the table. "I've had enough excitement for one day," she said. "I feel grungy. I'm going home. Have fun at the sex emporium."

Michael watched her leave, then sat back in the booth and ordered another beer and a bacon burger. He had to get on a better diet, he told himself. Better yet, he needed to get a life.

He hadn't been at The Courier five minutes before he had been propelled into this major story and he was disappointed in his performance. He'd been given a golden opportunity with the job at Ravena Ventura's estate and he'd been an eyewitness to three attempts on her life. But he hadn't come up with much beyond theories he couldn't prove and questions he couldn't answer.

All he needed was one little break. Then he'd have one hell of a story. He'd be the new hero of popular journalism. And Jane would go gaga over him.

Except it wasn't happening. He was sitting here alone in a bar, drinking beer and eating artery-clogging food, doing nothing that would take him closer to his ultimate headline.

He looked around and spotted a few faces from the office that he recognized. But he didn't really know these people, nor did they know him. He was close to no one except Jack and Jane.

Thank God for Jane. She'd started out resenting him without realizing how much he needed her approval. He'd worked hard to earn it and she'd thawed out a lot, though he still sensed a solid wall between her professional and personal lives. He still didn't know much about her. He didn't even know if she had a boyfriend tucked away somewhere. She never talked of one. Perhaps, like him, she was a prisoner of her job. The Courier did that to you. Like most female journalists she had a vocabulary that would make a truck driver blush but she could turn on a dime and go from spitfire to sweetheart. Sometimes she even seemed to be flirting with him.

Michael checked his watch. She'd probably be home by now. He toyed with the idea of calling her, asking her for a real date, maybe buying her that dinner. The strip club could always wait until tomorrow.

The arrival of his burger brought Michael crashing down to earth. He decided he probably had more chance of success pursuing Ellerby than Jane.

He gulped down his meal, finished his beer and checked his watch. Seven-thirty. South Florida's night owls were probably still closeted behind closed doors, primping themselves for whatever the evening had to offer. It was a little early to hit the Keyhole Club, but so what? He was looking for information, not entertainment.

The burger was a lead weight in his stomach. The thought of poking around asking questions at a strip joint began to play havoc with his nerves and his digestive system.

He took a deep breath. What the heck? If he had to ogle strippers as part of the job, so be it. He would tough it out. Someone had to do it. He pulled out his billfold, paid his tab with a flourish, and slid a generous tip under his beer glass. Then he headed for his car and the southern reaches of Boynton Beach, where the Keyhole Club awaited him—a neon beacon of hope in one corner of a dingy shopping center.

Chapter 47

The Keyhole Club was a glitzy looking building that would have looked more at home in Marrakesh than Boynton Beach, Florida. It stood alone in a corner of a rundown and nearly abandoned strip mall. It has started life as a barbecue-rib restaurant that went belly-up after a couple of years. Now the building was an entertainment Mecca for men with too much disposable cash and an overabundance of testosterone. But at eight o'clock on a midweek evening it wasn't drawing much of a crowd.

There were only half a dozen cars in the parking lot when Michael arrived. All were clustered near the main entrance, reflecting light in all directions from a flashing neon sign. This was a pack Michael didn't want to join, so he steered into a corner parking spot in one of the darker and weedier recesses of the lot. He didn't want to start feeling like a customer.

He pulled out a tiny notebook and a pen and copied down the names being promoted on the club's huge sign: "Top XXX-rated stars Aimee Ashleigh and Jenny Johnson." Apparently alliteration was a plus in the porn business.

Michael gritted his teeth. Feeling a little apprehensive and a lot foolish, he pulled open the heavy wooden door to the club.

He was instantly enveloped by darkness. The only lighting in the cramped entranceway winked at him enticingly around the corner of a wall that shut off any view of the club's interior.

He had expected someone to meet him and greet him at the entrance but no one did. He'd been hoping he could ask his questions in the doorway, then leave. But that apparently wasn't going to happen so he stumbled around the wall into the heart of the club.

He found himself in a huge dimly lit room which unfolded around a semi-circular stage that was the main source of light. Two scantily clad girls writhed around poles of tarnished brass to the accompaniment of blinking bulbs and canned music.

As Michael's eyes grew accustomed to the dark, he realized that the girls were only slightly outnumbered by their audience. Fewer than a dozen customers huddled together near the stage, drinking in the desperate spectacle and swilling Budweiser from the bottle.

Michael urgently needed to talk to someone, then get out of there. He looked around for a bar and spotted it in the far reaches of the room, a subtly lit oasis that had been carefully designed not to compete with the stage. It had no customers. Drinking was not the main attraction here.

But there had to be a bartender. That would be a good place to start. He began to feel his way toward the bar when a figure loomed out of the darkness.

"Good evening, sir. Would you like a seat?"

His path was blocked by a well-endowed girl in a pink halter top, a thigh-high skirt and a bare midriff. Michael wondered if she ever took a turn on the stage.

She gestured around with the palm of her hand, sweeping from the stage to some invisible regions behind her. "It's early yet, so there's plenty of room," she said. "What would you like to drink? There's a five-dollar cover, but we've got twofers on domestic beer and wine until nine o'clock."

"Uh, thanks," said Michael. He felt his way to the nearest seat and sat down at a small circular table. "I'll just have a beer."

"Don't you want to sit closer to the stage?" she asked.

"No thanks. That's okay."

She looked at him suspiciously. Hadn't he come in to eyeball the strippers? "I'll be right back," she said, and vanished toward the bar.

She returned in less than sixty seconds, plopping a couple of sweating bottles of Budweiser on the tiny table. Michael pulled out two twenty-dollar bills and handed one of them to her. "Thanks," he said. "Could I ask you a question?"

"Ask away." Her tone suggested she was used to being asked questions to which she never produced answers.

"I'm looking for either Aimee Ashleigh or Jenny Johnson."

"So are those guys down by the stage. That's what they're all here for. They're our headliners this week. Lookin' for a lap dance? We have private VIP rooms, you know."

"Uh, no. I just wanted to talk to them. Or at least to one of them."

"Which one?"

"Either one. I just have a question for them."

"Are you a cop?"

"No. I'm a reporter. Looking for someone."

"Well, I'm sorry sir, but you aren't going to find them here." Her change of attitude abruptly ended any threat of global warming. "There's nothing newsworthy going on here. And our dancers don't chit-chat with the customers."

"I understand that. But I know they're in the adult film business and they could help me."

"Well, you're out of luck. They don't hit the stage until ten o'clock. And we don't encourage interviews. Whatever you're looking for, you're not going to find it here."

Michael pushed the other twenty-dollar bill into her hand. "Perhaps you could arrange for me to talk for a few minutes with one of the other girls," he said, nodding toward the stage, where both dancers were now down to G-strings and caressing themselves to a chorus of half-hearted whoops and hollers.

"Enjoy your beer," she said and vanished with his money. The girls onstage were finishing their set. Perhaps she'd gone to intercept one of them. Hopefully his Jackson would carry some weight.

Less than thirty seconds later two men were at his table. They didn't look happy. He smiled at them. They scowled back. Apparently Jackson didn't carry much weight after all.

"You the guy lookin' to talk to the girls?" asked the taller and leaner of the two men. He was about fifty with square-cut features, a military haircut and a five-o'clock shadow from some other time zone.

"Yes. I'm looking for someone. Maybe you can help me."

"I'm the manager here and I can help you out the door, kid. We don't need no reporters nosing around in here. There's nothing to report. We run an honest, clean business, obey the law and pay our taxes so I suggest you take a hike."

"You're throwing me out?"

"No, son," said the other man. He had the nose of an ex-boxer and was carrying two hundred and forty well-distributed pounds. "We're not throwing you out. We're showing you out. Nice and quiet. We don't want no scenes here."

"I'm not here to report on your club, or create scenes. I'm just trying to find someone. Perhaps you know him. David Ellerby. Sometimes he uses the name David Elfman. He's in the adult movie business."

"I don't know him," said Tall and Lean. "He ain't here."

The other man gestured for Michael to leave his seat and the two of them walked alongside him to the door.

"Sorry we can't help you, son," said the manager. "We're a respectable gentlemen's club."

They closed the large wooden door behind them, leaving Michael outside, feeling rather ridiculous and glad there was no one to see him. He trudged to his car wondering if there were other, friendlier "gentlemen's clubs" he could investigate.

He fumbled for his keys in the darkness and was trying to locate the lock on his car when he heard a rustle behind him. He turned to see a girl in a T-shirt and shorts leaning up against the wall of the club pulling on a cigarette. It was one of the girls who'd been dancing when he arrived. Her eyes darted around as though she was doing something illegal.

"Hey, kid," she said. "You the reporter looking for Elfman?"

"Yeah. You know him?"

She took another drag on the cigarette, dropped it on the asphalt and crushed it under a well-worn sneaker. "You could say so. I worked for him a couple of times."

Michael's heart started to beat faster. "I need to talk to him. Do you know where I could find him? Where he lives or where he has his studio, maybe?"

"Don't know if he's still there," she said, "but he had a studio on a little ranch up in the Acreage. It's actually a small horse farm with a house and stables on it. He had no horses, though." She sniffed. "Just chicks."

"Do you have an address?"

"Nah. But I could tell you where it is."

Michael fumbled around in his billfold and produced another twenty-dollar bill.

"You know the Acreage?" said the girl.

"No, but I've heard of it. North part of the county?"

"Yeah. It's out in the boonies. Swamp and alligator country but it's quiet up there, which is why Elfie liked it. If you go west on Orange Trail you'll come to it. About six miles northwest of Royal Palm

Beach; can't miss it. It's the only spread with a white fence. Big house facing the street, stables on the west side and a huge barn-like building out back that he used for indoor sets."

"Thanks," said Michael. "You've been a big help."

"No prob. Don't know what you want him for but I'm sure it's not to make him Time magazine's cover boy of the year. He stiffed me out of half what he said he'd pay me. He'll get what he deserves. They always do. Look, I gotta go. They'll be lookin' for me inside. And I need this gig."

Michael nodded and watched as she melted back into the shadows, then disappeared through a small door at the rear of the club.

This was the seamy side of Palm Beach County. It could have been Detroit or Anyplace, U.S.A. not the glittering Palm Beaches featured in Chamber of Commerce literature. But it was here, just as it was everywhere, clinging to the grimy fringes of the American dream.

Chapter 48

Ravena spent the early evening cleaning Ellerby's gun. Then she carefully loaded it, caressed it, felt its weight and its power in her hands, checked that the safety was on, and dropped it into her purse. She was ready.

She changed from a simple red shift dress to dark blue jeans and a plain black top. No jewelry, except for her Cartier watch. She went into the powder room and examined her makeup carefully. Minimal. That was good. She pulled back her hair tightly and tied it up. It might have taken five years off her looks but it didn't. It sharpened the angles of her face and made her features more severe. That was good, too. Now she looked like any other suburban West Palm wife, perhaps out to the supermarket or Wal-Mart, or wherever suburban West Palm wives went. She didn't even need a wig to hide the fact that she was a woman with the world at her feet. Now she was Mrs. Nobody, fulfilling the tedious obligations of her pathetic second-class existence.

She had told Carla, the new live-in housekeeper, that she had a headache, would be retiring upstairs after an early dinner, and instructed her to field any phone calls. Then she called security to tell them to lock the front gate, shut off the visitors' phone and close the guardhouse for the evening. She didn't want to be disturbed. Not under any circumstances. *And she didn't want to be seen leaving the property.*

She waited until dark, then went quietly downstairs, slipped into the garage and opened the roll-up door with the remote. The Lexus purred quietly as she rolled down the driveway, and the garage door closed slowly behind her with an almost inaudible whir.

The front gate swung open when she hit a button on the dash and she turned north on the coastal highway.

Ravena smiled grimly to herself. She was on the loose among the proletariat. And she was on a mission. She picked up the Interstate and romanced a steady flow of slow-moving traffic to West Palm Beach. There she exited and drove west, away from the city.

She knew exactly where to go. She was not far from where her sister had been pulled out of the canal in Loxahatchee. Yes, this scrub and swampland dotted with surprisingly handsome real estate was Ellerby country.

At the town of Royal Palm Beach, just a few miles inland from the real Palm Beach geographically but light-years away from it culturally, she headed north again, then west on Orange Trail, a two-lane strip of asphalt that was losing a battle to remain rural. If there had ever been orange groves around here they were long gone.

Now Ravena had to concentrate. She passed mini-mansions perched in the middle of five-acre tracts. Some of the parcels were plush little horse farms, some were scrubby and neglected. All the tracts had ponds, testaments to the drained swamp from which the real estate had been claimed.

She came to a four-way stop. Straight on. Now she had to look for a "Deer Crossing" sign on the left, though no one in the neighborhood had seen deer in years. "Alligator Crossing" would have been more appropriate, but the Realtors wouldn't have liked that.

Her headlights picked up the sign in the darkness then she strained to spot a white fence on her left. Suddenly it was flashing by. This was Ellerby's property. She glanced over at the house, a modern Mediterranean-style home that looked out of place in the middle of a farm.

She had been here before. Ellerby had brought her here to shower and pull herself together after her sister's death.

Now, as then, the house stood shrouded in darkness. Two unlit floodlights sat atop high poles, one by the gate and one between the empty horse stalls to the right of the house and a large wooden barn at the rear of the property. These lights were carefully positioned to illuminate the small pastures surrounding the house, but without horses the pastures were captives of the night. The only visible illumination was little more than a glimmer in the gloom—a tiny security light by the front door of the house.

Was Ellerby home? *He'd better be!* Ravena had called to tell him she was on her way to see him. She could see no vehicles except a small ancient tractor parked by the horse stalls, and assumed his car was in the garage.

Ravena slowed as she drove by the farm and continued west until she came to a dirt road. There she turned left and left again. Now she was heading back to the rear of Ellerby's property.

She pulled over onto the edge of the swale and parked the car at a precarious angle, trusting that it wouldn't get stuck in mud or slide into the ditch.

She checked her purse for the gun and pulled out a flashlight. Then she got out of the car, kicked off her shoes and replaced them with a pair of old sneakers. She started walking, flicking the flashlight on and off until the beam picked up Ellerby's white fence.

He probably had some kind of security system to protect the house, but the fence had been designed only to keep horses in, not to keep humans out. The little rat was in for a surprise.

Ravena ducked between the fence rails and found herself in the back pasture, behind the huge windowless barn that had the architectural appeal of an airplane hangar.

She decided to head up to the house, hugging the wall of the barn until she reached the corner. Then she stepped briskly toward a thicket of scrubby trees.

She clutched her flashlight tightly but declined to use it, just hoping she wouldn't disturb any wildlife. Snakes were common in this area. She didn't know if they were abroad at night but it would be just her luck to step on a water moccasin.

She got her bearings from the fence line and kept inching forward carefully until she was parallel with the house. To her left was the stable, an open wooden structure with eight stalls that had once been home to someone's show horses. There had been no horses here since Ellerby took over the place but the building remained, along with a wash rack, a now-empty manure pit and a small office at one end that had also functioned as a changing room, tack room and storage area.

The stable was stuck in a time warp, a reminder of someone's adulation of equestrian sports. The horses and their riders had moved on, but the sickly sweet aroma of horse feed and manure lingered as though their ghosts were still there, watching over the property.

Ravena turned toward the house. The land rose up to the center of the property and the house stood atop a man-made hill, looking down on a pond to the rear, and to the outbuildings and a maze of fenced pastures.

In the daylight Ellerby's estate looked like something it no longer was, a family horse farm. It was now the hub of Ellerby's porn business, but Ravena doubted if any of his neighbors knew what went on behind the walls here. And if they did, it was unlikely they would care.

When Ravena reached the house she edged her way along the wall, cursed silently when she walked into an air conditioning unit, then stepped onto a cement patio. Faint slivers of light were filtering through blinds behind a sliding glass door. So Ellerby was around here somewhere. But she could hear nothing save the gentle hum of the air conditioner. No TV. No music playing. Where the hell was he?

Ravena pushed gently on the sliding glass door. It was locked. She tried to peer through the blinds but could see no signs of life. She rapped on the slider. No response. Obviously Ellerby wasn't there. Perhaps he'd run out for beer, cigarettes, condoms, or whatever other products men deemed vital to survival.

Where the hell was he? Was he trying to intimidate her? He was always trying to prove her need for him. But Ravena was no brain-fried female and she held the trump card. She had control of all the money.

The little slug was probably on the property somewhere, no doubt practicing some grandstand performance for her benefit. But she wasn't going to be his private audience. She was the hunter, not the prey . . . and suddenly she realized where she could find him.

Chapter 49

Ravena clutched her purse tightly, feeling the comfort of the gun through the leather. She flicked her flashlight on and off quickly to create stepping stones of illumination around a hot tub and a hodgepodge of patio furniture. She paused when she reached the edge of the patio. Here the terrain dropped off sharply toward the pond. She flipped off the light as she traced a mental path across the property. She certainly didn't want to walk into that pond in the darkness and she had to use the flashlight sparingly. Even in the Acreage strange lights flashing across private property could raise questions from passing motorists.

Ravena plotted a path in her head back to the barn where she had climbed through the fence. This was where Ellerby had to be, lurking in that monstrosity he called his studio.

The main entrance to the massive rectangular structure was at one end, where huge double doors opened up almost to the entire width of the building. They had been designed to accommodate horse vans, tractors and other farm equipment, but they were rarely used during Ellerby's tenure. Most of those who had business here now came and went through a simple wooden door in one corner of the building.

It was here where Ravena stopped and curled her fingers around the knob. She pushed the door open and a flood of pale yellow light spilled out into the darkness. A high ceiling, carefully situated lighting, and more up-market trappings than Ellerby had in his house prevented the windowless building from being claustrophobic. She had to admit that he'd done a commendable job transforming an equestrian storage area into a high-quality movie studio.

Like a loft, the building had not been partitioned off, except for two sizeable bathrooms and a makeup and dressing room. The focal point of the layout was a well-appointed bedroom area at the far end. It was open to the interior, guarded by a phalanx of klieg lights and cameras awaiting their next project.

Right now the only well-lit area of the barn was a section set up as an office near the entrance. Here, on a desk, sat a state-of-the art Mac with a forty-eight-inch monitor, the focal point of an impressive array of expensive electronic wizardry. This was where Ellerby personally transformed his porn pictures into a profitable enterprise.

He was sitting at the monitor when Ravena opened the door and he swung around in his chair to greet her.

"Hello, Ellie," she said quietly.

"Sweetheart," he said, "what a surprise!" He got out of the chair and reached out to hug her and kiss her on the cheek. She turned her head aside and his lips brushed her earlobe.

"I've missed you," he said. "It's good to see you. But I could have come down to Manalapan, you know."

"I'm not your sweetheart," Ravena reminded him. "And I told you I didn't want you at the house. It was never a good idea for you to be hanging around there all the time. We've been through all that. I'm here on business."

"Ah, yes!" Ellerby sat back down. "Make yourself at home," he said, indicating a solitary chair at the side of his work station. "We are going to be a great team. Ravena Ventura and David Ellerby. Ellerby Studios, or something fancier if you like with both our names. Ellvena maybe, or how about Ravella?"

Ravena ignored the offer of the seat and moved toward him. "Cut the prattling," she snapped. "I'm not here to talk about that bullshit. There's not going to be any joint business enterprise."

Ellerby smiled through thin lips. "I keep telling you we are a team," he said. "I know what you know and you know what I know. We need each other. Neither of us would survive without the other. Think of it, perhaps, as each of us holding half of a treasure map."

Ravena snorted and moved closer to him, leaning over, pushing her cleavage under his face.

"Get this straight, Ellie," she said. "We're not a team. I don't need you. It's you who needs me, or at least the money and the clout that I represent. You saw my sister's death as a way to get your greasy hooks into a fortune. There's no we, there's no us, there's no team. In fact, darling, there's not even going to be a you."

She stepped away and whirled around in a circle, pulling Ellerby's gun out of her purse as she did. When she faced him again it was firmly in both hands and the safety was off.

Ellerby tried to stand up, but his legs had turned to rubber. He sat back down with a thud as they collapsed under him. "What the hell are you doing?" he croaked. "For God's sake, stop waving that gun around. Is that my gun?"

"I'm not waving it around, Ellie," she said. "If you pay attention you'll see that I'm pointing it at you. And yes, it is your gun. You're going to shoot yourself with it."

"Huh?"

"I'm here to tell you that you're fired as my manager. I will tell the police that I finally found out the truth about you, about your background, and that you had lied to me. You aren't fit to shine my shoes, let alone be my manager. So I phoned you tonight to tell you that you're out. Unfortunately you didn't take it very well. You launched into a tirade, threatening all kinds of things, so I decided to come up here to calm you down and reason with you. I didn't realize how much you were in love with me and that you found the rejection so unbearable you blew your brains out."

"What? Don't be ridiculous. Are you crazy?"

Ellerby tried to stand again but Ravena took one hand off the gun and pushed him firmly in the chest. He sat back down with a thud.

His eyes widened in panic. "Look, sweetheart, we can work something out here. I don't know why you're doing this. I told you we were a team. It's simple. We just keep to ourselves and move on with our lives together."

"You really don't get it, do you Ellie?" she snapped. "I don't need you to help me move on with my life. I've got the money and I still have the looks. I've had time to step back and analyze the situation and it's obvious that you bring nothing to this partnership other than blackmail. And I don't need some little weasel like you trying to bleed me dry."

"I'm not blackmailing you. We have the same things to gain and the same things to lose. I really care about you and I can bring a lot to the table. You know I have movie production experience. And I'm certainly not going to kill myself."

"Wrong, Ellie," said Ravena. Both hands were back on the gun and she raised it slightly toward his head. "And to make sure you don't fuck it up I'm going to help you."

"You'll never get away with it."

Ellerby's eyes darted wildly as Ravena stepped toward him. Now she had the gun only inches from his face. He was making whimpering sounds.

"The police will figure it out," he said. "They'll find the master disk. And they'll realize—"

Ravena screamed. "What? I have that."

Ellerby shook his head. "That was just a copy."

"You lowlife prick! You stinking, lying son of a bitch!"

Ravena was boiling. Her grip tightened on the gun and her finger jerked on the trigger. She staggered back from the recoil and the shock as a shower of blood and brain tissue erupted in front of her. Her shirt was splattered with Ellerby's vital fluids. His body slumped in the chair. Part of his head appeared to be missing.

She had fired too soon. He had rattled her. She had to have that master disk. She needed to ask him about it. But it was too late for that now.

She ran to the bathroom and tore off her top. She should have figured that something like this would happen. That it could be messy. She looked in the mirror and spotted specks of blood and tissue on her neck and her ears. She washed them off quickly then scrubbed her hands. That would have to do. She checked her jeans. No blood on them. Good! She rolled up the bloody shirt. She could burn it later. In the meantime she'd find something to wear in the wardrobe that Ellerby kept on hand for his porn stars.

Moving quickly, she picked up the gun and wiped it clean of all prints. Then, averting her eyes from Ellerby's head, she folded his fingers around the weapon and let it drop to the floor.

Now she had to find that master disk and any other copies he might have around. They would be around here somewhere. That movie was one of the holds Ellerby had over her, but she doubted that he would have gone to any great pains to hide it efficiently. The little bastard had been too proud of it to squirrel it away.

Chapter 50

Michael glanced at his watch. Eight-forty. He was alone in the parking lot of the Keyhole Club. And he was wired.

He mentally ran through the directions to Ellerby's place that the girl had given him. Then he pulled the street map from his car and traced the route to the Acreage. It wasn't far from where Ravena's sister had been found in the canal. Was it coincidental that Ellerby had a pad around there?

Michael knew he should call it a night, go home then discuss a plan of action with Jack Iverson in the morning. But he was being guided by his impulses. He'd hit a brick wall with his fancy theories and story ideas. He'd put in a lot of work on this story with only mediocre results and he was frustrated. He had to do *something!* And there was no reason to wait.

He pulled out his phone and punched in Jack's cell number. He was instantly forwarded to voice mail, but didn't bother to leave a message. Perhaps Jack was at home. He called his editor's home number and got an answering machine. Strike two!

In desperation he called Jane and excitedly filled her in on the Keyhole Club, his meeting with the girl in the parking lot and the directions she'd given him to Ellerby's movie studio.

"I'm going to drive up and see if he's there and try to get to talk to him," he said. "Now I've been pulled off security detail I don't have to worry about my cover getting blown. If I can corner him alone I might be able to get him to open up."

Jane was alarmed. "You're going to do that right now?"

"Yeah. What's the point in waiting? Perhaps he's out of town, or even out of the country, but then again, maybe he's not. And I'm curious. I'd like to get a look at his place. The guy is creepy and we know he's got a history. I'm gonna head on up there. I'll talk to you later."

"Wait," cried Jane, "what about —"

Too late. Michael had gone. She stared at the phone and shook her head.

Jack would not be happy to be left out of the loop. And Michael had apparently forgotten that blowing his cover would also blow his opportunity to be Ravena's chauffeur. She knew what she had to do.

* * *

Michael slid behind the wheel of the Mustang, contemplated his street map again then brought the engine to life. He'd been lucky to get to talk to that stripper. Maybe his fortunes were changing.

Orange Trail was easy to find once you knew where you were going. But Michael wasn't sure where it was taking him. The road cut a narrow swath through the jungle to connect the fragments of habitation where humans had fled to escape urban sprawl. There were no street lights and the thickets of ever-encroaching wilderness cast ghostly shadows in the moonlight.

There was no traffic to keep up with, no trucks pushing him to drive faster or move out of the way, so Michael maintained a careful twenty-five miles an hour as he squinted ahead, looking for a tell-tale white fence.

Suddenly his headlights picked it up, a gleam in the distance that grew in size and intensity as he approached. The only white fence in town. This had to be Ellerby's place.

He braked as he spotted the metal gate in the fence line, set back from the road by little more than the length of a car. Rather than pull up to the gate, Michael carefully angled the Mustang off the pavement and parked parallel to the fence.

He cursed as he found he couldn't get out of the car. The fence was blocking the driver's door. Irritated, he slid over to the passenger side of the car and climbed out awkwardly.

He looked across at Ellerby's farm. It was pretty much as the stripper had described to him. In the gloom he could pick out the roofline of the hulking barn at the rear of the property and the horse stalls to his right. Across from them, on the other side of a fenced pasture, was the house, a typical sprawling suburban home stuck in the middle of a rustic farm.

Michael checked the gate. There was no lock, no button or bell, no apparent alarm system. Just a simple chain to fool the horses, even though there had been no horses here for some time.

He unhooked the chain, carefully replaced it behind him, and then warily followed the shell-rock driveway as it wound a circuitous path to the house.

Whoever had torn this piece of land from the grip of Mother Nature had lovingly designed it as an equestrian paradise. From what he knew of Ellerby, Michael found it difficult to believe this was his home. At the same time, it was secluded. All manner of activities could take place here without any eyebrows being raised. In fact, there didn't seem to be any eyebrows around.

Michael muttered to himself, angry that he hadn't thought to bring a flashlight, as the driveway brought him to the garage. Cautiously, he stepped out of the shadows and around the corner to the front entrance.

The measly porch light didn't reveal much, but it was enough to guide his finger to a doorbell. He pushed it and heard a faint ring somewhere inside the house. He waited. No one came to the door. There were no voices, no footsteps, no scuffling noises.

He tried the bell again then hammered on the door. Still no answer.

Michael began to turn away from the door when a noise stopped him in his tracks. A thud. A dull crack breaking the night's cloying silence. Something falling? Some wild animal? It could even have been gunfire. Whatever it was, one thing was certain. Michael was not alone.

He stopped and listened. The night was as silent as a monastery full of Trappist monks. The sound was not repeated so that probably ruled out a wild animal. The more he thought about it the more Michael became convinced that it had been a gunshot. Guns were probably de rigueur around here anyway.

The sound had come not from inside the house but behind it, somewhere toward that night-shrouded barn to the rear of the property. Something inside him told him to leave and wait for the sun to melt away the eerie shadows. But he was a reporter and good reporters don't leave when the going gets spooky.

He stepped carefully around the house, running a hand along the stucco walls. He stumbled and cursed as he scraped his ankle on something. He felt around carefully with his hands and found himself embracing an electric pump. Just something servicing a swimming pool or drawing well water into the house.

At the rear of the house Michael stumbled onto the cement-slab patio, stopped to let his eyes grow accustomed to the darkness, and looked across to the barn. There was no sign of life, but there was little light to detect any. He noticed the small pond in the hollow below him that might have been lying in wait for unsuspecting trespassers like him. He wondered if it harbored any alligators. Did alligators patrol at night? He didn't know and he had no desire to find out.

Gravity sped him down the hill, but he regained his footing at the bottom and carefully gave the pond a wide berth. He paused and listened again, but the silence was deafening.

The barn loomed in front of him like a refuge on windswept plains. Maybe Ellerby used it as a backdrop for movies with names like Little Whorehouse on the Prairie. Perhaps he was in there now, doing whatever it was Ellerby did. Was he responsible for the gunshot? And if so, who or what had been the target?

Michael reached the barn and ran a hand along the rough-hewn wall to guide him until he could find an entrance. He could see little in front of him and breathed a sigh of relief when his fingers found a doorframe.

He fumbled for the knob and the door yielded to his touch with a creak. He stepped across the threshold, temporarily blinded by a sudden flood of light. He blinked instinctively then recoiled in horror at the scene in front of him.

Chapter 51

Michael stood in the doorway, his mouth agape. His first instinct was to flee, but he was paralyzed by what he saw.

Ellerby, or what was left of him, was slumped in an office chair turned away from a desk where he'd apparently been working. A sizeable portion of his head appeared to be gone and blood, brain tissue and bone were splattered around him, and around a gun that lay on the floor beneath his outstretched arm.

But somehow the real horror was not the sight of Ellerby bloodied and dead but of Ravena Ventura, in a bra and jeans, leaning past his inert body, rifling through the desk drawers as though nothing was amiss.

Michael startled her. She looked up, froze, and then backed away from the desk. She was breathless.

"Michael!" she gasped. "Wha . . . wha . . . what are you doing here?"

Michael stopped in his tracks. He had no desire to get any closer to the scene. "I came to talk to Mr. Ellerby," he said. "I see I was too late."

"Wha . . . what about?"

"I uh…had some questions for him."

"Well thank God you're here. I thought you'd gotten a new job and moved on. I just got here. I wanted to talk to him, too, and found him like this. I just called nine-one-one. The police should be here any minute."

Michael's eyes narrowed. Ravena was jumpy. Finding a dead body could do that to you. Especially if it's someone you know. But why would it make you take your clothes off? And her eyes were darting around the room. She was in panic mode. And she had been frantically searching for something in Ellerby's desk.

"I don't think you should be touching anything, Miss Ravena," said Michael. "It might screw up the police investigation."

"Investigation? What's to investigate? It's obvious that Ellerby blew his brains out. He'd been under a lot of pressure lately and I'd just fired him as my manager. He'd lied to me. He wasn't the man I thought he was—or the man he told me he was."

"You just told him you'd fired him?"

"Yes."

Michael stared at her. Things were not right here. His blood ran cold and a ball of fear was gnawing at the pit of his stomach. He licked his lips to fight off a wave of nausea.

"I thought you said you'd just arrived and found him like this."

"Yes . . . yes. Actually I'd phoned him to tell him he wasn't working for me anymore. He was broken up about it so I decided to come up here and talk to him face-to-face. That's when I found him. You must have been right behind me."

Michael took a step backward toward the door. He needed to get away from there, away from her. Had she really called the police?

"You were looking for something in the desk?" he said.

"Yes . . . uh, I wondered if he'd left a suicide note. I haven't found one yet, but I figure there's probably one around here somewhere. Don't most people leave notes before they kill themselves?"

Michael continued to edge slowly toward the doorway. Why would Ravena be standing in her underwear, ignoring a dead body while she looked for a suicide note? If Ellerby had written one he'd apparently taken the time to hide it before he blew his brains out. Things definitely did not add up here. He heard no sirens and there was no sign of any cops. Ravena's story wasn't making much sense and his gut told him he was in harm's way.

He fumbled for his cell phone. It wasn't there! Then he remembered he'd tossed it onto the passenger seat when he'd clambered out of the car. It was in the Mustang, way up on the roadside.

"The police should be here by now," he said. "I think I'll go look for them."

He began to back slowly toward the door and braced himself to make a run for it. But the door opened behind him before he reached it.

A woman stepped into the room. An attractive blonde, dressed in sneakers, well-worn jeans and a white T-shirt. She bore an uncanny resemblance to Ravena, except she was taller and older––and brandishing a gun.

"Well, well," she said. "What a mess we have here. What the hell have you been doing, sis?" Then she turned to Michael, cold eyes boring into him from head to toe. "And who the hell are you?" she said.

"Emily!" cried Ravena. "Thank God it's you. This is Michael, my bodyguard. We need your help."

Emily didn't appear ready to help. Instead, she waved the gun at Michael to direct him over to where Ravena was standing. She stared at what was left of Ellerby and curled up her nose.

"At least you took care of that asshole," she said.

Ravena gasped. "What do you mean? What's going on here?"

Emily sneered at her sister. "Cut the crap, sis, it's over. I know exactly what's going on here. That's why I came to visit you at your house. Just had to make sure I knew who and what I was dealing with."

She touched Ellerby's body gingerly with her toe. "He was trying to squeeze me out. He and I figured a Ravena porn flick would help us tap into those movie-star millions. Unfortunately that deadly mishap kinda screwed everything up. Then David hit on another idea that would make you his puppet while he pulled the strings. But that was leaving me out in the cold. He was going to screw me out of my share. There was only one way left for me to benefit. As Ravena's solitary heir."

"You mean—"

"Yes. Sorry, sis, but both my sisters have to die. I've waited a long time for this. Playing second fiddle as a child while my twin siblings became the little darlings of Hollywood, watching the name Ravena Ventura rise to the top of the Hollywood heap. Did either of you ever give a shit about me? I suffered years of anguish in Mexico, went back to L.A. and tried to reconnect with my family roots, but the Ravena Ventura Revolutionary Guard thought I was a crackpot and kept me away.

"Then I met David and helped manage his adult enterprises. He was a jerk but he seemed to keep landing on his feet. After he met you I knew I'd finally hit pay dirt."

Ravena started to sob. "Emily! What are you saying? What are you planning to do?"

"Looks like we're going to have a murder-suicide. Pity I wasn't able to take you out of the picture before this. It wasn't for want of trying. I actually thought I'd hit you in that parking lot in Delray. And how a bullet didn't find you on your patio is beyond me. Guess I'm not the markswoman I thought I was. But I did a good number on your limo on the freeway, didn't I? Somehow you have a charmed life, but like all good things, it's coming to an end."

Emily waved the gun at Michael again. "Get over there and kick that gun over here, away from David. Now!"

Michael stepped over to where Ravena had placed the gun by Ellerby's hand. He slid it across the floor with his foot, moving closer to Emily as he did so. He knew he had only one fleeting chance of getting out of there alive.

Emily waved her gun slowly between her sister and Michael. Her eyes shifted between them as she stooped down to feel for the weapon on the floor. Michael flew at her as her fingers curled around it. He hit her full force with his shoulder. She stumbled, off balance, and crumpled to the floor facedown. Ellerby's gun skidded out of her grasp but she still kept a death grip on her own weapon.

Michael reeled away from her and dived for the exit as she staggered to her feet. He crashed into the door then yanked it open as a bullet splintered the wood over his head.

Suddenly he was outside, enveloped by the cloying darkness, which was now a comforting shield. He heard more gunfire behind him. He had to get to his car quickly, drive to safety and call the police. It seemed very doubtful that they were on their way.

Chapter 52

It was starting to rain and the meager moonlight had disappeared altogether. Michael needed to let his eyes adjust to the overpowering darkness. But he couldn't wait for that. He had to get out of there. He tried to establish his bearings, painting a picture of the farm in his mind. The rain suddenly began to intensify, stinging him with liquid pellets driven by an angry wind that tore through the trees. He ran blindly toward what had to be the road and the safety of his car.

Emily was somewhere behind him, not too far. She still had her gun. And she wasn't afraid to use it. She had worked out a course of action and was intent on following it. He had been in the wrong place at the wrong time and she couldn't afford to let him get away.

Ravena had obviously shot Ellerby and set the stage for it to look like a suicide. Then Emily, who had probably heard the shot from the house, had appeared on the scene to finish the job. With Ellerby, Ravena and Liz dead, there would be no one standing between Emily and Ravena's fortune. Except Michael, the solitary witness.

Michael yelped as he ran into something solid. He had hit something with his knee and his whole leg started to burn. The place was littered with either farm or movie-set bric-a-brac, and there was no telling what lay in his path.

His cry had identified his position, and he heard another gunshot. Emily was aiming blindly in his direction but she was way off target. Thank God she really wasn't much of a shot. The darkness and the pelting rain were giving him natural cover. But he could hear her cursing and calling out to him as his feet swished through the soggy grass. He wondered where Ravena was and if she were still alive.

It was a long way to the road, much farther than it had seemed when Michael had arrived. But at that time he wasn't being chased by a lunatic with a firearm. He needed to find some cover. Emily may be lousy with a gun, but if she kept firing there was a good chance she'd get lucky.

He was somewhere between the stables to his left and the house to the right. He knew he had to keep to his left or he would probably wind up in the pond.

Perhaps he could reach the stables, lie low there for a while, either in the horse stalls or in the wooded area behind them. Then he could creep toward his car.

He could dimly make out the stables. He was closer to them than he thought. Running as fast as he could, fighting to keep his footing in the mud and the slick grass, he veered toward the building—and gasped at the force of a sudden blow to his chest.

The crack of the impact sounded like a gunshot. Had one of Emily's bullets found its mark? Was he going to die ingloriously in a muddy field? He doubled over in agony then realized Emily hadn't been that lucky. He had run full force into a fence. Now he wasn't sure whether the sound had come from the wood splintering or his ribs breaking, and he didn't have the time to find out.

With his every step now punctuated by stabbing pain, Michael ducked between two rows of fencing. As he did a bullet whistled over his head. Emily was getting closer, and so was her aim. Bent double, he staggered blindly across the small pasture that fronted the stables.

Desperately gasping for breath, he tripped over the edge of the shed row, a covered dirt walkway in front of a row of horse stalls. There was another bank of stalls behind them, and the shed row encircled them all.

He crept down the aisle, wondering where he could hide. Emily obviously knew where he was. She would be on the scene any second. He could jump into one of the stalls and lie down in a corner. It was so dark there was a chance she would never spot him. But if she did he would be as helpless as a fly in a spider web. There had to be a better hiding place than that.

Going into the stables had been a mistake. It offered no secure place to hide. He'd be better off in the woods behind them, even though there may be unfriendly animals lurking in there. And it was very low-lying land. There could be swampy areas where he could get sucked in the mud. But the trees would also shelter him in the darkness. He could probably slide between them quietly until he hit the road then backtrack to his car.

He also knew that the pounding rain and the cover of night could work against him. He could easily lose his bearings in that dense wilderness, and who knew how far it extended?

The rain abated briefly and he heard a noise in the pasture. Emily was still on the move out there. She was heading toward him. He desperately wanted to talk to her. But negotiation was not an option. Not while she was waving a pistol around and firing it at will.

If he wanted to stay alive he couldn't stand still. He had to keep moving and hope he could reduce the distance between himself and his car.

He slid along the stable wall, past a couple of stall gates, and then his elbow hit a doorknob near the corner. This wasn't a stall. He turned around, twisted the knob
and pushed on the door. It opened with little resistance and Michael was met with a smell of musty hay and leather. This had been some kind of storage or tack room. Perhaps he could block the door with something and lie low in here, but he could see nothing. Then he heard it, a spine-chilling sound that changed his mind. A scratching on the wooden floor and a high-pitched mewling. The room was overrun with rats!

He quickly abandoned the door, leaving it ajar, and turned toward the back of the stables where the woods lay waiting in the darkness. They were his best bet after all.

A gunshot stopped him in his tracks. A bullet clanged on some unseen metal over his head. Michael prayed for no ill-fated ricochet and it thudded harmlessly into woodwork.

Emily was in the pasture, barely thirty feet from him now, suddenly bathed in a tiny pool of light. She could have passed for an angel who had slid down from heaven on a light beam; except angels didn't carry semi-automatics. And where had that light come from?

Michael's heart raced. There was a car moving slowly on the road beyond the stable. Its headlights cast a warm beam across the grass as it grew closer. Emily was trying to melt into the darkness, but the light seemed to follow her.

The car was stopping. Thank God! Maybe it was the police. Perhaps Ravena had called them after all. He needed to buy time.

"Emily!" he called. "We need to talk. But please put the gun down."

She answered by firing wildly in his direction. The bullet tore through leaves in the trees behind the stable.

Suddenly there was more light cascading all over the small pasture and throwing pale yellow stripes across the side of the stables. The car had turned into the tiny driveway. The headlights were now aimed directly at the scene.

"Michael!"

A woman's voice, but not Emily's. It sounded like Jane. It was Jane! Michael heard a car door slam and he could see her outline as she stepped toward the gate.

"Michael," she cried. "Are you all right? What's happening?"

"Jane!" he shouted. "Get out of here. And call the cops. I think there's been a murder. And there might be another one any minute."

It sounded like a joke but he prayed she would realize he wasn't kidding.

He tried to dodge out of the light. What was Jane doing here? Now she was in danger too, and she was distracting him. He had to keep his eyes on Emily, who was getting closer and closer. Soon she would be so close even she couldn't miss.

"Emily. Wait," he pleaded. "Don't shoot. We must talk."

"There's nothing to talk about?" she yelled. "Who's your girlfriend up there? She can't help you."

Jane's car lights still bathed the pasture in front of the stable but Michael could no longer see her. He wondered if she was in earshot.

Michael had his back to the wall, literally and metaphorically. He had run out of options. Emily was now only about twelve feet away from him and stepping into the shed row. He could see her clearly, which meant she could see him.

He looked her squarely in the eye and raised his voice over the rain, now rattling relentlessly again on the stable's metal roof.

"We need to talk," he said. "I'm not really a bodyguard. I can help you."

She replied with a laugh, but it was drowned by the sound of sirens, swiftly getting louder and louder. The police had arrived.

If Emily had heard them, she paid them no heed. She raised the gun again, slowly and deliberately. She was close enough and in enough light that he could see the end of the barrel, pointed at his chest.

"Sorry," she said. "I'll tell them that you killed Ellerby and Ravena and that I managed to stop you as you were trying to escape."

"Don't do it, Emily," he begged, but his voice was little more than a breath of air lost in the turbulent night. He heard someone yelling in the distance as he turned away from Emily and closed his eyes in anticipation of the bullet he couldn't avoid. So this was how it was going to end.

A burning pain exploded on Michael's left side. He clutched at it with his right hand and crumpled to the dirt in the shed row.

Chapter 53

Michael could hear a voice. A woman's voice, soft, quiet, caressing. But he couldn't react to it. He couldn't move, or open his eyes. He wasn't sure he wanted to. But she was calling his name. It must be Ravena. There had been some terrible misunderstanding but everything was going to be all right now.

He was lying on his back and his entire body was sore and burning from pain. He fought to see, struggling to understand why his eyes had been super-glued shut.

Slowly, he concentrated on forcing his right eye open. Everything was white and hazy. He couldn't make anything out, but he could still hear the female voice calling his name. Was he dreaming? Was he dead? Maybe they were checking his credentials at the Pearly Gates.

He blinked, grimaced, and worked on raising the other eyelid. The white haze slowly gave way to blinding light. Everything in his view was still white. Where the hell was he?

Then a figure came into view. A face. A face he recognized. It wasn't Ravena. It was Jane.

"Hello, Michael," she said quietly. He could feel her soft breath on his cheek as she leaned over him. It was warm and comforting. He thought hopefully that she was going to kiss him, but she just smiled and said, "Welcome back."

Back from where? Where had he been?

He tried to smile and to say something, but the best he could muster was "Hi." His facial muscles didn't seem to be working properly and the smile felt like a leer. He began to mumble gibberish.

"Just rest. Don't exert yourself," said Jane. But Michael had to know what was going on. Apparently he wasn't dead, unless Jane had decided to accompany him to the Great Beyond, something he found encouraging but rather doubtful.

The pain in his body was not subsiding, but he gritted his teeth and pulled himself up. He looked around and realized where he . . . in a hospital room.

"Wha…what happened?" he croaked.

"You were shot. You've been out for some time and you missed the exciting part where they cut you open and fixed you up."

"Gee, thanks for sharing that with me. Ravena's sister was shooting at me."

"Yes, we know. But it's all— "

She fell silent and turned her head as the door opened and Jack Iverson peered around it cautiously.

"How's he doing?" he asked.

"He's awake and doing fine," said Jane, "but you know he's not supposed to have more than one visitor at a time." She didn't try to hide her irritation. "I'd better leave you two to talk. I'll come back later, Michael."

"No, don't leave," he implored.

"I'd rather leave than get thrown out. It was tough enough getting in here."

Jack patted her on the shoulder. "Quit bellyaching and sit down," he ordered. "I got tired of cooling my heels."

He put his rear end down carefully on the edge of the bed and inspected Michael. "So how are you feeling, kiddo?" he asked.

"Like shit, but I guess I'm gonna live. What the hell happened? The last thing I recall was being at Ellerby's farm with that crazy bitch chasing me and shooting at me."

"Nothing wrong with your memory. Anyway, you were lucky. If Jane hadn't followed you out there and arrived in time to call nine-one-one, you'd be dead meat by now. As it is, you took one bullet in your side and another one grazed your arm, but the docs say you're gonna be okay. You also picked up a cracked rib from somewhere. What the hell you were doing to get in a mess like this I'll never know but you're currently getting VIP treatment from the cops. There's a uniform on guard in the hallway and Jane and I had a hell of a job getting visiting privileges. We tried to convince 'em we were family but Henderson showed up and recognized Jane. We talked him into giving us a pass anyway, only because he thinks you're still out of it. The cops are waiting to grill you and as soon as Henderson finds out you're awake he's going be in here."

"Can hardly wait," gasped Michael. The talk about his injuries had suddenly made the pain worse. "Can I get some painkillers or something?"

"I'll ask the nurse on my way out," said Jane.

"What about Ravena?" asked Michael. "Is she alive? Is she all right?"

"She's in surgery," said Jack. "Took a bullet in the abdomen but they say she'll make it."

"What about her sister, Emily?"

"Cops winged her in the shoulder when she ignored their demands to drop her weapon. That saved your life, I guess. She's in another room down the hall; in custody."

"It's like a bad dream. Did the police fill you in on what happened?"

"Not much. But we did some checking on Emily. Seems she turned her back on the family when she was eighteen, ran off to Mexico and married a businessman named Hector Posada. He turned out to be a honcho in the Mexican Mafia and their marriage was turbulent, to put it mildly. She finally dumped him, ran back to California and eventually wound up as creative director of Phetish Publications, a producer of porn magazines. Phantasy was a subsidiary of Phetish Enterprises, one of Ellerby's many ventures. That's how she met Ellerby and she came to Florida with him when he moved his base of operations to the east coast.

"Somehow one thing led to another and you wound up on the receiving end of her gun. And you can thank Emily for your fifteen minutes of fame. Don't let it go to your head, Mikey, but you're going to come out of this smelling like a rose, even though you were a stupid asshole for racing up to Ellerby's pad like that. You're supposed to check in with me for advice, direction and assignments, not go flying all over the place on wild and dangerous goose chases. But unless Henderson finds a way to legally silence you, you'll be telling your first-person story in the next issue of The Courier."

"Thanks a lot," said Michael. "Now how about those painkillers?"

"Sure. We'll check in on you again later." Jack slid off the bed, nodded to Jane and vanished through the door. She followed him with a smile and a wiggle of her fingers.

Jack and Jane were replaced at Michael's bedside in less than a minute by a nurse, whose niggardly fussing and take-charge attitude he soon found annoying. But she gave him an unidentified pill and a fresh paper cup of water.

"It won't put you to sleep," she assured him. "And there's a detective waiting to see you. Unless you're seriously not up to it, I'll let him in. After all, you've been chatting with visitors already and I can't wait to get the cops and everyone else out of here. This hospital is a madhouse."

"Huh?"

"Cops everywhere; it feels like a prison. And all those reporters. The parking lot is full of hordes of people running around with cameras, microphones and tape recorders."

"Sorry," said Michael. "Didn't know I was so popular."

"Oh, it's not you they're interested in. It's that actress, Ravena Ventura. She's under very tight security. She's in surgery at the moment but the cops are all over the place, guarding her like she's Fort Knox."

She skittered out of the room and Michael could hear her talking to someone in the hallway.

It turned out to be Henderson. The detective walked in, closed the door behind him, leaned back against it and folded his arms. He analyzed Michael with piercing eyes gleaming under a furrowed brow.

"Well," he said at last. "You did it, hotshot."

"Did what?" Michael struggled to sit up in the bed.

"Got involved in one holy mess. I told you to leave the police work to us. You're lucky you're not pushing up daisies."

"What the hell is going on?"

"You don't remember? Ravena Ventura's manager was found dead at the farm where we found you. He'd been renting the place in the Acreage to make porno flicks. He was lying on the floor in the back barn with his brains blown out. Ravena was lying beside him with a gunshot wound. Top that off with her older sister Emily using you for target practice and you've got the rest of the story."

"Has Ravena told you anything?"

"Nothing much. She's been busy getting serious medical attention."

Michael's stomach was churning. His mouth was dry and he wanted to vomit. "What does Emily have to say?"

"She claims she arrived to find Ellerby and Ravena dead. At least she thought Ravena was dead. She says Ellerby's gun was on the floor and you were standing over his body. She was scared, and you turned and ran when she asked you what you were doing there. She chased you across the farm, firing warning shots to get you to stop. Says she thought you'd killed them both."

Michael wrestled around in the bed, plucked a handful of tissues from the nearby table and dry-retched into them. He was being accused of murder?

Henderson's eyes were slicing into him.

"That's bullshit," Michael said at last.

Henderson pried himself off the door, grabbed a chair with one hand and straddled it next to the bed. "That's what we think," he said. "The gun that killed Ellerby wasn't the same one that wounded Ravena or yourself. I suspect we have a murder or a suicide plus two attempted murders. Anyway, right now I need a statement from *you*. I want your version of what went down at Ellerby's farm."

Henderson pulled out his miniscule notebook and started writing laboriously as Michael told him what had transpired. After he'd finished the detective snapped it shut with a dramatic gesture.

"Thanks," he said. "I'll be back to see you later. Looks like you've got yourself a whale of a story."

Michael nodded and smiled. "Yeah, to match my whale of a headache."

Chapter 54

Michael was propped up in his bed at noon the next day, hammering away on a laptop when Henderson poked his nose around the door.

"How ya feeling?" he asked.

"A lot better now I can get things down in writing. What's new?"

The detective closed the door behind him and pulled a chair to the side of the bed.

"Enough to make your head spin. We may never know exactly what happened on the night that car went into the canal, but we do know a lot more than we did. Turns out that Ravena Ventura isn't Ravena at all but her twin sister, Elizabeth Thomas."

Michael beamed. "I knew it! I was——"

"Don't start with the 'I told you so,' hotshot, unless you know the next winning powerball numbers. After we advised Emily that Ravena was alive she told us we had Liz, not Ravena. So we checked the fingerprints of our Ravena with Elizabeth Thomas's in LAPD files. They're a match. Elizabeth Thomas and her sister Rachel, known to the world as Ravena Ventura, were mirror-image identical twins. They looked alike, except——"

"Except everything is reversed! I knew there was something strange about her after seeing all those Ravena movies. With mirror-image twins, if one has a mole on the right side of her body, the other will have one on the left. Usually one is right-handed, the other left. Comparing their natural hairstyles would be like looking at one of them in a mirror. Their hair curls or parts the opposite way, but no one would notice unless you saw them both together. There were just too many things that weren't exactly right, but I could never put my finger on it. The real Ravena was left-handed, wasn't she?"

"Actually she was ambidextrous. You'd be amazed how difficult it was to get that seemingly simple question answered. But we finally tracked down a former assistant from her L.A. days, and she confirmed that. The handwriting was a tough call, too. Elizabeth had been working on the signature. That's pretty much all the writing she had to do, for signing checks and autographs."

Michael was as excited as a kid with his first computer. That explained the doodles on the scrap of paper he had taken from the office wastebasket.

"There were no identifying moles, by the way," Henderson added dryly.

"Did you check her internal organs? I hear that sometimes the heart of one mirror-image twin is on the right."

"Huh? Contain yourself, hotshot. A thorough medical examination found nothing like that. Anyway, I'm not even sure she has a heart."

"What does Liz have to say about the deaths of her sister and Ellerby?"

"She's kinda sticking to the story she told you, that Ellerby had killed himself and she found the body. Then you showed up, her sister Emily showed up…and the shit hit the fan. The last part of her story seems to be the truth, but she's already told stories that have more holes in 'em than my roof after last year's hurricane. And gun-residue tests show that Ellerby never fired the shot that killed him."

Henderson paused and looked at the floor. "Funny thing is," he said, "Elizabeth keeps insisting she's the real Ravena Ventura. Maybe she's going for the insanity defense."

"Elizabeth was the weak twin, always in Rachel's shadow. When Rachel died, she just assumed her alter ego, clothed herself in Ravena's mantle. In a strange way Elizabeth really is Ravena Ventura now."

"Makes no difference who she is, or thinks she is, she'll be going down for a long time regardless of the outcome of the murder investigations. We're already looking at conspiracy, wrongful disposal of a body, forgery, embezzlement and a slew of other things your fertile mind has probably already thought of.

"She's blaming Ellerby for everything and there's no doubt he was a prize scumbag. She says he starred her in a porno flick with the idea of using it to blackmail Ravena. When Liz sent a copy of it to her sister, there was a confrontation in Liz's apartment. She says Ravena went ballistic, pulled a gun and started firing wildly. She insists Ravena's death was an accident, claims the two of them were struggling over the gun when they fell and Ravena whacked her head on the corner of that ugly-ass metal table. Apparently that was the 'weapon' we were looking for."

Michael stared at Henderson. "It was probably Ellerby's idea for Elizabeth to take over Ravena's life," he said. "But why would she go along with it? Didn't she realize he was just using her to get at Ravena's money?"

"She says she was scared. Ellerby had already shown his enthusiasm for blackmail and she knew she could be accused of murdering her sister. So it was easy for Ellerby to get her to help him dump the body away from the real crime scene. This gave Elizabeth time to establish herself as Ravena and get rid of any help that might realize she wasn't the real McCoy."

"You're starting to make me feel sorry for her—mostly a hapless victim of circumstances, just caught in the middle."
"I wouldn't go that far. But if she's smart maybe she'll find a way to cut a deal and hang Emily out to dry."

"And that takes us to Emily. My biggest headache. Is she still trying to pin everything on me?"

"Yup. But I wouldn't worry about it. My guess is the real story is pretty much as you told it. Liz says Emily was the one who shot her. Seems Emily had been staying at Ellerby's farm and was in the house when you showed up. We searched the place and found a Browning SA-22 rifle under one of the beds. Her prints were on the stock. It's probably the weapon used in the shooting incident in Manalapan."

Michael nodded. *And the shooting incident at the medical center.* "With Liz out of the way Emily would be in line to inherit all of Ravena's money," he said. "And with Ellerby out of the way there'd be no one to testify against her."

"Except you. Did I tell you that you were very lucky?"

"Not as many times as you told me I was a pain in the ass. One more thing. Where does Ravena's murdered dentist fit into this?"

"Some dentist. He was a drug dealer, a real dirtball. A typical friend of Ellerby's trying to get in on the action when he learned what was going on. That was his big mistake. He was shot with Ellerby's gun."

"Have you made any statements to anyone else in the media?"

"Nothing beyond a routine release explaining that Ravena Ventura is recovering in the hospital and that the investigation is continuing. We're still up to our eyeballs trying to nail everything down and I'm making no major announcements until we do."

He winked almost imperceptibly, stepped over to the bed and pumped Michael's hand. "Go ahead and write your story. Just don't name me as a source."

He turned, walked to the door, then looked back and nodded at Michael. "Thanks," he said, and was gone.

Michael stared after him for a few seconds then reached for the phone.

* * *

Jack Iverson growled and grumbled about deadlines, but Michael was excited at a level he had never experienced before. Prospects of a Pulitzer Prize paled in comparison with life at The Courier.

It took him another hour of furious typing, interspersed with arguments with two nurses and a doctor who insisted on interrupting him with meals, examinations, bed checks and questions.

Finally he was done with his story, an emotional tale of two sisters who took wrong turns in their lives and lived in the shadow of their famous sibling. One had met her downfall by trying to step into Ravena's shoes and the other had been overpowered by jealousy and greed.

It was a story to die for…and Michael would have died for it, but for Jane. He read through his copy and e-mailed it to Jack. Then came the anxious wait for the phone at his bedside to ring. His hands shook when it did.

"This is incredible," Iverson told him. "JC wants a first-person sidebar on your escape from death and he's ordered Peterson to send a photographer over to take shots of you in the hospital. When are you getting your ass out of there? JC wants to see you as soon as you're released."

"They're saying they might release me tomorrow. So JC isn't going to fire me?"

"Nah. He's probably going to give you my fucking job."

"I'd sooner have a raise."

"You're gonna need one. Jane's on her way out the door here. She can't stop talking about you and she's on her way to see you. She's already babbling something about a fancy dinner. Just remember that she's high maintenance."

The heart that had been thumping wildly in Michael's chest was doing it again; but for a different reason now. "How do you know she's high maintenance?" he asked.

"Kid, one day you're gonna learn that I know everything."

Jack laughed and hung up.

Michael put his head on his pillow and closed his eyes. He couldn't wait for Jane to breeze through the door.

THE END

About the Author

Malcolm English was a tabloid editor for more than 30 years. He lives in Boynton Beach, Florida.

For more information,
ninespeakers@usa.net

Find more books from Keith Publications, LLC At

www.wickedinkpress.com
www.dinkwell.com
www.dreamsnfantasies.com

A information can be obtained at www.ICGtesting.com
d in the USA
'011825240113

25BV00011B/85/P